I0622125

THE

UNWONTED HEROES

JESSICA GRIMSLEY

Written by Jessica Grimsley

Copyright © 2018

ISBN: 978-0-6481818-3-5 paperback

ISBN: 978-0-6481818-4-2 e-book

The rights of to be identified as author of this work has been asserted by them in accordance with the copyright, Designs and Patents Act 1988

All rights reserved. No part of this publication may be reproduced, stored in or introduced into a retrieval system, or transmitted, in any form or by any means (electronic, mechanical, photocopying, recording or otherwise), without prior written permission of the writers. Any person who does any unauthorized act in relation to this publication may be liable to criminal prosecution and civil claims for damages.

Published with the assistance of: www.loveofbooks.com.au

Dedication to my Granddad

In loving memory of my Grandad William Henry Grimsley
who loved to read.

Contents

Prologue: Disappearance

Jonathan decided to make another stop that night instead of driving straight home. He had been away at Harvard University for a year and looked forward to seeing his family in New York again, but felt it wise to rest and wait one more night.

He had left late because he had to work another shift at Toys "R" Us, his part-time job while studying.

He recovered from a mini heart attack after almost driving into a sign that said "Slow down, stupid" with an angry man pointing at him and he parked his car next to a train track before hopping out and taking a few deep breaths. Gazing around the town, he searched for a place to stay for the night, as well as somewhere to get a bite to eat.

He was too tired to see what the town was called, but, it was obviously quite old and not much to look at or be excited about. It was just a town for resting on a road trip.

He approached an old motel called "Sleepy for Weary" and checked in for the night. It was clean and tidy inside, and some renovations made it look new, although the outside was rather sad and old looking.

The young receptionist greeted him warmly and introduced him to the motel. She took an interest in him and was rather flirty, asking him many questions and speaking fast like an auctioneer. He was too worn-out to listen, so he politely asked where the nearest place to buy food was.

As he left, she blew him a kiss and he caught a glimpse of her in the reflection from the window, picking up the phone on the front desk in a hurry, still watching him with a large smile.

There was an English pub just next door and around to the other street. It wasn't the place you'd expect to find such a pub. It was beautiful and dark inside due to the lighting and dark wood used on the walls and bar, and there was dark blue carpet. It was packed with people, most of whom were gathered in a corner watching a sport on the TV. Jonathan couldn't quite see what it was with all the people standing in his way, but he didn't really care. His tummy was very demanding. People were sitting and chatting and occasionally glancing at the television, but they seemed more interested in listening to Journey playing from the speakers.

He ordered a glass of red lemonade and a large plate of hot chips with gravy before choosing to sit in a place away from all the noisy people; he didn't really like big crowds. There was another little TV near him, turned to a different channel. A news broadcast was on, covering a story that had interested him for years.

"After thirty years of Danny Smitt being behind bars for 8-year-old Denise Youngbird's disappearance, new evidence has been found to prove his innocence."

The waitress arrived with his chips and drink. "Would you like me to change the channel for you, love?"

"No thanks," he replied, eager for her to get out of the way. "I ordered gravy with my chips."

"Oh sorry, I'll get that for you now, love."

"There have been many mysterious disappearances over the years, just recently an English man, age 26, went missing and was last seen going to the loo at a friend's party. Why is it so difficult for the police to solve these damn cases?"

"Yeah, you just sit on your arse, mate, and have a go at others!" Jonathan muttered as he sipped his drink.

"Find the individuals responsible and give these families justice!"

"There's your gravy, love. You enjoy that." She glanced at the TV. "These stories scare me, I'd hate to be kidnapped." She walked off again, taking the plates and cups from the people who had previously sat at that table.

Jonathan finally ate his first chip which was covered in gravy. He was fascinated by these stories; he loved mysteries. It was obvious that none of the disappearances were connected. The young girl was taken thirty years ago, and this young Englishman was taken just recently, and he was 26, not 8. Also, he was from England, not the United States. It was the same with all the other disappearances; the people and circumstances were very different. Why the man on the news was even comparing them? Maybe he'd missed the beginning of the story, and they'd said something about new evidence that suggested a link between the cases.

Jonathan noticed the pub had grown quieter because the game everyone was watching had finished and just about everyone had left. Now it was just the people that worked there and a few old drunk men singing to themselves at a corner table.

It's probably time to eat up and drink up, Jonathan thought. It was getting late, and he wanted to get up early to finish his journey home.

"Thank you did you enjoy that?" the waitress asked with a nice smile as Jonathan got up.

"Yes, thank you." He gave her a thirty dollar tip.

"Oh, you are too nice, love. Have a nice night!"

It was a nice pub, he thought as he left. When he returned to college, he would be twenty-one so he could have a beer there next time.

Surprisingly, he was enjoying his night in the town, although he noticed a few people snickering as they walked behind him. He looked over his shoulder to find seven tough-looking men almost touching his heels. They were all probably in their thirties and wore old clothes and had beards. Typical. Jonathan, slightly concerned, tried to ignore them and keep walking, but they started to surround him. Realising this was serious, Jonathan became scared, although he did his best to act confident.

"Staying at a motel are'yer?" the one closest by an inch asked. "That's a nice, cozy place you chose. But what were you thinking, son? Going to a pub without your mummy or daddy?" The others all agreed and grinned at one another.

"Can I help you with something?" Jonathan asked as two of the men overtook him to stop him walking any further. "I'm really tired, and I've got a long drive tomorrow."

"Oh, don't worry. We won't keep you long, will we boys? Oh, no, son. Just give us some money, and we'll be on our way."

"Money? I haven't got any money."

"No? You look like a rich little college student to me. Nice clothes and nice hair."

"Nice car!" One of the other men pointed at Jonathan's car, a dark blue 1984 Camaro Z28 5-speed. It was a gift from his dad for being a straight-A student.

Admittedly, his parents were pretty rich, but they never spoilt him or his sister, Ruth. They used their money as a reward. If they did well at school, they got something nice. If they got a terrible report card, then Dad would make them scrub the toilet for two hours, calling it preparation for their future job. Jonathan understood why the men would assume he was rich, though. He did have nice brown hair which he kept combed nicely and held with some gel, and his clothes were nice, and his tie matched his grey eyes.

"That's not my car," Jonathan lied.

"Really? Then why did Sandra see you pull up in it?"

Sandra? Jonathan thought. Then he remembered the name tag on the receptionist at the motel. *That's why she picked up the phone in a hurry.* She thought he was loaded with cash.

"Look, I haven't got any money on me. I swear. I used most of it up." Jonathan reached into his pocket and clutched his car keys.

"Not good enough, son," the main guy said, shaking his head disappointedly. "If you don't give us any money, then I'm afraid you're not allowed to leave until you come up with a solution to this problem."

"Ok well, you see that bank over there?" Jonathan pointed, and as the men looked, he pushed the one who was doing most of the talking and sprinted to his car.

As he reached out for the door handle, he saw the big guy from the back of the pack lunge towards him. He hadn't even grasped the handle when he felt himself tumbling, then pinned on the pavement. Struggling to catch his breath he noticed the big guy who'd tackled him spring back upright and join the rest of the guys pouring petrol over his car. Jonathan couldn't believe it – that car was his most-prized possession. But what was worse, after they had covered his car in petrol, they walked over to him with the can.

He knew they were going to pour it on him, so he got up and took off like a rocket. He ran faster than he ever had down the road beside the train track.

He didn't want to look back, but he had to. They were chasing him and gaining fast! Jonathan was already panting hard and was almost out of breath. His tie kept whacking him in the face as he ran. Fear kept him going. Fear that he would be burned to death. Fear that he would never see his family ever again.

Soon he had a stitch, jabbing him in the side like a knife. He looked back again and saw the men were closer. He hadn't slowed down, but he was just about to. He was about to give up. Then, Jonathan felt a strange sensation as he noticed the storm that had emerged around him. Fast swirls of bright lightning surrounded and poked him all over his body. He stood still and watched in horror. He felt his dinner shifting around inside him, making him feel uncomfortable, and a very brief thought of it coming back up crossed his mind. His bladder wasn't strong enough, nor was the confidence he had tried to display earlier. He panicked, he screamed for help. He saw that the men hadn't noticed any of it. By the time Jonathan had thought he caught one of the guy's attention, he blacked out.

The thugs stopped chasing after Jonathan, and just stood there, awestruck. They had thought he'd stopped to give up. They rubbed their eyes to check, but he really was gone. He had completely disappeared into thin air. They hadn't noticed what had happened, so could only assume one thing.

"Aliens!" one of the smaller and skinnier men yelled as he ran away screaming in fear. "Run for your lives!"

Chapter 1:

"Come on, girls! I'm falling asleep here!" the coach yelled sarcastically. "Get the bloody ball!"

The girls were doing awful. The pitch was wet and muddy, and they kept falling over, but the coach said the boys don't slip so neither should they. The grass was uneven and bumpy. There were holes in the pitch filled with puddles from the rain they had earlier that day. But worst of all was the mud which Alice, their goalkeeper, kept sliding in.

"Oh for goodness sake!" the coach yelled again as they lost the ball. "Tracy, you're off! Leonie get in there!"

Finally! Leonie jumped up off the bench and waited to whack Tracy's hand. Tracy was a shy girl with glasses and wore her light brown hair up into two plaits. She was nice, but she always lost the ball. She was also very small though, and the other team was quite brutal. Leonie was a reasonably good player, she was a bit shy too, but she wasn't afraid to tackle.

Once Leonie got in on the pitch she immediately got the ball from Stacey who took the throw in. She dribbled the ball down the field but was faced with two defenders, so she saw that Camilla was open and passed it to her. Camilla then kicked the ball to Stacey who was wiped out by a stocky girl on the other team. A yellow card was given to the girl, and a penalty was given to Leonie's team.

Leonie's best friend Cody took the penalty. She was very good at taking penalties and often took the kick. As usual, she scored.

Cheers filled the old metal stands with the girls' families in them, and the Coach went nuts doing a crazy dance. Cody ran over to Leonie and jumped into her arms almost knocking her over. They were soon joined by the rest of the team, and it became a group hug. Stacey then did a perfect cartwheel.

The game continued. The other team did really well, too well. Camilla jockeyed a bit, but the other girl got past. Soon out of nowhere, Cody came charging in with a slide tackle and managed to get the ball away from the girl without making any contact. The girl on the other team simply jumped right over Cody and looked rather angry.

Leonie took the ball and ran up the pitch with it towards the other goal. As the same girl who took out Stacey came at her, she passed it to Camilla who ran up further before passing it to Stacey who immediately passed it back to Leonie who then took a shot and scored.

Again the girls gathered up excitedly for a group hug, and Stacey did another cartwheel. This time, the coach did a sort of Gorilla dance.

The referee blew his whistle which meant the game had ended. Leonie's team had won with the final score at 3-2.

In the changing rooms, after the girls had showered and changed, the coach came in for a talk sounding very chuffed.

"Well done girls, victorious yet again!" This time he did a really bad Irish dance.

Of course, as usual, he had something bad to say. This time it was to Tracy. It was pretty horrible, it included him telling her to reconsider her choice of sport and perhaps take up golf. All the girls expressed their anger at him, Cody booed him. Tracy was still new, and they all agreed that what she needed was some encouragement and practice, not to be yelled at like she was in the military. So all the girls often gathered up to their home ground, back in Maryborough, to practice on any night, except for Tuesday and Thursday which were normal training nights with the coach, to help Tracy and to work on their own skills. It was working quite well.

Like after every other victory, the girls went to McDonald's to celebrate. Leonie usually has two cheeseburgers and a medium fries with a chocolate milkshake. She often thought she was a bit of a pig when she has that, but that's nothing like what Cody has.

Cody has a big Mac with a large fries, chicken nuggets, a snack wrap and a large sprite. After all that she has a McFlurry like the rest of the girls.

Even though Cody ate a lot, she was still in surprisingly great shape because she was very active (unlike Leonie who was a tad plump). Along with soccer, she did swimming, tennis, and volleyball. She was also very funny and often told jokes. Leonie couldn't really hear the joke she told just then because she was cleaning up the pickle off her cheeseburger she'd dropped on her lap, she hated pickles! She did catch enough of Cody's joke to know it had something to do with a nun and a blind man. All the girls roared with laughter so it must have been a cracker.

Cody's jokes were usually a bit crude, but they are seventeen-year-old girls, so that sort of thing was hilarious. A lot of her other jokes were killers too. Leonie had a similar sense of humour, but she was shyer by nature and not as confident in her jokes. She couldn't help it and often wished she was more confident and goofy like Cody, but Cody's parents wished she was more like Leonie. That rarely bothered her though, she was so content with just being a teenager and playing soccer all day with her friends. She could see them all being best friends forever.

Camilla, the Brazilian girl, came back with the McFlurries as it was her shout today. Everyone had to have an ice-cream shout except for Tracy and the newest member of the team, Shani, she was from Africa and was a very good defender, but the coach wanted to try her on the right wing as she is very fast and good with crosses. Leonie plays on the left wing, Cody is a striker, Camilla is a midfielder and Stacey is also a striker. The other girls on the team often rotate positions. Stacey wasn't happy when the coach made her a sweeper once, she said that was the reason they lost that game.

Alice, the goalkeeper, had finally arrived. She was late because she forgot a change of clothes and she was the one who got covered in mud the most, incredibly. She was a right grot, and her mother was always angry about having to put in more of an effort into washing her soccer kit than necessary. None of the girls minded her messy habits because she is a fabulous goalkeeper, the best one they've had. She only started playing soccer last year.

"I so can't believe this is the last year of school," Shani said excitedly. "Anyone know what they're doing after school yet?"

"Nah," Alice said loudly as she sat down with her kid's meal. "I haven't really thought about it."

"My dad wants me to be an optometrist like him," said Stacey, "but I'm more interested in Law."

"Yeah I want to be a Medical examiner," Camilla said enthusiastically.

"That's gross." Stacey cringed.

"Nah, just kidding. Maybe a chef or something in IT."

"What about you Leonie?" Shani asked interestedly.

"I've always wanted to be a pilot. So I'm aiming towards that. Dad takes me to flying lessons now after we've been to the firing range. We haven't been on the holidays though."

"Your family and guns," laughed Cody. "I only know Black Ops."

"Well, what's your dream job, Cody?" Leonie asked sarcastically.

"Hmm," Cody then smiled as she knew the answer. "A Manchester United player!"

All the girls cheered in agreement. Manchester United was the girls' favourite team. They often had a friendly battle with the coach who liked Arsenal. Leonie enjoys approaching him when United beat Arsenal (which is often) and saying something like *"Oh isn't it a lovely day today in the football world. Oh, not for those Arsenal people though."*

Their all-time favourite players were George Best, Sir Bobby Charlton, Ryan Giggs, Valencia, Rooney and many others. They often dreamed of playing for Manchester United even though it was a men's team. They even go as far as saying they could beat them but Leonie knows they would all cower if they ever did get the chance to play against them, which was highly unlikely. Cody is often nicknamed Scholes because she always slide-tackled everyone, even when it wasn't necessary.

After they had finished their many meals they had ordered from McDonald's, they did their usual let's start eating better from now on talk and left to go home. Stacey had organised a night out that night and expected them all to join in. While she was explaining her plans for the night to everyone, Leonie turned to Tracy and smiled as she asked her a question.

"What job do you think you'd like to do when you leave school?"

"A clairvoyant."

Leonie forced herself to keep smiling until Tracey had walked off, then she dropped the smile and confusion spread across her face.

Cody, who had heard what she had said because she didn't want to listen to Stacey, had the same look on her face but you could say she was almost cracking up.

"I think she was joking," Cody giggled as they walked through the park on their way to Leonie's house. "I mean she's a smart girl, she gets the best grades. She doesn't strike me as one of those psychic freaks."

"Yeah I know I just wasn't expecting her to say that."

They didn't really say much more after that, they weren't really into gossiping much. Leonie had been really lucky to find friends who were laid back and didn't expect too much from you, except of course in soccer. None of them like arguing and if they ever did it would only last five minutes. All the girls agreed if any of them have any beef, to lay it out there and then and be done with it. Then, they would all go get an ice-cream and get back to enjoying life. Leonie hoped it would always be like this.

Suddenly Cody's phone rang, and she almost dropped it as she went to answer it. "Hello? Yes. You're kidding? Yeah alright. Well, we'll just have to make it another time then won't we? Right, bye."

"What happened?" Leonie asked curiously.

"Tonight's cancelled. Stacey has to go to a family thing."

"Oh dammit."

"I might just go home and rest anyway. My mum is making her roast beef tomorrow, by the way, want to come?"

"Sure! I'd love that. It is ok though right? I don't want it to be like Easter where you're Aunties were asking me which kid I was."

"Nah it's fine. My Aunties are up in Rome."

The next week was pretty dull for Leonie. She didn't really even try to find anything to do, school started in a week, and she always got nervous on those last few days leading up to school.

She didn't do badly in school, in fact, her grades were pretty perfect. She wanted a good job when she grew up, becoming a pilot was her goal, so ever since grade ten she's been putting in a big effort and it has paid off, almost. What she didn't like was some of the teachers and the other students.

Leonie used to get bullied all the time in primary school and middle school because she was shy, nerdy and a tall geek. She pretty much grew to the height she is now when she was a lot younger, and the rest of her didn't really fit. Thankfully by the time high school arrived, she grew into a more beautiful young lady, with her long golden hair, gold hazel eyes, and clear pale skin. However, she still expects to get picked on even though she hasn't for ages.

She finally made friends for the first time when she started high school, with the girls from her soccer team. Cody, is her best friend, she was originally from Detroit (or as Cody calls it, Detroit Rock City) but moved to Australia when she was nine. She's kind of crazy but means well, she introduced her to the soccer team where she met all her other close friends.

Leonie, Tracy, and Alice were the only ones out of her friends who were actually from Australia. There's an American, Brazilian, African and Stacey is from Brighton, England originally. Leonie thought it made the group more awesome and they each shared many stories about their homes with each other. It was cool to have people from different countries; Leonie often wondered what it would be like to meet people from other time zones too. Leonie cherishes her friendship with each of her friends, they have a lot of fun together and have similar interests, although their personalities are quite different for example, Cody was very silly, and Stacey was a control freak. But they seem to tolerate each other well, and it doesn't bother Leonie one bit. Mostly because she'd never had any friends before and now she did, and she didn't want to lose them, ever.

Chapter 2:

"Come on Leonie," Camilla yelled from the car. "Get in!"

"I'm coming!" Leonie yelled back as she ran down her front lawn with several large bags.

They were having a slumber party at Stacey's farm for the weekend before school starts up again. Leonie had one bag full of the stuff she will need for the next three nights and goodness knows what's in the others. Before Stacey had picked up the other girls in her dad's four doored Ute, she made a trip with Leonie and Cody down the backstreets (a really quick way to Stacey's farm) with a bag containing some of Leonie's dad's firearms before dropping them back home to pack normal things. They were camping out in Stacey's huge backyard, and it was, of course, Cody's idea to bring the guns.

Leonie's dad was in the United States Marine Corps back in the day, before moving to Australia. He now spent most of his time at his club called "Decamp" (it's named that because it's mainly filled with men trying to escape their wives). They have firing ranges and even archery. Leonie often got to go along and practice too. However she would spend all her time there, and her dad wanted her to do something different on the holidays and banned her for a while. She was angry at first, but in the end, she was thankful because she got to hang out with her friends a lot.

Leonie was especially good at archery although she wasn't overly fond of it because she liked modern day weapons and not arrows and swords. She would rather drive a tank than ride a horse, although if her dad offered to buy her a horse, she most certainly would not refuse.

They also taught several different kinds of martial arts such as Tang Soo Do, Judo, Taekwondo, Eagle Claw and Muay Thai. Leonie trained in Taekwondo and Eagle Claw and advanced very slowly, but she enjoyed it very much. She even enjoyed the harsh discipline, her father prepared her for that. (Stacey practised Martial Arts there as well and was extremely impressive at it, Leonie would never want to get into a physical fight with her, not that they'd ever had any reason to. Stacey was very kind, but she was tough and knew her stuff. Although she wasn't a very fast runner though, Stacey, when they play soccer she was really slow, Cody often said it was because of her large breasts. Leonie just knew that she was slow yet powerful.)

It was a very nice place; it was hard work but very satisfying.

Leonie was going to teach Cody and Stacey a thing or two about guns because they had no clue and wanted to learn. She knew it was pretty stupid to steal her dad's guns and go out with them without him, but Cody assured her it was for a good cause.

While Camilla and Leonie tried to squeeze all her stuff in the boot of the car along with Rocco, Stacey's German Shepherd, and Rufo, Stacey's Rottweiler, the other girls were arguing about which music to play. At that moment "She Sells Sanctuary" by The Cult was blasting through the speakers but soon they were hooning through town blaring "Street of Dreams" by Rainbow followed by The Angels music.

It was clear that it was going to be a great weekend, despite the fact that when they stopped at the red light the car that pulled up next to them had Camilla's grumpy parents in it who didn't look happy to see them. Camilla dropped to the floor of the car to hide, and Cody who was in the passenger's seat rolled her window down and smiled. Stacey turned the music down.

"Is Camilla going to this party?" her father asked furiously.

"Camilla?" Cody checked. "No, I think she's got a bug and doesn't want to speak to us."

Mr Moretti drove off without saying anything, and Camilla popped back up laughing. Stacey turned the music back up and screeched off down the road.

"Whoa," Leonie shrieked as she clutched on to Cody's seat. "I think I need to go back for my head you maniac!"

"Yay there's the drive-in," Shani cheered as this was the reason they went to Stacey's house through town and not via the backstreets. "I'm starving, and Alice is on tonight! We can annoy her!"

Immediately, Stacey scarily jerked the car in the direction of the drive-in and hurried the girls to tell her what they wanted. Leonie just wanted a burger as she wasn't very hungry and wasn't surprised when Cody asked for nearly the whole menu.

Leonie smirked when Calum, a short, stocky Rugby player from their school was there to take their order. He rather fancied Stacey, and all the girls enjoyed teasing her about it because she didn't really like him.

"Is Alice there?" Stacey asked, avoiding eye contact.

"Don't like me do you, princess? That's a surprise. We'd better fix that, perhaps you should come watch a real football game."

"Rugby," Cody blurted out, "are you taking the piss?"

"Shut up, Cody. No one likes you."

Cody laughed. Calum and Cody were archenemies, in a friendly bro way. They just enjoyed calling each other names. Calum often called her a tosser and would ask her when she was joining the men's soccer team. Cody would often hide things in his locker, like posters of half-naked men.

"That stuff you do shouldn't be called football," Cody explained, "You rarely ever use your feet."

"Yeah? And you're in the wrong game, Cody. All those tackles you do, rugby tackles, stupid git!"

"Shut up, Calum," Stacey finally interrupted while furiously sticking her knuckles into Cody's mouth to stop her from responding. "Just get Alice!"

The whole conversation had been so fast that Leonie struggled to catch each word. The car behind them had started angrily honking their horn.

Finally, Alice, the goalkeeper, came to take their order as well as their comments on her uniform. To repay them, Alice dropped the bags of food onto the road as Stacey went to take them and Stacey made Cody get out and retrieve them. Stacey started to drive off without Cody but she just happily waved the bags of food and ate some of Camilla's fries. So Stacey realised she shouldn't leave her behind with all their food. Camilla wasn't happy either and ate Cody's fries to make it even while they were cruising down the highway.

Everyone was excited when they arrived at Stacey's farm. It was the best house to have sleepovers at. It had a lovely big Old Queenslander house with a large veranda going around the whole house, and there was a gym underneath the stairs of the balcony. There was a lot of land for them to play on, filled with many huge trees. Leonie was afraid of the chicken pen though, as there's an angry overprotective Rooster who chases everyone except Stacey. Currently, Stacey's rich parents are overseas with her two younger brothers on holiday, Stacey had to stay behind because it's halfway through grade twelve and they want her to get a high OP. So they have the whole house to themselves.

The girls struggled to get all their stuff into the house. Camilla tried to walk Rocco and Rufo in through the gate but they pulled so hard on their leads, and she fell face first into a puddle of mud. Everyone roared with laughter, and Camilla stormed into the house to have a shower (but she was smirking too).

The party started off with listening to Def Leppard and Kiss while playing Ginger Beer pong, which Shani, who hated Ginger Beer, didn't join in. She and Cody were having a brutal pillow fight though, and somehow Shani managed to whack Cody so hard that she fell to the ground and didn't move for a minute.

Next, they all took turns playing a new online Zombie game. Camilla got into a fight on the microphone with some guy who was calling her a hacker. Eventually, they all agreed to play FIFA 13 instead.

At 8:15, Tracy finally arrived looking rather nervous as usual. Leonie helped her with her stuff and dragged her over to join the other girls who welcomed her frantically.

"What now?" Stacey asked as she sat on top of Camilla.

"How about those guns Leonie brought?" Cody grinned evilly in a way that made Leonie rather uncomfortable.

"I don't really like the idea of using guns," Stacey explained obviously taking a second thought, "my dad would kill me."

"How is he going to kill you all the way from Italy? Besides they're only paintball guns."

That settled it. Everyone gathered outside in the huge forest that was Stacey's backyard. Stacey's neighbours were a long way away, so they didn't need to panic about them, they knew that Stacey's parents were away, they told them because they didn't trust Stacey's friends. Just in case, they turned the music up really loud.

Just as Leonie was about to start telling the rules, Shani shrieked "Someone's coming!"

Cody swore, and they all worked together to hide the bags filled with weapons and paint in a Forsythia bush next to the barbeque. This wasn't the best hiding place, but five desperate, panicking teenage girls wouldn't notice that.

Suddenly Stacey's neighbour Jane, a middle age woman who breeds border Collies, rather nice lady but comes off a bit snappy, walked through the gate. Her husband followed, and he was all wet, probably walked through the sprinklers again, he didn't look happy.

"Hi girls," Jane chirped, and she had a quick look around. The girls made weird noises that meant they were saying hi back. "Just wanted to check how things were going and make sure there's no drugs, alcohol, boys, guns, drugs."

Did she really think we were that bad? Leonie thought. She knew Stacey's parents weren't particularly fond of her friends and the same with Camilla's parents, but they really thought they would have those things? They had weapons alright but none of those other things, drugs, and boys! Leonie wasn't quite into boys yet, she hadn't even had a date or anything. Some of the other girls had boyfriends before, but they shared the same views, they'll wait until after school to worry about boys. Cody doesn't even acknowledge boys in that way, she is a bit childish, but she's never had a boyfriend and doesn't even want one yet. It's great though, they can all just focus on soccer. Anyway, all the boys they know are pricks too, and why would they want a bunch of pricks at their party?

Jane's husband stared right into Leonie's soul. It was a cold stare that made you want to shiver and wonder why the heck he was looking at you. "They probably guessed we would come and are saving the trouble for later, dear."

Cody pulled a face at Leonie as if to say *what's with him?* Leonie half smiled and nodded in agreement.

"Oh, what harm could a bit of fun do," Jane squeaked excitedly, "just make sure you don't mess up the house, don't take any drugs or drink any alcohol."

"And no guns," Jane's husband said bluntly as he stared into the bush the girls hid Leonie's bags in, how'd he know? "Guns are for men, not little girls."

"As if they'd have any guns, you silly git!"

"Hey, I'm just helping out our neighbours. They're good people, and we need to take extra precautions."

"Extra precautions?" Jane yelled as she and her husband had a full on argument. Tracey, Shani, and Stacey were frozen to the spot whereas Camilla and Cody were facing the trees, their bodies shaking because they were silently giggling. Jane's poor husband was trying to make things better with his wife but ended up saying the wrong thing.

"You wanna fall out with me today, Earl? You and I gonna go home and we're gonna dish it out the old fashion way. Let's go!"

After the pair went home with Jane practically dragging Earl by the ear, the girls quickly gathered together to see if anyone knew exactly what the *old fashioned way* was. No one did.

Everyone agreed that playing with guns during the night was a bad idea and they didn't want to risk Jane and Earl coming back with their foul tempers. So they decided to play murder in the dark instead. Cody's idea, of course.

Whenever they had a sleepover party, they always played murder in the dark, to make Cody happy. She always brought with her a little toy rubber axe for the person who was playing the murderer to use. It was supposed to be safe for kids to use, but Leonie still thought it really hurt when you were whacked by it, out of nowhere, in the dark. One time, they watched a scary movie before playing Murder in the Dark and as Camilla jumped out from behind a tree when the night was pitch black at Stacey and hit her with the axe she screamed really loud and ran all the way back to her room. Leonie and Cody were in a tree hiding a fair way away, bored from the wait and swore it sounded like she was being murdered for real.

Tonight, Shani was it, and she grinned evilly during the countdown after they'd blindfolded her, so she didn't cheat, even though it was too dark to really see much.

Cody and Leonie always hide together or nearby in case they get bored and can talk about something. They had to change their direction of choice tonight because last time Shani was hiding with them too and might suspect they'd be hiding there again.

Almost immediately into the game, as Leonie and Cody just got settled up in a tree, they heard the scream of Stacey. Leonie gave Cody ten dollars because she bet she'd be found first. A while later they heard Camilla scream. The screams seemed more intense than usual, especially Camilla's, her scream was usually half laugh. All that remained was Leonie, Cody, and Tracy.

It was about five minutes later when they heard footsteps close by. Giggling, Leonie and Cody slouched down into the tree with their hands over their mouth so that Shani couldn't hear them. It went silent for a moment until suddenly they were both hit on the side of the head by an axe. Leonie got a heart attack and shrieked while Cody fell out of the tree and landed face first on a pile of leaves. Shani roared with laughter, and Leonie and Cody joined in instantly.

The three of them trotted back to the house laughing their heads off. Cody had leaves stuck all through her light brown hair along with several knots, not that it was tidy, to begin with.

"Right," Cody clapped her hands together, "that just leaves sly Tracy then."

Shani, still giggling finally caught her breath, "and Camilla and Stace."

"You haven't caught them yet," Leonie asked. Shani shook her head. "Give me my ten dollars back!"

Cody threw the money back at Leonie, "but we heard them both scream."

"Yeah!"

"Really," Shani said looking confused, "I thought you were all mucking around when I heard the screams."

Within seconds their eyes were on the woods as they heard another scream of horror which could only be Tracy. They never heard her voice that much, but it had to be her. Cody had to check Shani was still beside them because who else could be terrorising the girls. Leonie thought of Earl and how he was strangely staring at her earlier on. Was he a maniac or something? Maybe he had a real axe!

That thought was enough for Leonie to sprint to her bag of weapons and pull out her dads Desert Eagle Mark XIX and load it carefully. Her father had taught her all about safety with weapons and her first lesson was to never point a gun at someone unless she was going to kill them. She felt bad about stealing these weapons as it was a bloody stupid thing to do especially with Cody around. Weapon safety was important to her dad and to him misusing a gun was the same to him as animal cruelty was to animal lovers. Leonie knew what she did was terrible, but at the moment she needed to focus on her three friends who could be hurt. More than likely it was nothing though and probably no reason to bring a gun into it.

"Whoa!" Cody shrieked, "You have a real gun!"

"You never know, Cody."

What it was, Leonie took her dads paintball rifles but forgot until they were at the drive-thru that he keeps a Mark XIX in the side pocket of his bag.

The three ran off into the woods with a mixture of feelings, scared, confused, excited, pumped and nervous. If this was a prank by the other three, it was working well.

As they reached the east of Stacey's woods, they came to the fence that meant if they went over it they were going on to Jane's property. However Leonie thought they'd gone too far because Tracy seemed closer than what they were, but there had been absolutely no trace of anything on the way. Cody, who was searching passionately for blood, had walked into a large spider's web and looked like she was wrestling with an imaginary ninja.

To the girl's slight relief Jane and Earl pulled up in a truck to the fence. Their side of the fence had very few trees so they could easily drive there and could have easily seen something.

"What on Earth are you girls playing at," Jane yelled furiously, "all that screaming and carrying on!"

"Wh-what?" Shani asked looking completely perplexed.

"We heard them scream too," Leonie said urgently as she tucked her Mark XIX into the back of her jeans. "We were playing murder in the dark when. We thought Shani got them but. We can't find them. The others! We can't find them!"

"Calm down sweetheart," Jane said after the girls explained everything, her tune changed to calm. "Let us all go back home and we'll call someone to help, okay?"

Leonie couldn't stop shaking, Shani's whole face was blank, and Cody was completely silent for once.

Chapter 3:

The whole thing wasn't a prank. Leonie tried telling herself this to stop herself from worrying but now she couldn't because it was real. Jane had called the police and told them there were three missing teenage girls. The police turned up quickly along with all the parents, and many people combed the backyard and further beyond that. There was no trace of Stacey, Camilla or Tracy. It was like they'd disappeared. Cody had gotten her voice back and was flapping her gums.

"It's got to be predators, there's no other explanation."

"They weren't armed, Cody. They're fine, they probably just got spooked and took off. They'll catch up with them soon."

"Pretty sure Stacey would run back to the house, not away from it. And Camilla doesn't get scared. Now, Tracy, she doesn't talk so why would she suddenly start screaming?"

Leonie didn't want to hear it. She didn't like how serious things were getting so she ignored Cody and just stared into space.

The police were very concerned and serious as they were walking around very fast and more people were turning up. A lady had called Stacey's parents who were over in Italy, and by her reaction on the phone, her parents were screaming at her. Stacey's parents weren't the only ones furious and asking a lot of questions. Shani's mother and father were going off at some guy who wasn't listening, and her dad looked like he was going to thump him one.

Camilla's parents pointed the finger at Leonie and Cody, saying that "Those two girls are trouble!" and "Camilla should have never hung around them! I knew this would happen someday!"

The only calm parents around were Leonie's. Her father, George, was a Marine back in the United States and is now a police officer after he met her mother on a visit here many years ago. Leonie's dad has gold hair like Leonie, blue eyes and is over six feet tall. He's very strict, but he's loads of fun when he's not working and likes spending time with Leonie. Her mother, Samantha, was in the Royal Australian Air Force as a nursing officer but left and became a psychologist, she's very beautiful and has Leonie's eyes, although she has red hair and is very small and petite. Her mother is more quiet and sweet, like Leonie, as compared to her loud father.

Her parents knew panicking wouldn't solve anything, so her dad just did his job there along with the rest of the police and her mother tried to comfort all the distressed parents of Leonie's friends.

Leonie was worried though because neither of her parents had spoken to her at all since they arrived. She wondered whether they knew she had accidentally stolen her dads gun. Either way, she knew it would only be a matter of time until they found the bags in the Forsythia bush which wasn't very concealing.

Cody's father finally arrived as they were being questioned by a young police officer from Nepal. Cody's father was a hilarious little fella with a pot belly and never seemed to have a clue what was going on around him. He spotted Cody and waved at her as if he had just arrived at her swimming carnival. Cody hid her face in Leonie's jacket to hide.

Leonie turned her head away from Cody just in time to see her dad slowly walk up to her looking very disappointed. He had the bag which contained *his* paintball guns in it. Frowning, he shook his head and walked off to hand them in. Leonie buried her face in her hands. She felt so stupid and ashamed. She had let her dad down, and it was a horrible feeling.

Leonie's dad didn't speak to her for the rest of the holidays, and her mother had a somewhat firm voice with her when she did speak, but she never spoke about the incident with her. Her parents were often like that, her father would go off and gather his thoughts and work it all out before speaking or yelling at her. Her mother would have to talk to her about other things like preparing for school. It was a really painful way to end the school holidays.

Today was the first day back at school. Leonie looked at the alarm clock which read 5:42am and thought *Oh no*. School was in a few hours, and she really didn't want to go.

She hadn't seen or heard much from Cody or Shani since the other three had disappeared. It was all a bit of a panic for everyone. There had been no sign of the girls for the past few days. The police had searched all around. There was not one single trace of anything. No clues.

All of this reminded Leonie of some other strange stories. In nineteen ninety-six, a twenty-year-old University student, Jonathan Morse vanished next to a railway track near New York. Even though that was seventeen years ago, she remembered hearing about it on the news when they talked about some Max Clark who went missing back in two thousand and nine. Other stories such as twenty-six-year-old Jamie Young from England went missing in nineteen ninety-five, last seen at a party heading for the toilet. The people investigating these stories made no progress at all.

Leonie got ready for school and checked loads of times to make sure she had everything she needed. Her maths textbook for this year scared the crap out of her and she'd avoided revising all holiday.

She then went on her dad's computer in his small office downstairs to try and find out more about the strange disappearances. After ten minutes, she found in one of her dad's files a list of names, some she was familiar with.

Warren Mitchel – Mysteriously disappeared in 1973. Last seen by his father in his office at work in Cardiff, Wales. The office door locked from the inside. Age 11 years and 10 months. Case never solved.

Max Clark – Mysteriously disappeared in 2009. An African American FBI agent, last seen by witnesses who saw him riding his bike before vanishing leaving his bike to crash into the vehicle, in Arizona. A story the law believes to be made up. Age 24. Case never solved.

Leon Tyrell – Mysteriously disappeared in 2005. Ex-Navy Seal and was currently working as a doctor in LA. Last seen leaving a pub. Age 54. Case never solved.

The next one really fascinated Leonie.

Emmelia Elliston – Mysteriously disappeared in 1889. Age 22. Caused panic among people. Case never solved.

Leonie thought if Emmelia weren't murdered she'd probably be dead now anyway of old age. She felt sorry for her anyway. Her dad put a little note beneath it saying *Not much known about her except she was very beautiful and was about to be married.*

The next 40 plus stories were similar, all the people vanished, and included the ones with Jonathan and Jamie. The last three her dad had added were of Stacey, Camilla, and Tracey.

Leonie realised this meant her dad thought the same as her. That there was something strange and similar with each of the disappearances, which was nothing, there was nothing about the stories except for they had all vanished and never been seen again.

"Maybe it's aliens," Leonie said to herself. Whatever it was, it took three of her best friends, and she wasn't happy about that at all.

*

The first day of school was terrible. Cody got detention before school even started, and Leonie didn't get to see much of her. She didn't know what she got into trouble for, but knowing Cody, it was probably for something really stupid. Once, she pretended there were ghosts in the girls' toilets, the school building is hundreds of years old and apparently used to be a prison or something, Leonie believes it still is. Cody actually likes the school, not the learning bit, except for Science which she's really good at, but she likes exploring the school and swears there are bodies somewhere.

So on the first day back, Leonie got yelled at by three of her teachers. She had forgotten her new Maths book (the one that scared her) and had to share with a cheerleader who complained about Leonie's breath.

She got yelled at in French class, but luckily Leonie wasn't too fluent in French, so she had no idea what Miss Caunes was on about.

Lastly, she got yelled at in sports because she was too scared of doing the high jump. She had long legs and could probably do it. She hated the metal bar because it might hurt to get hit by it on the way over and she was scared of the elastic one because she thought if she got her foot caught in it, it might be like a slingshot and send her flying. She got given laps, and the whole class smirked at her.

Leonie met up with Shani to head for their last class which was Biology. On the way, they saw Cody having a good old time dancing with a mop in the hall.

The first Biology lesson of the year started with dissecting a cow's eye. Leonie and Shani partnered up and played catch with the eye while the teacher was busy helping a fainted girl to a chair outside after seeing black stuff come out of hers when she picked it up. Cody would have loved this lesson.

When the first tiring day of school finally ended – with Cody having to stay behind for more detention for burping into the principles microphone which echoed through the school, amusing many – Leonie walked Shani to the bus stop and said goodbye. Leonie's mum had rung her to say she would be walking home because she was flat out at work. She wondered whether that was the real reason.

It had been a horrible walk home in the rain, and it was even worse when Leonie arrived home and saw her dad's car parked in the driveway of their nineties two-story brick house. She started feeling very anxious like she usually does when she knows she's about to be yelled at and punished.

Dad sat at his office desk, busily reading some letters. So Leonie thought it was best to head upstairs to her room and not disturb him. The yelling can wait a bit longer.

"Leonie," He called after her as she made it halfway up the stairs, "I think it's time to talk."

Leonie paused before slowly walking back down to his office with her head down. His voice seemed rather calm than she had expected. She hoped he wasn't too hard on her, even though she deserved every bit of punishment she'd ever been given all at once.

"I'm sorry, dad," she said quickly, hoping to ease things up by getting in first, "I know what I did was wrong, and I'll never do it again."

Her dad waved his hand for her to stop talking, "they want to talk to you down at the police station."

"Oh."

"Look," her dad had more of a softer tone, and his face looked sympathetic, "you know I'll always love you no matter what. You're my daughter. Yes, you did the wrong thing, but, I think you're getting old enough for me to not yell at you, and for

23

you to make your own decisions. And if they're the wrong decisions, then you'll have to take the consequences on your own and learn from your mistakes. And just know that when I do yell at you or am disappointed in you, it's only for that moment, for that situation. It doesn't and shouldn't impact our whole relationship."

Leonie was almost tearing up, tears of joy. His voice had been so warm and reassuring. He had never been so calm about anything else bad she'd done, and this was probably worse, besides other things she had done with Cody to disturb the peace.

"I'm sorry, dad."

"It's alright, love. Come here."

Leonie went over and hugged her dad tightly. She didn't like it when people gave her the silent treatment.

"Did you get into trouble?" she asked, taking in a deep breath.

"I just got told to make sure I kept my things safely locked up, and it wasn't to happen again. Everyone's more concerned about finding the girls. How are you coping?"

Leonie shrugged. If she said anything, she would start crying. She missed her friends so much and hoped they were okay. Her dad seemed to read her mind.

"They'll be ok, we'll find them, you'll see. We can't give up. That's why I've been doing a little research on my own."

Leonie wanted to tell him she already knew a bit of the information he'd found out but thought he might get angry at her for snooping around. She'd just gotten out of trouble and wanted it to stay that way. So she just pretended to be fascinated when he told her about the guy who disappeared into thin air, leaving his bike to crash into a car and about the beautiful lady from the 1800's.

"Whoever it is must be really clever," Leonie said trying to force some information out of her dad, "leaving no clues or anything. I wonder how long they've been doing this for and how many disappearances they're responsible for."

Her dad didn't reply straight away. He seemed to be thinking hard before finally saying, "so you also think someone's snatched them and have done it more than once or twice?"

"More than thrice," she said enthusiastically, "It's got to be someone or something. I mean, you should've heard them scream, dad. They were terrified."

"There is something fishy," her dad agreed, "but I only included the part about Emmelia Elliston because the story of her disappearance was similar, not because I think it was the same person. They'd be either too old by now or more than likely dead."

"And the similarity in the stories is that there is nothing but the disappearance, right?"

"Right."

Leonie and her dad agreed on most things, but like everyone else trying to solve these mysteries, well, it just couldn't be solved, not without any clues, and there were none. Their conversation eventually led to her dad's crossword he was having trouble with.

At 5:00 pm Leonie and her dad went to the police station to talk to Chief Mandson. To make Leonie feel less anxious Chief Mandson took her and her dad to his office to talk.

Leonie and her dad sat on two chairs, and Chief Mandson sat on the edge of his desk in front of Leonie, and by the expression on his face, it must have hurt his bottom.

"First of all miss Reine," he said in his strong Welsh accent, "I'd like to express my deepest sympathy. It must be so tough to lose your friends. I hear they were exceptionally good football players."

Leonie's confusion at the phrase *lose your friends* as if they were dead was soon cast out of her mind when she heard someone outside her friends and family call the game she loved so much by its proper name of *football* and not soccer. Leonie suddenly felt better about being there than before. She nodded.

"I just wanted to make sure myself that you can't think of anything, anything at all, that might help us out. What were you doing besides playing murder in the dark? Anything?"

Leonie looked up at her dad as if to make sure it was ok to answer, not that she knew what to say. They were just mucking around being kids. Her dad looked down at her with his eyes, same as hers, wide open.

"Well," she said before clearing her croaky throat, "we were just having a sleepover before school started."

"With your father's paintball guns?"

"I didn't mean too." –

Mandson chuckled and shook his head. He didn't seem bothered for some reason.

"Well moving on. Now I have been trying and trying to get in touch with your other two friends. Now Miss, er, Cody Malice is very difficult to contact, I rang her father, but he thought I was a telemarketer from India calling to sell him something. Can you ask her to drop in tomorrow for me, after school?"

Leonie nodded again. Unable to get much out of Leonie, Mandson decided to end the interview and asked her to wait outside while he talked to her dad.

Leonie sat there unable to control herself as the tears rolled down her face. She put her hands over her face as she cried uncontrollably. She had always been very sensitive and emotional. If someone were to raise their voice at her, she would start tearing up. She missed her friends and going to the police station and talking to Chief Mandson had stirred her emotions up.

A lady came over to see if she was alright but Leonie wouldn't take her hands away from her face. She felt really silly and knew lots of people were staring at her.

When her father came out of the room, he dashed over to comfort his daughter. Leonie held her dad tightly as she sobbed into his shoulder.

"I miss them," she whimpered, "I wish they'd come back home!"

"I know," her dad said with his arm around her as he walked her away from all the staring people. Chief Mandson was left gawking after them before tending to a constable who was almost crying himself.

Leonie spent the next long day at school mainly to herself. Shani wasn't there due to a tummy bug, and Cody was in different classes and only saw her at lunch and then she had to go see Chief Mandson straight after school.

When Leonie came home after a slow walk, her mum was in the kitchen making her famous delicious curry. She smiled at Leonie as she entered. Her mother had a beautiful smile that could warm up even the coldest of hearts. She looked so much like Leonie except with more pale skin and her red hair (and of course she was older). Leonie smiled back at her mum, but her attention was soon grabbed by her dad who was peering out of his office. He had a funny grin on his face waving for her to come over. Leonie quickly dashed into the office and sat in her dad's chair as he requested. He clapped his hands together.

"Right," he said still grinning, "I've been talking to a friend from the city today, and you'll never guess what I've found!"

"What?"

"Evidence! I was talking to some of the witnesses again via Skype thanks to a friend getting me through and some teenager had confessed to having a recording on his phone of Max Clark disappearing into thin air!"

"WHAT?" Leonie leapt out of the chair, but her dad pushed her back down before plugging in a USB stick to the computer.

"It just so happens that his girlfriend was dancing in the street at the same time. He was filming her, she wasn't that good, but then, then, here we go."

A video appeared on the screen of her dad's computer. A lady wearing not many clothes was dancing on the side of the street when suddenly a man on a bicycle soared past almost knocking the phone out of the boy's hand. Naturally, the boy swore and yelled out after him. The dancing girl was no longer in the spotlight because her boyfriend, probably drunk, was chasing after the man on the bike. He wasn't fast enough to keep up with the cyclist, who was Max Clark, but he did capture something extraordinary. Just as the Max Clark reached an intersection, he disappeared into thin air, leaving his bike to smash into a really nice looking red 1969 Mustang convertible. The bike landed in the back seat of the Mustang and the old man driving it continued driving, unaware of what had just happened.

"Wow," was all Leonie could say as she wore the same expression as her dad, "does your boss know about this?"

"No, no one believes things like this. They'd say it was a fake. And they'd wonder why the boy didn't show this to them at the time."

"He probably collapsed in a ditch and had a horrible hangover the next day. Can we show Cody?"

Cody couldn't get there any quicker. Although she cracked up laughing at the video, laughing at the bike landing in the Mustang without the driver knowing and saying, "that old guy shouldn't be driving!" She was also a bit serious and concerned at the same time, which wasn't like her.

"Why do you think that guy was flying along like a maniac," Cody asked as if she was coming out of the cinema discussing all her favourite parts of a movie, "and how much do you think that loser with the camera drank? He must've been hammered!"

Leonie's dad wisely ignored Cody's excitement and began writing in his notebook, but Leonie has never been able to read his writing to find out what. He then got up and faced the two teenagers.

"I think this is what happened to Stacey and the others," he explained, "since I first started working on cases like this I never would have believed it, but it's crossed my mind several times recently, and I really want to find out more. I need your help," Cody and Leonie leaned in eagerly, "now that we know that people are actually disappearing into thin air, that's something! Now, we should try and link all the other cases similar to this, including your friends, and find out some things like what were they all doing at the time they disappeared."

Leonie and Cody both looked at each other for some ideas while Leonie's dad raced into his desk draws, looking for something.

"Well," Leonie's dad said as he popped up from behind his desk with a file, "let's start with what we do know. Your friends, what were they doing when they disappeared?"

"Hiding," Cody said, "from Shani."

"Running," Leonie exclaimed, "when we play we usually try to run as far away as possible to hide."

"So they were running away," Leonie's dad muttered as he wrote it down.

Leonie suddenly thought of something, "That man on the bike was flying past, wasn't he? So maybe, maybe he was running from someone too?"

"Yeah," said Cody who had just been looking at the files on the computer that Leonie had read earlier, "and this guy that disappeared at a party on his way to the toilet. Maybe he was trying to get away from someone too."

"And Jonathan Morse," Leonie's dad pointed out, "he could have been running away from someone. It was night time after all, and his car was covered in petrol. I'll look into that a bit more. Now I have to go to the office, and I don't particularly want you two girls involved in this much more, it's already been hard on you. I just wanted some help with your friends. Focus on your schoolwork."

Leonie's dad made it clear to them not to get distracted with this case even though they both tried to protest because they wanted to help, they knew he was right and eventually accepted it, and then they helped him take his work files to his car.

Leonie and Cody spent the rest of the afternoon at the park kicking the ball around. After they got the ball back from a playful Lhasa Apso that ran off with it, they headed to some swings to sit where they usually sit to talk.

"It's sad isn't it," Cody said, looking at the ground, "I wonder where they are and if they're alright. There's no football without them."

"They're tough girls. Hopefully, they're together so Camilla can keep them safe… But you know, they were just running from Shani, these other guys were probably running from something important, like that Clark guy was an FBI agent. So it doesn't really make sense."

Before Cody could compute what Leonie had said, three cars pulled up in the car park. Leonie recognised them from all of those Saturday games and sometimes at training nights to drop off their girls.

Chapter 4:

The parents of their three missing friends got out of the cars and stormed over with Camilla's in the lead. They didn't look happy.

"Oh crap," Cody whispered, "you know they blame us, right? I say we make a run for it."

Leonie pulled Cody back when she tried to run off, "they can't really blame us, we're kids, and we didn't do it."

"Tell *them* that."

Camilla's mother did a sort of old woman run up to Leonie and poked her in the chest, her face full of rage, "where's my daughter! You two girls bring her back! What did you do! Oh Lord!" She was pointing back and forth between the two of them and cried as she spoke, mainly in Portuguese, "my beautiful Camilla!"

The rest of the parents joined in at pointing and shouting all at once, and Leonie couldn't understand a word any of them were saying. To onlookers, it would have looked like they were two murderers who got away with it and were facing the wrath of the victim's parents, or at least that's what it felt like to Leonie. She got more and more uneasy as the longer it went on, the angrier and aggressive the parents became. She thought Camilla's mum was going to whack Cody at one point.

Finally, Leonie grabbed Cody's arm, who had started yelling back at the parents, and ran off with her through the park. To her amazement, the parents chased after them along with the

Lhasa Apso that wanted their ball. She could make out some of the yells from the parents, especially from Stacey's mother's loud, high pitched voice, "Running away! Proves you're guilty! I'm calling the police! Hooligans!"

Cody looked back at the parents in disgust, probably because she caught a few of the words they said too. Cody actually looked really upset which Leonie had never seen before. It was pretty horrible though, she couldn't believe how childish and scary the parents were being, blaming them. She could understand they were sad, but they were taking it too far.

After about twenty minutes of running for their lives, they made it to Cody's street. They hadn't looked back for ages, but Leonie was sure they lost the parents and the dog ages ago.

"No way," Cody snapped as they stopped so Leonie could get her breath back, "I can't deal with this, this is madness! They're insane! Sorry Leonie but I'm going home now, I need to be alone. Later buddy."

Cody hugged Leonie, who was still panting like mad, then ran off down the road to her house. Leonie watched her go inside before heading off to her own home where she was greeted on the front lawn by her panicking mother who ran over to her and hugged her.

"Are you ok," her mum yelled. "your father rang me, I was so worried, they can't do that, how's Cody?!"

"Mum we're fine," Leonie reassured her, "really it was a bit scary and all but what can you do. Their daughters are missing. I guess they're doing what they think is right by them."

Her mum took her inside and made her some hot cocoa with marshmallows, cream, and a flake. She then made her some really nice nachos.

When she'd finished her delicious food and drink, her dad arrived looking exhausted and hungry.

"What happened," Leonie's mum said rushing over to help him with his coat, "did they get arrested?"

"Nah we just took them to the station to cool off. They'll be fine."

"They'll be fine," Leonie's mum cried, "they'll be fine?! What about our Leonie!? What about Cody!? How do you think they'll be!? Those people should be locked up!? Threatening two girls like that! It's a disgrace!"

Leonie could imagine her mother taking on all those parents at once and believed it could be a reality if given a chance. Leonie's dad sent her upstairs while he tried to calm her mum down, who by that point had steam coming out of her ears. Leonie wished her mum would settle down, but gathered it was better than if she didn't care and half an hour ago Leonie was feeling the same way. So Leonie cranked up "Wasted Years" by Iron Maiden and played FIFA 13 on her PlayStation 3.

Later on that night, Leonie's parents were still arguing. Leonie was watching Rocky III when Cody's face appeared at her window. Leonie shrieked and fell back off her bean bag, and Cody laughed.

"What are you doing here," Leonie chuckled as she helped Cody through the window, "my parents aren't in a good mood at the moment."

"Why do you think I came in through the window?" Cody joked, "anyway I came to get you for the play Shani's in."

"That's tonight!? I completely forgot about that."

Shani was doing a school play that she'd been practising for all holiday. It was something to do with Romans, that's all Leonie knew.

"Yeah, and she also needs us for the play to stand on stage and hold stuff."

"I don't particularly think this is the best time to ask my parents if I can go out though," Leonie sighed.

"Well just leave them a note then. Come on we're gonna be late. Hey, it's Rocky!"

Cody watched some of Rocky III while Leonie wrote a note to her parents.

"It doesn't have to be fancy or anything," Cody called over her shoulder, not taking her eyes away from the TV, "I guess we could just stay here though and watch Rocky. We could watch the fourth one with Dolph Lundgren! You know he has a master's degree in chemical engineering! Nah Shani needs us."

"Ok let's go," Leonie said as she placed the note on her bedside table then put her jacket on, "how the heck did you get up here without breaking your neck?"

"I didn't want to, but it's for a good cause. Shani's play."

"Oh, I thought it was because you love me."

"Yeah, that too," Cody joked, and the two of them laughed and pretended to vomit like they did when Calum flirted with Stacey.

"Sorry about before by the way," Cody said through gritted teeth as she helped Leonie out the window, "it just hit me hard, all this stuff that's been going on."

"Don't worry about it," Leonie replied as she almost fell to her death, "everything's so weird lately."

As they reached the ground, Leonie took one last look at her parents through the living room window; they were angrily throwing her mum's new purple cushions at each other. She shook her head as her dad copped one really hard in the face. She then ran off with Cody into the night.

Her mind was blank as she jogged behind Cody because she had been thinking lots over the past week about everything, and her mind must have wanted a break. She had thought a lot about the things her dad had shown her earlier. It all seemed too difficult, even for all the smartest people in the world to figure out, and her dad wanted to solve it all by himself. Then again, so did Leonie.

They stopped at Alice's house to steal her brother's bikes because they were too exhausted to continue running. Leonie thought she was having an asthma attack, but Cody assured her she was just unfit and a few kilo's overweight.

The school was busier than what it was during school time. The car park was full, more than at drop-off and pick-up, and had a few drivers arguing over parking spaces, which was nothing out of the ordinary. Although to Leonie's astonishment, one guy was trying to push another car into a ditch so he could take their parking space.

The halls were filled with families trying to find their way to the right place. The actual theatre room was worse, it was crammed with people pushing and shoving. A lady walked past with a little kid who started screaming in Leonie's ear, and she was sure she'd gone deaf.

"Whoa," Cody said, wide-eyed, "I never knew theatre was still liked by so many. I mean look at all these kids."

"Let's go find Shani," Leonie said, rubbing her ear.

They pushed their way through a crowd to the other side of the theatre. It was a massive theatre because the school takes drama very seriously and they've won many awards for some of the plays they've had. Leonie hates drama because she always gets the role of the lady who doesn't do anything. Shani always got the big star role, she was very good at acting though. Cody always fell asleep during drama class, and Mrs Oliver would have to poke her with a pencil or something to wake her up.

Shani was waiting with some of the other people in the play. When she saw Leonie and Cody, she raced over and grabbed their arms and took off to the dressing room with them, saying nothing.

"Ah girls," said Mrs Oliver, their drama teacher, a middle-aged hippy woman who talked in a loud opera voice, "it was so nice of you to take out your own time to come and help us in this wonderful piece of art. I do hope you consider putting in more of an effort in class though." And she danced off over to a group of boys in grey tights.

"She's a nutter," muttered Cody.

Shani dressed them up in what Leonie first thought looked like Monks clothes. Leonie got a soft cottony white robe and looked like someone who was going to give fruit to a King. Cody got a thick brown robe and looked like a Jedi Knight.

While Leonie and Cody mocked each other's costumes, Shani's parents walked in to wish Shani good luck. They had with them her father's Border Collie assistance dog. Following behind them was Cody's clueless father and her drunken mother. She wasn't usually drunk, but she'd just received a big promotion at her office job, Cody had told her on the way there, and what better way to celebrate than to get sloshed and embarrass your daughter. Leonie knew she'd enjoy this, better Cody than her.

"Ah hello, sweetheart," Cody's mum smiled funnily and hugged her daughter, "did you hear the good news. Mummy got promoted so that she can earn more money and buy her little princess nice fings!"

"And I can go play golf," Cody's dad smiled.

Cody was paralysed with fear and embarrassment, her mum was so loud that everyone, which was fifty plus people, was staring. Cody tried fixing her mother's shirt which was half revealing her lacy bra. Leonie smirked as Cody's mum turned her attention to the Border Collie.

"Aww, is that the dog that herds sheep!" She stated loudly before passing out, her husband not realising until he heard the loud thud.

"Dad get her out of here," Cody begged, after checking her mum was ok, "I'm supposed to be doing a play here."

Shani's parents helped Cody's dad get the drunk lady out of the room. Once they were gone, Leonie and Shani burst out laughing, and Cody whacked them both several times.

Leonie couldn't believe how amazing Shani was during the play. She stole the whole show - to Leonie and Cody's relief as they felt they'd both sucked and were an eyesore - and everyone's eyes were glued to her. She had always been great but this was her best by far, Leonie thought. Although Shani had also been a bit gloomy lately from what had happened to their friends, you wouldn't have noticed if you were watching her.

Leonie still didn't know what the play was about even when she learned from Shani it was called *Julius Caesar*, but she did know that Shani played a guy who talked to a dead body.

After the show, Mrs Oliver came over to congratulate and praise everyone, except for Cody who had roared with laughter when a boy fell off the stage. Mrs Oliver took Cody aside to have a few words with her and made her apologise to the boy.

Leonie was sitting with Shani, waiting for Cody to come back.

"Tracy was going to do what you were doing tonight, Shani said blankly, "and a boy was going to do what Cody did. But he was sick."

"Oh," Leonie replied.

"You know Calum's been acting weird lately too. I think he really likes Stacey. Even though she's always mean to him."

"Okay," Leonie nodded but was a bit hesitant to say anything more. She wondered where Shani was going with this.

"But thanks for helping out tonight," Shani smiled, "it must have been scary being chased by all those parents. I mean how could you and Cody have had anything to do with it?"

"You did a great job tonight Shani," Leonie said quickly, wanting to end the subject there, "I wish I could act like you."

"Thanks, Leonie."

Leonie and Shani briskly hugged each other, then Shani went over to her parents because they had to go home in a hurry. Their usually well-trained Border Collie assistance dog was playing up. It was barking like crazy and growling at a man who was at a table making himself a coffee. Shani's parents looked very concerned and shocked because their dog had been very well-trained, and it wasn't like her to play up. Leonie thought the dog must have sensed something about the man that it didn't like.

"Lucy stop it," Shani's dad ordered anxiously to his dog, "enough!"

Cody came over to Leonie after she'd said goodbye to Shani too and looked back at the man that Lucy didn't like, he was now helping himself to some biscuits.

"I wonder why Lucy didn't like him," Leonie said, "Maybe she could smell his dog or cat on him."

"Nah," Cody replied as she stuffed her mouth with some crisps, "she's well trained. She wouldn't just bark like that just for that reason. Although, I'd bark at him too. He looks like a right prick."

"Don't be rude."

"Well she's a smart dog, she'd know an asshole when she saw one."

Leonie rolled her eyes, and Cody shoved some more crisps in her mouth. They both stared at the man, and as he passed them, he glanced at them with a very cold look on his face. He made Leonie feel uncomfortable because he didn't really seem right. She never felt comfortable with strangers, but he was different. As soon as he looked at her, her throat dried up, and she started shivering. She looked at Cody to find her shivering as well, not as much but she was definitely uncomfortable.

"I'm thirsty," said Cody, swallowing several times and licking her lips, her throat must have dried up too, "let's go get something to drink."

As they were getting their drinks from the vending machine, Alice appeared and ran up to them, panting.

"Alice," Cody cheered, "haven't seen you in ages. How ya been!? Still got the shits?"

"Look," Alice said desperately, "Calum and his mates are looking for you. It seems the girl's parents blaming you have influenced lots of people. I'd get out of here if I were you. He doesn't seem happy. He saw you in the play."

"What's he up to," Leonie asked, "why is he looking for us?"

"I don't know," Alice sighed, "apparently, Joe said, it turns out he really loved Stacey and is sad" –

"Love," Cody laughed, "I knew he had the hots for her but, *love*. Calum's a teenage boy for crying out loud."

"Look just get out of here, before he finds you."

"Thanks, Alice," Leonie said, tugging Cody's arm as she heard the sound that could only be Calum and his gang storming around the halls in search of them.

They both jogged away from the loud footsteps, looking back several times to make sure they weren't gaining on them. To Leonie's absolute disbelief, Cody wanted to stop to go to the loo.

"I won't be long I promise," Cody said as she closed the door of the cubicle she'd entered, "besides we'll be safe in here because this is the girl's toilets and they're boys. They can't come in here."

"What a relief," Leonie said sarcastically.

Leonie stood at the sinks and looked at herself in the mirror. She stroked her long golden hair that her mum creepily describes as a beautiful mane. Sometimes she wanted to cut it really short into a pixie cut, but Cody who cut it short a few years ago assured her she'd only want it to be long again. So she often kept it up in a bun.

"You haven't fallen in have you?" Leonie called as she checked her teeth in the mirror. Cody didn't answer, "Oi! Cody! Are you deaf!?"

There was still no answer, so Leonie decided to bang on the door of the cubicle that Cody was in. When that didn't get a response, she went and got some paper towel and threw it over the door. There was still nothing. So she went into the next cubicle and stood on the toilet to peer over the top.

"I said! You haven't fallen in have you – Cody?" as Leonie got a peep into the next toilet she saw that Cody wasn't there. She thought for a moment that she must have snuck out while she was daydreaming about herself, but she saw the door was still locked from the inside and there was no room for even a toddler to squeeze out the bottom.

Leonie scratched her head, all confused. At first, she thought it was a prank that her best friend was planning for weeks as usual… Then she started to think. Could Cody have disappeared as well? For some reason, she thought about how Stacey, Camilla, and Tracey all screamed before disappearing. None of the other disappearances had anything about screaming, they just vanished. If Cody had disappeared, then it was very quick and quiet.

Leonie started freaking out. Where was her best friend? She couldn't lose her best friend! She started getting really worried.

This usually happened if she wasn't with Cody or her parents. They were like her safety cues. If they weren't around, she would get really bad anxiety. Even walking to and from school by herself would be fast-paced and not looking at anyone she passed along the way. This was worse though, not only was she alone, she had no idea if Cody was alright.

After pacing up and down the restrooms thinking and being uptight, she finally made the decision to leave.

She was fearful that Calum and his buddies were right outside the door waiting for her, but there was no one there. However, she jumped when she heard a noise. It turned out to be her English teacher, Mr Starbird, a ginger. He came strolling down the hall and smiled when he spotted Leonie.

"You alright Miss Reine," he asked as he walked past, "you look lost."

"No I'm fine," Leonie replied in a really soft trembling voice.

Mr Starbird kept going, humming to himself. Leonie was now stuck on what to do. There were people after her, possibly to beat her up, and Cody was missing. She thought she should have told Mr Starbird when he asked her, but he's probably long gone now to try and catch him, and she didn't see which way he went down the corridor.

She decided to walk towards the big hall used as a gym. That's where she and her friends usually mucked around if it was too wet to play football outside. They usually played handball which would trigger arguing and ultimately turn into a game of brandy which involved pegging the tennis ball at each other. It hurt more if the ball was wet (which Camilla and Cody often did). Once, Stacey was sent home after Alice pegged the ball at her head and it bruised badly. Alice was the best at the game as she could catch the ball most of the time and had a huge throw. Even Cody snuck out once to hide in fear.

She walked left and right down corridors until finally, she made a bad turn. She walked around a corner to find Calum and his gang heading in her direction. There were seven of them, all rugby players. She stood frozen to the spot, fear stopped her from moving, and her eyes stared at the boy's wide open. They had stopped too but didn't look terrified like Leonie did.

"There's one of them," Mike a big guy with a shaved head pointed, "where's that moron one?"

Calum stared at her, he was quite big himself. Leonie thought he might have suspected Cody to be hiding somewhere with a trap. Leonie used this as an advantage.

"Cody now!" She yelled before bolting back in the direction she came. She could hear many loud running feet behind her and several yells but decided to focus on what was in front of her and how to get out of there.

She came to the music room on the first floor and struggled to slow down and ran into a drum kit. She opened a window and climbed out. Once out, she looked back to see one of the boys had almost grabbed her foot but wasn't quick enough.

Unfortunately, the music room was at the back of the school, so she still had a bit of running and climbing to do. She stumbled away in the rain, sobbing, as one by one the boys climbed out of the window and continued to chase her. She was sure her heart was going to burst out of her chest at any moment.

Leonie almost had a panic attack by the time she made it to the basketball courts. She had to keep going, though, because she knew her heavy breathing would give her away at any hiding place she tried.

She forced the gate opened and ran through and slammed the gate right in Peter Moore's face, making him yelp and curse. She chained up the gate and ran off out the other side. She made it just in time because some of the boys had run around the side to try and catch her.

The boys still chased her out of the school. Leonie sprinted across the main road, which was quite busy at the time, and down through the park. She didn't have to look back to know they were still running after her, she could hear the car horns going off on the main road and some screeching cars trying to avoid seven idiots running across in front of them.

Exhausted, she reached the now empty corner shop, across the road from the training ground for her soccer team. She was almost going to collapse so decided to hide around the side.

She sat against the brick wall, shivering, with her knees held to her chest with her arms. It didn't seem to be her year so far.

After a few minutes, she heard the boys arrive at the other side where she had been. They were chatting to one another, trying to work out where she was. They started unwrapping wrappers by the sound that Leonie heard. They stopped to have a snack.

Leonie, still sitting down turned her head to the right to find Shani standing there with a soccer ball. Leonie felt slightly relieved, slightly more concerned. There were two of them now which meant she was safer. But now Shani could be in danger as well.

"What are you doing," Shani whispered looking confused, "where's Cody?"

Leonie suddenly remembered that after the play, the three of them were going to kick the ball around. She'd forgotten all about the play, so of course, she'd forgotten all about this too. "She's gone." Leonie sniffled, looking up at an even more confused Shani who crouched down next to her.

"Gone where? Home? What's the matter? Why are you crying?"

Leonie struggled to speak. She was feeling the same way she was at the police station when she burst into tears. Only this time it seemed much worse. However, she did feel a bit stronger than before because she had more information then about what was going on. She had cried a lot before and knew it got her nowhere, and now that she had a bit more to go on she realised she can't sit around feeling sorry for herself, she had to get up and try and find her best friends of whom their friendship she cherished so much.

After taking in a deep breath, Leonie managed to stop with the sad face and replace it with a much stronger and serious one, "Alice warned Cody and I that Calum was looking for us. So we were going to run off. But Cody needed the loo so we went and she disappeared in there."

Shani leaned back onto her bottom, "So Cody vanished on the toilet?" She half giggled a little, "You sure she didn't flush herself?" She then saw the seriousness on Leonie's face. But Leonie managed a smile herself somehow.

He had to cough to indicate he was there. Leonie and Shani looked up to find that Calum and his buddies had been listening the whole time. Leonie felt a bit scared again for a moment but realised his face had relaxed a bit and he didn't seem so angry or insane.

"Cody disappeared too?" Calum asked softly, "Like Stacey and the other two? It seems like whoever is around you disappears Leonie. Are you a psychopath?"

Leonie's fear of this boy turned to annoyance. So she decided the best she could do was to tell them all about what her dad had discovered about all the disappearances. She went into every bit of detail possible until she was satisfied with what she had told them. When she had finished, Shani looked as though it had put her mind at ease, Calum looked stunned, but he seemed to believe her, and the other boys laughed, especially at the part with the bicycle and the Mustang.

"So it's not me," Leonie stated, "this has been happening for years. It's just the people in charge don't want to believe things like this even if there's no other explanation."

Calum sat down next to the girls and nodded as he accepted what he had been told, "I'm sorry Leonie. I guess because there was no explanation and the parents said it was you, I just got a bit" –

"It's ok Calum," Leonie smiled, making nervous eye contact quickly.

"I want to help you though. I mean, I want to find Stacey. And I'll be missing that Clown too."

Mike suddenly made a yelping noise as he was fiercely pushed aside by Camilla's dad. He looked just as angry as he did when he chased Leonie and Cody earlier along with the other angry parents.

Without thinking, Leonie took to her feet and bolted to the pitch – a shortcut home - She looked back to find Camilla's dad chasing after her along with Shani and Calum who were trying to stop him.

It was very sudden, about halfway across the pitch, when she saw a strange light around her. It was like lighting on the pitch. She was sure that none of the others could see it because they were still chasing after her the same way. Leonie stopped dead in her tracks. She turned around in circles, trying to figure out what was going on. She heard a sort of zapping noise which was soon joined in by a loud noise which sounded like a screaming kettle and then there was a loud noise like thunder. Leonie was petrified and automatically screamed at the top of her lungs. Then the now confused looking Calum and Camilla's dad vanished from her sight, and the shrieking Shani was also gone, and she blacked out.

Chapter 5:

Time Freeze

When she woke up, she felt a bit groggy and had a slight headache. The first thing she noticed was a mark on her arm where some sort of needle had been. She examined it a bit, ignoring all the voices she heard, they didn't register to her that they were real voices. Then she looked up to find that sitting next to her was a handsome young man with grey eyes staring down at her and smiling gently. Leonie only made quick eye contact with him before looking away. She looked down at what she was lying on; it was a wooden bench, like the one in the changing rooms. Then she saw the room *was* a changing room and that there were other men in there as well. She thought she must have passed out in there or something, in the men's changing room. She looked at the handsome man again hoping to recognise him from the men's team, but she'd never seen him before. Not in person anyway but he looked familiar somehow.

"How are you feeling?" he asked her in a soothing voice. Leonie noticed a very slight trembling in his voice, as if he was also a bit scared but trying to hide it, he also had an American accent, "I know you will probably be a bit confused and frightened but just try to relax, even though it's hard."

"That's great advice," came another voice from a man behind him. He had an English accent and sounded very cheery and calm, "Oh don't worry we're in a strange place but don't worry because this happens all the time." He said that in a sarcastic voice that made the handsome man in front of Leonie roll his eyes.

"I just meant we don't need to worry her... What's your name? I'm Jonathan."

Jonathan! Leonie thought. That's how she recognised him. He's Jonathan Morse. The man who went missing next to the railway track in New York back in ninety-six. A complete mystery and yet here he is, wherever this was. She couldn't believe it. This is where he got to, a Changing room.

Jonathan was very good looking, tall and athletic. Leonie examined his gorgeous looking brown hair brushed very neatly and very beautiful clear grey eyes that were complemented by his shiny tanned skin. He looked a bit posh and very intelligent, and he made her feel warm. It was strange seeing him dressed in nineties clothes, but she probably looked strange being from the twenty-tens, although she dressed more eighties style.

She then looked around at the other men standing around her. The English man that spoke also seemed familiar. She then realised that he was the fella who went missing on his way to the toilet at a party. Jamie Young. He looked like the happiest person she'd ever seen. He had dark brown hair that parted in the middle and came down to his chin. His eyes were a darker brown than his hair. For some reason, she couldn't help but notice he was wearing thick white socks in his drift strap sandals under his trousers which looked like they were tailored too much. He also looked very cheeky in a Cody kind of way, and judging by his cheeriness and his sarcastic comment earlier (and the fact that his disappearance also involved a toilet), he *was* the male version of Cody. There were other men around, but Leonie didn't have time to analyse them

"I'm Leonie," Leonie said softly, "Leonie Reine."

"Hello Leonie!" Jamie said, "I'm Jamie!"

Leonie nodded. She wanted to tell Jonathan and Jamie that she knew about them and what happened to them but she was too shy to say. So she just sat there gazing at the ground. She was tearing up a little bit for lots of different reasons but did well to keep the tears from falling from her eyes.

Leonie hated being alone without her family or friends and hated being somewhere she didn't know. She had so many questions she wanted to ask, but every time she wanted to speak, her anxiety got the better of her.

One thing she never thought would happen while looking into all the disappearances and while being sad about her friends disappearing, is she never thought it would happen to her. Not even when Cody vanished. She wondered where they were, all her friends. They weren't in the room. She thought there must be lots of different rooms and they were in another. Then she started questioning how she got there in the first place and remembered the lightning and Shani's face during it. The more she thought about things, the more her eyes watered and she panicked. She wondered whether Shani had vanished too since whomever or whatever is causing all the disappearances seemed to like her and her friends. And her parents too, she couldn't help wonder whether her dad had found out she's gone too and is freaking out. Or perhaps her disappearing is enough for him to go to his boss and slam all his information in his face. She also wondered how long exactly it had been yet.

Leonie managed to pull herself together and focus on what's happening around her instead of what might be happening back home. All the men had backed off a bit to give her some space. Some were chatting on the bench on the other side of the room, some leaning against a wall. Jamie was the only one still sitting next to Leonie. He was talking to a little boy who was about ten or twelve and looked like he was from the 70's.

The two noticed Leonie and Jamie swung around to smile at her again, "this is Warren," He said. Warren smiled at her.

Warren Mitchel. Leonie remembered this kid too. He disappeared in 1973 when he was 11 years old (and 10 months). His bright green eyes and dark brown hair really made him look beautiful and innocent. Leonie noticed he looked a bit sad and scared.

Leonie decided to look around at the other men to see who else she's heard of and immediately recognised Max Clark. He was the man whose bike smashed into the Mustang after he disappeared. He was a tall, thin and serious looking man who had a slight shyness about him as well, and he must have had a bad landing because he had a few bruises on his arms and his nose looked like it had seen better days too. She felt sorry for him because it must've really hurt and she felt bad for laughing about it before.

There was another man, in his fifties that Leonie thought she might have recognised. He had short grey hair (with some evidence that brown once existed), blue eyes and was tall, strong and very intimidating. She thought he must be Leon Tyrell. He was ex-military and became a doctor. He looked very solemn, and Leonie made a note to herself to try and avoid him.

It was a very strange place to be, and Leonie couldn't get her head around it. Nothing made sense so far. These people seemed somewhat relaxed somehow.

"Don't worry," Warren said, possibly sensing how Leonie was feeling, "they haven't come for anyone in years." Leonie gave a confused look that Warren understood, so he explained, "They come and take some people. The guards do. I think they need people for something. You never see them unless they're taking someone. Our food gets delivered through that shaft." Warren pointed at the shaft on the wall. "And if you need the bathroom, you can request permission by speaking into that camera." Warren pointed to the camera on the roof in the corner of the room. "And the door will open to the bathroom. It's only small, and if you spend too long in there, they gas you out."

Jamie interrupted with laughter, "gas you out! Ha! Get it!?"

Warren sighed before continuing, "They haven't taken anyone for ages. Not since Leon arrived, these guys only just came into this room too, not long before you, they were being held in another. I don't know why. In fact, there's not much I do know, but I do know that some people can skip the line to go through though. If they think someone is more important than you, they'll take them first. You could be like me and never get taken in for years because someone better keeps arriving."

Leonie shook her head, unable to take in what the little boy had just said. He was definitely more mature for his age, in fact, Leonie thought he was more mature than many adults, particularly Jamie.

"So you want to get taken?" Jonathan asked.

"Well, I've been here for ages. I think I'm more curious as to what's been going on all this time. What they're doing. Why they're doing it. What they're doing!"

"Why are you still a kid," Leonie burst out. Everyone stared at her in shock. Not only because *how would you know* but more so *hey she talked!* "I mean, you disappeared in nineteen seventy-three, right? Wouldn't you be in your fifties?"

Warren smiled again, "When you hang around as long as me, you get to learn a few things. Ok. All of you – and me – are in like a time freeze."

"A what?" Jamie asked.

"A time freeze. That's what I call it. It's where until you get out of the time freeze, you stay the exact same age as you were when you entered it. I was eleven and ten months, so I am still that age."

"So that's why you're so smart," Clark laughed, "you're still technically eleven – and ten months, sorry – but you've been alive for much longer than that, so you're like, old at heart and full of knowledge."

"That's right," Warren grinned, "couldn't have said it better myself. I ask everyone who comes in what year they vanished as well. Leonie?"

In a shy voice, Leonie replied, "two thousand and thirteen."

"Right, see, everyone who arrives in this room is from a later year each time."

"This information is all going right through me sorry," Jamie said, putting his hands in his hair. *You and me both* Leonie thought. Although she did understand what Warren said, it's just hard to believe it, even though she does, so it's more wondering how it's all possible.

"So Warren," Leon joined in, "Since we all seem interested in talking here. Do you have any idea at all what's going on? Who's doing this and what they want with us?"

"Are they Aliens?" Jonathan asked.

"Well I don't really know," Warren said as he got into a more comfortable sitting position, "I don't know how to answer any of those questions because I don't have the answers. It could be Aliens, I suppose, but I was leaning more towards future humans."

"What do you mean," Leon asked, turning his head a little.

"Well, just a thought. I mean, time freeze, grabbing people from all different time zones. That's all really extreme, even for our time. I think its extreme even for people of the near future. No, I'm talking way, way in the future, humans might be able to do this stuff. And maybe they need us for something."

"Maybe to stop some big mistake we made," Clark suggested.

"Or going to make," Leon said blankly.

"However time travel could exist in our time," Clark explained, "it is a theory, those who know it may just not want to share it with us. It doesn't have to be people from way in the future."

"That's an excellent point, Max," Warren agreed.

Just then, two big doors slid open. Leonie never noticed them before, and by their reactions, neither did anyone else, except for Warren.

Three huge masked men (or Aliens) came through the doors. They wore strange looking armour and the only skin exposed was their thighs, chest, and arms. Everything else was covered either by clothing or armour. The armour was an expensive and impressive looking blue and gold. They walked straight up to Warren and grabbed him.

"I must've finally impressed them," Warren said proudly as he willingly got up and walked off with the guards. The doors didn't close straight away, because the guards came back for Leon and Clark who showed more of a hesitation than Warren, but were curious too, so they eagerly went as well. All that took about two minutes tops and Leonie, Jamie, Jonathan and the other few men were left stunned, confused and worried.

"Well," Jamie said, not taking his eyes off where the doors had been, "Warren seemed positive about it. But what if it doesn't turn out to be something good, and they just want his blood?"

"It's better than staying in here forever," Jonathan pointed out, "we should try and get in there too."

"Why?" Jamie asked, looking nervous.

"Look how long Warren was here for. That could be us."

"Ok then. All we have to do is say something smart."

"Shouldn't be too difficult for you then," Jonathan smirked.

"Hey, hey, now you're the one wanting some help here," Jamie said defensively with his hands in the air again.

"Yeah, yeah, I was just joking. Anyhow, who else is in?"

The other men still had their eyes glued to the door and just made weird grunting noises in response.

"Leonie," Jamie asked, "you wanna get out of here? I know you just got here, but, it's not that exciting, I can assure you."

Leonie took a moment to process what they said before smiling and nodding. This made Jamie and Jonathan cheer.

"Wait," Jamie said before pausing, "what do we do if they *do* want our blood?"

"Panic," Jonathan suggested. Jamie nodded as if Jonathan had just solved all his problems.

"Ok," Jamie said in an overly loud voice so that whatever was watching through the camera could hear them (as if they couldn't hear even a whisper). "People of the future have brought us here for something. Maybe for something we've done. Maybe for something we're going to do. And maybe to take our blood. No matter. We'd like to get in now."

There was a quick, intense silence before all the other men roared with laughter.

"It didn't work," Jamie said looking disappointed.

"And you wonder why?" Jonathan chuckled, "you silly twit. It's obvious to them you just copied what Warren and that said. You didn't learn anything. They're not stupid."

"Actually, I did learn something after Warren told us all that stuff. I didn't know anything about time freezes until he told us. So yeah, I did learn something. I thought I was pretty clever, actually." Jamie said.

"Yes, very clever. But it's not going to work I don't think. I don't think wittiness is the type of smartness they're looking for."

"So they're after academic smartness then?" Jamie asked.

"Common sense smartness," Leonie interrupted, still hesitantly, but too keen to let it stop her, "I think Warren, Leon, and Max had a lot of common sense. I'm not saying we don't, just that they displayed it."

Jonathan nodded and then sat down.

"What are you doing?" Jamie asked.

"Waiting for the moment we display some common sense. It has to come naturally to work."

They spent the rest of the day chatting to one another about themselves. Jamie told Leonie he was a mechanic back in England and also worked in a pub. Jonathan was studying Physics and Computer Science at University and worked part-time in a bookstore and Toys "R" Us. Leonie told them she was in grade twelve and wanted to become a pilot after school. Jamie told her some stories about plane crashes with good intentions but only made her uneasy about her dream.

It wasn't long before the conversations led to sports. Jonathan was a basketball player and a competitive swimmer. He also did Shitō-ryū, a form of Karate.

Jamie played football, "that's all I've ever enjoyed," he had said, "I mean I never understood cricket or anything." This pleased Leonie, apart from the fact that he supported Arsenal like her coach did. They ended up having an hour's long conversation about football and their favourite team, while Jonathan took a nap.

Leonie quickly became friends with Jamie and Jonathan, they seemed like such simple, easy going guys, like she and her friends were. They were the sort of people she liked to be friends with.

When Jonathan woke up, Leonie decided to ask them about what they were doing when they disappeared. She already knew what Jamie was doing, although apparently, he was trying to get away from his ex-girlfriend as well. He described her as a *nutter.*

Jonathan explained how he was being chased by a group of thugs who wanted his money after an attractive receptionist told them about him and his 1984 Camaro Z28 5-speed. – *"Oh, you're 1984 Camaro Z28 5-speed,"* Jamie mocked in a posh voice, "Ooh la la, look at me just casually driving around in my 1984 Camaro Z28 5-speed."

Leonie told them all about what her father, Cody and she had been looking into about the disappearances, and how she thought what everyone was doing at the time they disappeared might have something to do with it.

"Well Clark was a spook, who collaborated with the FBI," Jamie explained, "he knew something he shouldn't have, and people were chasing him. I guess they wanted him to disappear, just not literally like he did."

"What did he know about?" Leonie asked curiously.

"He didn't say," Jamie shrugged, "he doesn't give away too much. I'm actually surprised he told us what he did. But it must have been serious if they wanted to take him out for knowing about it."

"And Leon," Jonathan said suddenly, "he told me he was leaving a pub when he saw an old military friend who was thought to be dead."

"And he attacked him or something?" Leonie questioned, half knowing the answer.

"Well, he was an *old* friend. Yes. He went a bit crazy, murdering innocent people and they left him in a place they were going to bomb. But it turns out he escaped. And wasn't too happy about it."

"He told you all this?" Jamie asked looking astonished.

"Not all of it. Clark told me about the bombing. He's a spook after all."

"Well I know Warren was hiding under his dad's desk in his office while he was being yelled at by his boss," Leonie informed, looking back and forth at Jamie and Jonathan, "I thought maybe something happened, and he had to run. Did he say anything to you?"

There were a few moments of silence before Jamie asked, "What about you, Leonie? What were you and all your friends doing?"

She told them about Stacey, Camilla and Tracy disappearing during the murder in the dark and about how Cody disappeared on the toilet (Jamie chuckled) and then how she had disappeared when running from Camilla's angry dad.

"But wait," Leonie gasped, "most of what all you were running from was serious, except for Jamie," –

"Yeah well, you don't know her! She's nuts!" –

"Anyway. Cody wasn't running from anyone. She was sitting on the toilet. And even my other friends. That wasn't too serious, it's just murder in the dark."

"Yeah, I've played that," Jamie announced, "with a real murder. Well, we were all drunk."

"I don't really think it has anything to do with what anyone was running from," Jonathan stated, ignoring Jamie, "I think they're just choosing important people. If they really are from the future, maybe they know what we're all capable of in the future and want to use us for themselves. Or, maybe they want to stop us from doing something in the future like Clark and Leon said."

"Hey, that's smart, Jono! Maybe you'll get taken now." Jamie laughed. And only about three seconds later, the door slid open again, and the same guards walked in, "Oh look at that, I must be psychic! The guards will now set me free and give me one million dollars!"

Jonathan punched Jamie in the shoulder then took a gulp of air and seemed to be bracing himself for whatever would be behind those doors. Hopefully, it's none of the things that Jamie suggested where they take your blood, dissect you, eat you or torture you.

But the guards didn't go towards a prepared Jonathan. Instead, they approached a not nearly ready Leonie.

Chapter 6:

Leonie panicked and squirmed as one of the guards picked her up and threw her over his shoulder as easily as she would a stuffed toy. Jamie, Jonathan and the other men looked just as confused as she was. She didn't say anything smart, it was Jonathan. Maybe they were wrong about this, maybe they just pick you at random, when they want you.

Jonathan and Jamie were yelling at the guards and trying to retrieve Leonie from the guard's strong grip. It was useless, mainly because it only caused Leonie pain as the guard forced his grip even more. One of the other guards kicked Jamie really hard in the side, and he went flying across the room. Leonie looked up at Jamie who looked really hurt and winded and curled up into a ball, but he still managed to keep his funny cheery facial expression. Meanwhile, Jonathan had given up on trying to help Leonie and tried to dart through the door but was caught by one of the guards who picked him up by the scruff of the shirt and threw him across the room where he landed next to a dazed Jamie.

As if none of that had happened, the guards casually left the room with Leonie hung over one of the guards shoulder.

Fear ran through her over and over again. She had a similar feeling as she did when going on a roller coaster that goes upside-down for the first time, unsure whether it was going to be good or bad. The things that Jamie had said about Aliens, taking your blood and dissecting you made her chuckle a bit before. But now she felt scared. She was afraid that all of those things would come to pass.

What happened next was a complete blur. She could only remember parts of it. She was lying on a metal bench similar to what they use in an autopsy. She was in a round room full of terrifying medical equipment she prayed she'd never have to see. Most of it was extremely advanced, and she had no idea what any of it was for, but she didn't exactly want to find out.

The mad scientist was the scariest out of everything in the room. He was a creepy looking man with dark brown hair which was long at the front with very fair skin. She didn't get a good look at his eyes, but she noticed his really long nose. He dressed in light blue jeans, a black business shirt, and a brown cowboy hat which he removed and replaced with a surgical cap. He was a cowboy scientist, only his long white jacket with pens in the front pocket made him look a bit like a typical scientist. Leonie knew that if she and Cody had seen a picture of him back home, they would have laughed and seen him as a joke. But in real life he made chills go down her spine. He is the type of person you would avoid making eye contact with as you walk past him in public. He's the sort of person you don't want to be alone with, and she's stuck to a table by what she just realised to be leather Velcro straps which are surprisingly difficult to get out of. Yes, she's tried. He had a small chilling smile that she knew she would never forget. Leonie made it clear to herself that she was going to die, probably in a horrible way. This is what made the tears roll down her face. He never said anything, which made him seem scarier.

She didn't remember much else. Although she was sure, he injected a needle into her a few times, and at another time she saw some bloody instruments like scalpel's leaving her body. But she felt no pain.

When Leonie woke up next, she felt like she had been out of it for ages. She felt a bit strange and bleary, probably because of all the drugs they probably gave her, she thought.

She was in another room with walls that had a glowing grey, and she wasn't sure whether the floor was just a big hole she could fall through, so she stayed on the bed that hung from a chain. She slowly looked around the room, until she came to a statue of what she believed to be Sekhmet.

She got out of the tiny bed and wearily walked towards the statue. She couldn't focus properly, and her vision was blurry. As she reached out to touch the statue, it disappeared, and instead, the Mad Scientist stood there looking serene and warm.

As he held out his hand, Leonie automatically took it, and he guided her out of the room. They walked down several glowing corridors before stopping so she could vomit on a poor man with a clipboard and then he led her into a room where she found Warren.

Warren was sitting on a really nice leather lounge with a glass of cold water. He was watching some sort of advanced 4D screen that floated in the air and was screening a horrible war that Leonie had never seen before, but it looked real.

Warren managed to jump out of the way in time as Leonie collapsed onto the lounge. She needed to lie down while the drugs wore off and she could gather her bearings. Then all the confusion would hit her, and she would have many questions to ask.

The Mad Scientist had a brief conversation with Warren -that Leonie couldn't understand because she wasn't with it and they were too quiet- and then he left the room after one last glance at Leonie. Leonie caught the glance and couldn't work out whether he was mocking her because she was spread out gracelessly on the couch in her disgusting white fifties themed nighty, or if he was feeling sorry for her state. But she wondered how he could feel sorry for her when he was the one who did it, whatever it was.

Warren kneeled down beside Leonie's face, and Leonie looked up at him with serious eyes and a numb mouth with her tongue hanging out like a dog.

Warren gave a small, caring smile and said, "Don't worry. I know everything will be okay."

Leonie tried to mutter a sarcastic *thank you,* but it ended up sounding like "Dinkuuu" because of her numb mouth.

Leonie stopped looking at Warren, but accepted the cold glass of water he poured for her with a straw. They spent the next hour or so sitting in silence.

Leonie's head was about to explode. The silence had only made her mind race with millions of different thoughts and feelings every minute. It was so full of information that made no sense, as well as confusion, anger, anxiety, and sorrow. She wanted to throw the glass of water across the room, and because the grogginess was wearing off, she feared she might.

She took a much needed big deep breath and thought of happy moments with her friends who she missed so much. *They must be safe* she thought as she recalled memories of them.

Last year the girls spent an entire day at the arcade in Bundaberg. Cody spent most of the time car racing and got a sore bottom. Leonie always thought Cody was such a goofball yet so full of life and despite her rough manner, she had a pure heart.

Leonie, on the other hand, spent most of the day shooting bad guys. Camilla tried too but ended up furiously throwing her gun at the screen and then got thrown out by the manager and spent the rest of the day in the food court.

Leonie didn't really know why she thought about this day above all others; she guessed it was just really happy and simple. They were just four teenagers having a good time at the arcade, and that was better than where she was now.

She played air hockey with Stacey several times, followed by basketball. Leonie remembered the basketball coming back and hitting her fair and square in the face. She chuckled at the memories of that day – Warren looked confused – especially at the sight of Cody finally getting off the racing game with a numb bum and then getting attacked by a self-serve slushy machine.

It was quite difficult to think of her friends after what she had just been through. She worried that perhaps they were suffering worse than what she was, being tested on or whatever and not having a clue why. She imagined their smiling faces from memories like that day at the arcade, and she knew that wherever they were at that moment, they weren't smiling at all.

She ended up giving in to her exhaustion and slept for a while. When she woke up, young Warren was still there in the same spot, he had been making origami and playing Sudoku.

"How are you feeling," He asked. Leonie felt weird being counselled by an eleven-year-old but tried to remember the fact that he's old and wise one the inside, in a way. "I know it is scary, but you must understand that things aren't always what they seem. Sometimes for things to be good, it's better not to say."

"That makes no sense," Leonie said, trying to keep a calm voice for the little boy that she sees sake. "I was always raised to tell the truth no matter how bad or insane."

"But if you're told the truth now, you will go insane."

Leonie couldn't think of anything else to say. She just shook her head and then buried it in her hands. She felt stressed out and almost wanted to punch a hole in the wall. But Leonie always looked for an easier way to handle things than giving into anger.

There was something about Warren though that did calm her and she really wanted to trust him. That's why she allowed him to accompany her when she was called to another room (along with some guards). She had to enter alone because the gas only needed to knock her out.

It was exactly the same as before when the mad scientist stuck needles into her and goodness knows what else. Her body was paralysed so she couldn't move or fight and her mind was affected by the gas so she mainly just sang and pretended to be a butterfly.

Leonie nicknamed him the mad scientist, but she thought when and if she caught up with Cody soon that she could think of a better nickname.

After Leonie had come back to her senses she was led into a room with more stupid scientists with clipboards, apparently to assess her. This was when Leonie noticed a change in herself, she felt different and acted differently.

They served her up an ice-cream which she scooped up with her spoon and slung it at the man with glasses face and turned her nose up at the ice-cream. They brought out some more along with some pizza, and she then ate it as if she forgot about everything that had happened since she first got taken. The truth was, it was still in her head somewhere, but for about ten minutes, she didn't give a damn about the mad scientist or anything.

Leonie was confused when they said she was perfect.

They gave her and Warren clearance to go somewhere and were led into a hall filled with three long tables with many people sitting and eating at each. The guards took them to the end of one of the tables where they found Jamie munching away on a chicken carcass (that was cooked), Jonathan was next to him eating fish and vegetables, Leon was cutting up a nice, well-done steak with chips and Clark was halfway through a lasagne. They all looked up at the same time, and their expressions changed from shock to happiness to see them. Jamie yelled something joyful to them, but Leonie couldn't understand with all that chicken still in his mouth. They all looked like they had lots to ask them both but decided to keep quiet when Leonie was served up a special meal. Pizza, a proper one. It had three sections with lots of nice stuff. Leonie didn't know everything it had but noticed some notable toppings. One had zucchini and cheese. One had basil leaves and mushroom. The other part was her favourite, chilly and pepperoni. Jamie eyed her pizza off the whole time she ate it.

Warren was served up a plate of fruit and nuts.

Leonie scanned the room several times with the hope that maybe Cody and the others were there. But they weren't, and it was mainly men in the hall scoffing down their food.

Finally, Jonathan leaned in and whispered, "so what happened to you two? What did they do?"

"Shh," Clark hissed, "I don't think we're supposed to know."

"I don't even know," Leonie said softly as she sipped her cup of water.

After everyone ate, there was no time to chat before they were forcefully pushed along by the guards. Leonie, Warren, Jonathan, Jamie, Clark, Leon and another man called Dean were shoved into a tiny room which seemed to serve no purpose as there was nothing in there. On the other side of the room was a tiny opening to a normally sized corridor.

A guard pointed impatiently to the opening and one by one they entered it and edgily walked down the long passage. Their footsteps echoed down the corridor, and everyone jumped when Clark accidentally knocked over a random vase. When they got to another similar room, they all looked confused at what was laid out for them.

Clothes, the sort you wear when out in the bush. There was a black singlet, a green jacket and black cargo pants along with some hiking boots. Leonie and Warren were happy about changing from their white nighties; the others look annoyed but still changed into them. Leonie didn't even care that she was technically wearing men's clothes.

As soon as they were dressed, there was a flicker of the lights which sent Dean into a panic, and he tried to run away. As he ran back down the hall between the two small rooms, he vanished.

Leonie breathed heavily as fear ran through her. Another disappearance, where do they go this time? She wondered. And where is *she* going?

Chapter 7:

A guard appeared in the room and grabbed Jonathan and pushed him towards a small door, big enough for a small toddler to walk through. The guard bent down and opened the door and Jonathan decided to try and attack him. But the guard was monstrously big and strong and anticipating his move, he grabbed him by the stomach, turned him sideways and threw him through the little door.

Leonie realised it must be a slide. *"Where the heck does this lead?"* She thought, well rather she panicked.

The guard chuckled a bit at Jonathan's slight, heartless, dull screaming and then turned to Jamie, who waved him away put his hands up willingly into the air and then dived headfirst into the slide from a metre away (Leonie knew he wouldn't try anything with the guard). He woohoo'd for ages before his voice faded.

Clark and Leon went next, almost on top of each other. Warren looked slightly concerned so Leonie – Who was also scared and didn't want to go alone – sat him on her lap as they went down the slide that was very long. It would've been a hit at McDonald's for all the kids, but here it was weird, and she hoped she didn't land into a water hole full of sharks or crocodiles or both.

Instead, they landed hard on a dirt ground after what felt like ages of sliding. Leonie's bottom hit a sharp rock that really hurt upon landing.

Jamie helped Leonie up while the others were gobsmacked by where they were. When Leonie dusted herself off and rubbed her sore bum wound, she too was in awe of the big beautiful place they were in.

They were on a large dirt hill (with rocks) In front of a large rock where the slide came out of, somehow. They could see a fair way away. There was jungle as far as the eye could see. It was so beautiful with many different colours including many shades of green. It wasn't the sort of place you'd expect to be killed or tortured.

"Maybe we took a wrong turn," Jamie finally said.

"On a slide?" Jonathan asked, "I didn't see any split ways."

"Where do you suppose we are?" Clark asked, specifically to Leon, "I don't see any guards. Maybe we could find a nearby town and call for help."

"Son," Leon said, "I've been all around the world, and I've never seen any place like this. The trees somehow clash. I've never seen any of these trees together before."

Leonie didn't know much about trees, but they didn't seem like the sort in the pictures of jungles she's seen. Some were normal but Leon was right, it looked like some inexperienced gardener picked a lot of nice looking trees and without thinking planted them all together. Although it was very pretty and they all seemed to fit well together in beauty. She couldn't quite work it out.

Leon continued, "I don't recognise this jungle at all. It's not right."

This news worried everyone. If it's confusing to survival experts like Leon, Leonie thought, and a survival expert is their best chance for them all to survive. Then they're screwed. So it's not a good thing for him to be confused.

"We'd better get moving," Leon said, "I can sort of see an opening down that way at two o'clock. So we'll try there."

"What time is it now?" Jamie asked before everyone glared at him, "What? I want to know how long until it's two o'clock, dummies."

They carefully made their way down the hill behind Leon. He had given them all a few words of advice and comfort. He made partners. Leonie was with Warren, Jonathan with Jamie because Clark was with Leon. He told them all to try and stick together but to make sure that they at least stay with their partner. He also told them all to relax and to not panic which made Jamie laugh sarcastically.

Once they were walking through the jungle, they spotted a few different plants that Leon wasn't sure of and warned everyone to stay clear of.

They passed a few ginormous spiders in spider webs so Leonie made sure to walk behind Jonathan who was tall and would clear the spider web path for her.

It was quite peaceful though, walking through the jungle - despite the spider webs. Warren had also pointed out a large white coloured python – it was very nice listening to the birds chirp and the wind in the trees. They even heard a stream somewhere which was good news. It was probably because she was so scared that Leonie looked for ways to comfort her. Hearing birds was always an easing noise. The key to survival is not to panic and to keep control of your mind, at least she thinks that's what Bear Grylls said.

They reached a slight opening which had the stream they were looking for right in the centre of it. Jamie and Clark were eager to get to the stream, but Leon put his arm out to stop them as he listened for something.

Leonie watched his face for any kind of sign. His eyes squinted, he slowly gazed around in front of them.

"What is it?" Warren asked, looking tired and thirsty.

"Shh," Jonathan hissed.

Leon took a few steps forward after taking his arm down from Jamie's stomach, but his body language still signalled something wasn't right. So everyone else watched Leon closely and waited.

Leon kept walking cautiously slow until he was right at the edge of the stream. It was then that the rest of them knew what he could hear. Leonie was shocked that Leon knew it well before anyone else. She knew he was great at what he did, but she thought he must have the ears of a dog.

There was a bush on the other side of the stream with something in it. It sounded like something quite large. Leon stood still and watched the bush with his hawk eyes. Jamie, on the other hand, was hiding behind Clark with his eyes wide open and trembling slightly.

After a few minutes, a very large wild Boar emerged from the bush and took off along the stream. Jamie was about to start laughing with relief when Leon hurried back to join them.

"What was it running from?" Jonathan asked.

"Exactly why I came back," Leon nodded, "Boars are very intelligent and shy. I think it just made a very wise decision."

Leonie gulped. That meant that something scary was coming. Only moments later, a sort of Antelope came charging out from the same bushes. It almost made it to the stream when a large Siberian Tiger proved to be faster and stronger.

Leonie turned Warren away from the gore while the men seemed mesmerised by it.

"Incredible," Leon said, "a Siberian Tiger attacking an Impala."

"What? Is it usually the other way around?" Jamie asked looking horrified.

"No," Jonathan said, "they should be in two completely different places."

"I beg your pardon?" Jamie asked as everyone slowly walked away up the stream.

"An Impala lives in the African wild," Leon explained, "and a Siberian Tiger is in Russia."

"Wow," Jamie beamed, "One of them got lost."

After all that the Siberian Tiger was suddenly spooked and ran away from its kill. Everyone tucked behind the rock and peered over to what was heading towards the dead Impala. Everyone shrieked, and Leon almost yelled in disbelief and excitement, "it can't be! No way. What? Guys, I don't believe it. Do you know what that is? It's not possible."

"What the hell is it?" Jamie asked in fear, "a lion? Or a tiger? Or both? I don't know."

"I believe"- Clark started before Leon interrupted.

"It's a Saber-Toothed Cat."

"Aren't they extinct?" Jamie asked.

"Yeah but this place is nuts," Leon replied, "wow it must've spooked the tiger. It'll come back though."

"I'm spooked by its teeth," Jamie cried.

"We better go," Leon said, "things could get nasty. I'm not an expert, but mixing animals from different times and places isn't going to end well at all."

"Not to mention adding the worst animal of all," Clark added, "humans."

"Oh blah blah," Jamie said as they all made a stealthy retreat.

Nothing more was said for a while because Leon was more worried about finding some shelter, protection, and water and hopefully some food.

Leon and Clark made some sort of bowls out of goodness knew what and filled them up with water from the stream after checking up further to make sure no dead animals were contaminating it. They each carried one ready for when they found a fire to boil it. Leon explained after Warren and Jamie wanted to drink it, that as soon as rainwater touches the surface, it's contaminated. Leonie was so thirsty, and Leon explained she was already dehydrated if she was that thirsty. Leon had managed to quickly make a spear as well and planned to make more with some extra sticks for everyone else once they had somewhere safe for the night.

They found a cave, to Leonie's horror. Nothing freaked her out more than a dark cave especially when they've encountered spiders, snakes, and tigers in such a short amount of time.

Leon threw a few large rocks into the cave to hopefully scare out any animals that might be inside. Once it was deemed safe, Leon was quick to rush everyone into their jobs he had assigned to them. This included Leonie, she had no time to fall apart because she and Jonathan were making spears and monitoring the boiling water. Warren was out with Clark gathering more wood, and poor Leon was with Jamie to try and find some food. Jamie lived on a farm and killed his own animals, so he had no problem with facing an African antelope. Leonie wouldn't be surprised if Leon himself had killed a bear with his fists.

"How are you coping?" Jonathan asked as he reached for his third stick, "I know I'm really confused and probably gonna go as nuts as Jamie soon."

Leonie chuckled, "Yeah same. Nothing has made sense to me for months. Not since my friends first disappeared. I've been hoping to find them here, but, I guess that's not going to happen."

"Well. If they're anything like you, I'm sure they're doing just fine."

"They're nothing like me," Leonie said shaking her head, "They're brave and smart. They're not so, nervous or shy. They

71

don't freak out if they're left alone. They can cope much better than me."

"Is that so?" Jonathan looked sideways at her, "I think you're doing just fine, Leonie. Look around you. Everything here is nonsense, and yet you're still quite calm and collected. We will find out what's going on. I promise."

Leonie smiled at Jonathan. This seemed to relax her a bit more. She believed Jonathan. He was just the sort of person who was pure and knew what to say and when to say it. Leonie's dad was exactly like that. If someone's head was all fuzzy and they didn't know what to do, one sentence from her dad cleared their mind and would set them back on track.

The next day, Leon had them up reasonably early. All he and Jamie managed to catch was fish. But Leonie loved fish, so she was fine. Apparently, Jamie found some chickens, but he couldn't catch any.

After they were walking back down the stream, they saw the same half a dozen or so chickens that Jamie had tried to catch. Immediately, Jamie was off running around trying to catch one. It was rather hilarious to watch. He was like a little kid running around after them. "Here chook, chook! Come on!" He'd say before falling over several times. Everyone laughed at the idiot, including Leon who eventually caught one within five seconds of trying. Jamie ended up being chased by an angry Rooster who came out of nowhere to defend his ladies.

Without really realising, they all learnt a lot that day. Leon found several different plants that didn't belong in the same country. They saw a few more unusual fights. There was one intense fight between a Eurasian Lynx and a Leopard. Also, an Elephant was charging at a Grizzly Bear. There was one sane fight between two pelicans though. This was at a lake they found. It was a huge lake with crystal clear water, just outside of the jungle they were in. There were mountains on the other side and massive big trees.

Jamie was at the end of the lake cheering on the pelicans, so the others sat down on some rocks and discussed their theories. Clark was on watch.

"This isn't right," Leon said straight away. "I think we're in some kind of enclosure or something. That's got to be it, and some scientist is experimenting with animals and plants being able to live in the same place. So we need to try and find the end. It can't be that big."

"Yeah! Go Peli one!" Jamie cheered over by the lake.

"So, it's kind of like *Jurassic Park*?" Clark asked.

"There better not be any bloody dinosaurs!" Jamie called out, "Otherwise that's me out, done."

"Why would they put some random people in an enclosure with wild animals?" Jonathan asked with a slight touch of anger in his voice, "Seems a little extreme and it's weird for the amount of effort they've put into capturing us, just for this. How did they manage to make us disappear like that? It's unheard of."

"There is a lot the Government doesn't tell us," Clark smirked, shaking his head from over by a big tree.

Leon had a quick word with Jonathan about something. Warren came and sat down next to Leonie. He was looking a bit more serene than before. They both watched Jamie and the two pelicans.

"What a moron," Leonie cackled at Jamie. She couldn't stop thinking about how much he reminded her of Cody. It was almost like he was her long lost twin. She also couldn't stop imagining if her friends were in this world too and had encountered some tigers or bears.

Suddenly, out of nowhere Leonie's heart nearly jumped out of her chest as a giant set of jaws leapt out of the water and grabbed the two pelicans and pulled them back down. It scared Jamie more than anyone else as he had only been about two feet away from the pelicans when the large Great White shark snatched them. "Shit!" Jamie had yelled as he bolted away from the lake like a rocket.

Leonie swiftly turned to Leon, Jonathan, and Clark who looked like mad people who had finally spotted an Alien they had been searching years for.

"When you think you've seen it all," Clark said quietly, "you think there can't possibly be anything crazier, and then a massive shark leaps out of a lake and almost has Jamie for lunch."

The three men cracked up laughing, and Leonie and Warren grinned too. Jamie stomped over pulling faces at them.

"Oh, haha!" he said sarcastically, "I'm glad you think it's funny. That bastard ate my two friends!"

"Okay everyone," Jonathan yelled as he patted Jamie on the back, "stay right away from that lake! And find Jamie a new pair of underwear, if you can."

Leon was cooking three chickens he had caught while Jonathan and Clark stirred Jamie up over how he ran like a girl before. Then, Leon shushed them when he heard something again. This time Leonie and the others heard it almost at the same time as he did. It sounded like many men yelling, and it even sounded like there were a few vehicles. Leonie stood up and tried to look up over the hill just ahead to see what it was. Whatever it was, it was getting closer and was making Leonie very nervous.

Chapter 8:

At the front was an army vehicle with a gun placed on the top slowly heading down the hill towards them. Behind them was a mixture of many different people. Some were on horses and wore old-fashioned military gear that Leonie had learned about during history class, and some were cavemen with machine guns.

There seemed to be a hundred of them all travelling in lines. It was somewhat a relief when the man in the passenger's seat of the military vehicle got out and smiled when they parked in front of them. He went over and shook Leon's hand.

"Tyrell," the man said, "It's been a long time, my friend."

"I was looking for you," Leon replied, "when I came here it crossed my mind that I might find you lurking around somewhere as you disappeared a couple of months back. Here you are with your own army."

"Yes. It's been quite a journey. But we should probably head back to base. There's a lot to tell you, my friend." It didn't take much convincing to leave with Leon's friend's army, not with what they've seen in their short time in the place.

Leonie got to ride on the back of a horse with a huge man. He wasn't fat, but he was built like a tank, although he was quite friendly and complimented her golden mane-like hair she had in her usual bun.

After about half an hour - or however long it takes to get a really sore bottom from sitting on a horse – they reached their camp. It was very nicely set up, and they did well especially if they arrived there like they did without any equipment.

They had many green tents set up. They were mainly small ones for only a few people, but they did have a few larger tents for the boss's to have meetings and to organise things. There was also a large medic tent because they get many casualties from wild animals and Leonie heard something about other groups of people.

First, the people got everyone something to eat and drink and gave them five-ten minutes before Leon's friend, whose name was Brian Hanson came in to talk.

They sat in one of the big tents on some wooden chairs. Brian was standing in front of them, and there were some other people gathered around too.

"First," Brian said seriously, lifting his gut to fit between his chair and the table, "I want to make it very clear that no matter how long any of us have been here. We know the what's and things but none of us are certain of the why's. Everything that we know comes from years of living here."

Warren put his hand up, and Brian let him speak, "I think I know something about what's going on."

"Well young man. Go for it."

Warren stood up on his chair in front of everyone and spoke confidently and enthusiastically. "I know about the time freeze and how I should be in my fifties, I think. I believe we're still in that time freeze right now."

"That's correct," said a lady of about twenty. She was standing next to a man, "I was taken from my home when I was twenty-two along with my husband here. The year was eighteen fifty-three, yet here we are still the same age. We have been around for a long time, could have had many lives."

"It is not too bad though," her husband explained, "I mean if you think about it. We're still young, but we've lived!"

Many other things were explained. Everything fascinated Leonie. They explained how the lighter green areas of jungle, forests, and land were safer than the dark green ones. There's something in the lighter greenery that the animals don't really like. So you're more than likely going to encounter a predator such as a bear or a wolf in the jungles or any place with the darker colours. It's the same in water. There's something in the lighter coloured water that animals like sharks and eels don't like so they stick to the dark coloured water. It reminded Leonie of her neighbours trying to stop her dogs from digging in one part of her garden, so she put some stuff there to deter them from it. Leonie wondered what it was.

Thankfully, animals like butterflies, birds, horses, even Zebras can still go into the lighter part. And little fish, Dolphin's and Dugongs can still go into the lighter coloured parts of water.

Everyone had to work, whether it is hunting or gathering food and other necessities. The rules were weird because all the people in charge were from different time frames. They weren't really told much else, that's Leonie, Warren, Jonathan, and Jamie. Leon and Clark seemed to be part of the leaders club and got to speak with all the leaders more.

Warren made a good point to Leonie on the way to their new tent home, "Why is Leon's friend a leader here if there are people who have been here longer? And suddenly Leon and Max are given top positions too?"

Leonie and Warren were going out that day with some expert hunter called Biff, a really tall strong guy from the 1700's. Jonathan and Jamie were coming too. Leonie really wanted to stay behind with Leon and Clark to find out more about what the heck was going on. She could tell the others felt the same way, but all of them didn't want to argue with Biff, the giant.

On the way out of the camp, a ruffled looking cat hissed at Leonie and then took off like a flash.

It was a very nice walk with lots of nice views. The unusual greenery mix never got boring and could easily distract them from danger like the big Black Panther that Leonie noticed after a while lying in a tree, watching them as they passed by. Leonie thought it had some human features on its face but was more worried about getting as far away as possible from the big black cat than to really care about its looks. It was beautiful though.

They had to walk through a stinky creek which made them nervous. Jamie mentioned what was on everyone's mind, "what strange animal that's not supposed to be in here are we going to find brushing against our legs? I'd actually prefer an anaconda than some giant creek Octopus."

"Shut up Jamie you big girl," Jonathan chuckled.

Finally, they came to some open African looking fields. At first, Leonie noticed a log on the ground in the long grass a little further in front of them, but then Biff pointed out that it was, in fact, a baby Giraffe that was hidden by its mother from predators that were probably nearby. So Biff led them away from the infant. After about fifty metres or so, Leonie looked back to find that the baby Giraffe was being dragged away by a Lioness and its mother was looking helplessly on. This really got to Leonie, it was worse to see something like that in real life than on TV at home.

After about twenty minutes or so, they settled down to watch Biff hunt. He told them that as soon as he killed the antelope, they'd have to be quick to help him get it back before someone tries to steal it. Apparently, Lions steal your kill if they find it and they do that all the time to Cheetahs. Biff also thought it would be interesting to tell them about a fight he saw between a Panda and a Hyena.

Jonathan and Jamie both fainted after seeing how Biff caught the antelope. It literally was like Biff was an animal and caught it with his bare hands and beat it to death. Leonie and Warren were too weak to help carry it, but Biff was so strong he didn't even need help anyway. They headed back to the camp through a forest with tall trees with Jonathan and Jamie trailing along behind.

Leonie wanted to ask Biff a lot about his time, but she was absolutely terrified of him so kept her mouth shut.

Warren had been quiet for a long time, so Leonie decided to talk to him instead.

"I miss home so much," Leonie sighed, "I bet you do."

"Not really."

"No?" Leonie looked surprised.

"No. It wasn't that nice. My dad worked for a criminal. He was about to kill him when I came here. I'm glad I didn't get to hear it…" Warren paused for a second, "I am sad though that my dad died too early," Warren said suddenly, "I mean he won't have much to share now in his talk."

"What do you mean?" Leonie asked curious and confused.

"Well, he always told me that when we die, we go to this place, it's like a big palace maybe, and all our family and pets are there, and we all catch up with one another and celebrate. He said life is just an experience we have and a chance to attain a good story to tell our relatives when we die."

"I see," Leonie said, "and what happens after you've all told your stories? What will you do for an eternity after that?"

"Oh Leonie," Warren sighed, "there's always more relatives waiting to join and tell their stories. It's never-ending."

"It's an interesting theory," Leonie said. It sort of touched her as it was a reminder that Warren *was* still a young, innocent kid after all. Even though he is as intelligent as they come and as grown up as possible. "Thanks for sharing that with me, Warren."

"I think it just helps me cope with the loss of family." Warren said before turning back to his serious face, "However, I am a man of science still."

Leonie didn't get time to react to what she just heard from the young boy because most of the trees around them were blasted and fell to the ground nearly squashing them. She couldn't hear or see anything for a moment except she could see dust and branches flying past her. After it cleared up, to her horror, a large silver, metal machine flew past with huge guns on both sides and a large laser gun on top. Several animals that ran by got disintegrated along with a person who she couldn't quite recognise in time. Someone grabbed Leonie and pulled her through all the dust and leaves, running. She didn't get a good look at who was with her due to the thick bushes and branches; she did catch a glimpse of their long black hair a few times. They ran for their lives until finally, the path stopped and Leonie fell off a large cliff into a big rock pool with a great thud. Leonie immediately jumped back up, she felt really disorientated and saw lots of stars. The sound that the loud machine was possibly getting closer encouraged Leonie to keep running. She slipped a few times as her feet were wet from the rock pool. The person who allegedly helped her before was nowhere in sight. In fact, no one was in sight, no animals. Just the loud noise of whatever that machine was.

After looking back to see if anything was behind her, Leonie somehow ran into a few dark yellow branches of a small tree, which stopped her in her tracks. It was horrible. Not the pain of running into the branches, but the slime that the branches were covered in burnt like crazy. It was stuck all in her long golden hair and all over her face, arms and chest. Steam came out of her burns. She became hysterical. It hurt excruciatingly for what felt like ages before it all stopped, and Leonie collapsed to the ground.

Chapter 9:

L eonie woke up moaning and groaning which was imitated
back to her by Jamie with a smile. Leonie jumped before
looking around and saw that Leon was there as well. They both
looked happy to see her as though she was an old friend.

She was in a hospital ward somehow; she was one of two out
of six potential patients in the beds. The other had their curtains
drawn. She had no idea how she got into a hospital, or really
any idea why she was there.

"How you feeling kid," Leon beamed, "you've had a rough
start to this game haven't you?"

"Yeah poor Clark has a horrible laceration to his left arm,"
Jamie said, "It's disgusting and nasty, but at least he wasn't
unconscious for four days."

"Four days?" Leonie asked softly.

"Well ten really, you were unconscious then came round for
a few days, a bit of Morphine, then you went downhill again
suddenly. None of the doctors had ever seen anything like it
before."

"Wow. What about the others?"

"Yeah don't worry," Leon said reassuringly, "Everyone's fine,
just those guards testing a new toy to everyone else's expense."

"Where are we?"

We're at the edge of this park or whatever it is. Turns out
Hanson and the others back at the camp we were staying at are

working as farmers for the guards here. They give them food and things in exchange for equipment they use for research."

"Research for what?" Leonie asked as she started to wake up a bit.

"Research to help us get out of here," Leon said blankly, "the guards are letting them try and work out how to escape."

"It's not a nice place this Leonie," Jamie sighed, "It feels like someone's opened us up in a box and placed us in a world and playing with us like I used to with Lego."

"Who is?" Leonie asked all confused.

"The guards and whoever they work for," Jamie replied impatiently. Leonie remembered the mad scientist.

"It's been a horrific couple of days," Leon said as he sat on a chair next to Leonie's bed, "Warren's working with the research team, the little trooper, and apparently, they've made some kind of breakthrough. Unfortunately for you, you walked into something bad."

Leonie tried to lift her head up but couldn't, "what do you mean? What happened, I can't remember, just that we were running."

"We're not supposed to tell her yet," Jamie mumbled.

"Well I'm sorry, but I can't wait I want to get back to the camp so we can get the hell out of here. I like you kid, but we don't know each other too well at the moment. So here it is. You walked into some tree branch, and the slimy stuff on it burnt some of your skin and hair off, and the rest of your hair had to be shaved off."

"Lovely," Jamie said sarcastically as he applauded, "Well done, you'd make a wonderful dad."

Leonie's eyes widened, and she demanded a mirror. Leon snatched one off Jamie who was trying to hide it and handed it to Leonie.

After wisely taking a deep breath, Leonie slowly raised the mirror her face. It was pretty awful. There was a horrible burn scar right around her left eye and travelled narrowly down her left cheek a bit. There was evidence of more burns on her face but had healed dramatically.

"Some of the future doctors used some technology and were able to repair a lot of it," Leon explained, "and they were even able to save the eyesight in your left eye. But even in the future, there are still complications."

Leonie moved the mirror further up to her head where she saw all her hair was completely gone. There was more evidence of burn marks that were healing on her head. Her right arm had a massive burn as bad as the one around her left eye. It trailed all the way from her shoulder to mid forearm. Her left arm had some more healing burns as did her chest.

Leonie said nothing for a while, but eventually, she decided to ask, "why could they not heal the two burns on my face and arm for?"

"Not sure," Jamie shrugged looking annoyed with himself, "my guess is they ran out of batteries or medication or something."

Leonie sat on her bed and stared down at her crossed legs. Jamie gave her a long warm hug and was very empathetic, while Leon gave her a pat on the shoulder and smiled a little.

The Doctor, a small, timid man, came in later to see how Leonie was going. She asked him if her hair would ever grow back again and he told her it most likely would not. When she asked questions about the tree, he told her a team of scientists was currently testing samples from it and that no one had any idea what the tree was or why it causes such horrific burns. Apparently, no one in this place had ever run into a tree before.

Leon decided to head back to camp after the doctor finished speaking with them. He was determined to find a way out.

Leonie still had to stay in the facility for a while to rest, so Jamie stayed behind with her. They mainly played cards and exchanged funny stories about their lives. Jamie made her feel comfortable and never mentioned her new look. When they had nothing to do they played with the buttons on Leonie's bed to make it go up and down and folded her head and legs up, so she was sandwiched together. Jamie got into trouble from the nurses a few times for playing with some wheelchairs and sneaking Leonie some food. At one time Leonie accidentally called Jamie Cody.

Leonie didn't know why (maybe because of whatever medication was being injected into her via IV) but she didn't seem too bothered by what had happened to her. Perhaps she's holding on to some hope that this place isn't real and just a really weird dream.

After looking at herself again in the mirror for a while, Jamie, who was asleep all curled up uncomfortably looking in an armchair next to the bed, woke up and started cracking all his bones back into place. Yuck.

"So was it a great party you were at," Leonie asked, "apart from when you ran into your ex."

"Huh?" Jamie said as he released his wedgie, "Oh. Yeah, it was alright, you know, just another wasted night after a crap day at my terrible job."

"So what's your dream job then?"

"Forensic Scientist," Jamie said proudly, "I think I'd be quite good at it, you know. What's yours?"

"A pilot. Always."

"Wow, have you ever flown a plane?"

"Yeah my dad's taken me a few times," Leonie nodded.

"Did he fly planes!?"

"Not that he's told me of for some reason, he's a Marine – he's American - and he took me to flying lessons and firing ranges and stuff."

Jamie swore, "Wow that's so cool! I've never even touched a real gun before. I mean I've fired Nerf guns and shit, but nothing like that. That's insane!"

Leonie cracked up, "yeah they're not toys, Jamie. Have you ever used a paintball gun? They're so much fun."

"Nah. But I do laser tag! Every Wednesday!"

"Do you have regular things on other days as well," Leonie smirked, "Ping pong Sundays?"

"Actually, I hit the driving range on Sundays," Jamie corrected, "but I do play ping pong on Tuesday afternoons. Or is it beer pong?"

"Hahaha, the only regular thing I have is school and football."

"Nice. Although, United, what a crap team. They should bulldoze Old Trafford."

Jamie took off just in time before Leonie could whack him one, the cheeky sod.

Finally, Leonie was given the all clear to go back to camp, wherever the hell that was. Jamie assured her he knew the way. The hospital was surprisingly large, it made no sense having a huge building like that in this sort of place.

It turns out they didn't need to know any directions as they were given some strange vehicle to drive back to camp in that knew the way to go. It kind of looked like a Chaimite V-200 APC, but not. It had no weapons, but it looked secure and as though nothing could break into it. Leonie was given a green bandana to cover her bald head with. She felt as though she looked like a pillock but went along with it anyway.

The journey was interesting. Leonie saw more strange things. There was a pack of Hyenas attacking a Zebra, which seemed normal enough. Wolves were watching nearby, and a Lioness got spooked by a big brown bear.

They passed through several villages as well. Each was very different. One was an old looking place full of houses right on the water where crocodiles were visible. To Leonie's disbelief, people still dove into the water.

Another village seemed even older fashioned, they were full of farmers.

There was a more flashy looking community full of modern looking houses. Jamie wanted to just stop and stay there.

The best looking town was one in the sky, obviously full of people from way into the future. Leonie almost lost Jamie for good. It was an epic place.

One thing all the towns and villages had in common was their biggest effort was in large fencing and security. Leonie understood this, it was to keep all the scary animals out. She was still waiting for a Tyrannosaurus Rex to show itself and if she saw a Megalodon, she could die happily. She remembered Cody being obsessed with sharks, and every year for her birthday her dad would take her cage diving with great whites or whatever they could find.

A lot of the villages had guard dogs patrolling either alongside a man or just by themselves. The most common were German dogs such as the German Shepherd, Rottweiler, Doberman, and Boxer. However, there were also a few pit bulls around along with some Irish Wolfhounds and Tibetan Mastiffs. There was even a little Chiweenie having a go at some guy stealing grapes.

Other than the strange villages filled with people from different times building what they knew, the rest of the land was the same as what they saw before when they first arrived and went exploring during their short time at the camp. Leonie did feel really sad at one point when a lion caught a Kangaroo in a field they passed.

Jamie who was playing with all the buttons that were in the vehicle found the music and somehow got "I Love It Loud" by Kiss to start playing. As he continued to press buttons, Leonie was about to tell him to stop when suddenly Leonie's seat was ejected up through the roof. Leonie screamed the whole way up, and the whole way down as Jamie looked up through the hole in the roof in horror. She landed painfully on the ground; she was unaware of the parachute release on her seat just like Jamie was unaware of the ejector button.

Jamie jumped out and rushed over to Leonie's aid.

"I am so sorry Leonie," he said looking astonished, "I swear I had no idea that was going to happen."

"Yeah me neither," Leonie groaned as Jamie helped her up, "man that scared the you-know-what out of me."

Before they even managed to start walking back to the vehicle, they were surprised at the sight of about twenty armed men that were starting to surround them. They wore old daggy clothes and most had long hair and beards. They smelt badly. Some went straight for the vehicle, they obviously intended on stealing it. However, the man who appeared to be in charge went straight for Leonie and stared intensely at her. At first, he looked as though he was about to say he recognised her, Leonie certainly didn't recognise him, but then his almost kind eyes immediately changed to unkind.

"Ew Yuck," He shouted as he scrunched up his face in disgust, "what is this?"

"It's disgusting!" A man somewhere behind the first man yelled.

"Hey shut up!" Jamie shouted angrily before receiving a smack in the chops.

Of course, Leonie knew they were talking about her, in regards to her new look. She didn't mind though because the adrenaline pumping through her, it didn't make her brave or able to defend herself, but able to block out all the comments. She was proud of all the comebacks she had thought of in her head, not that she said any of them out loud.

After many more nasty comments about her looks, too horrible for her to want to think about, Leonie watched on as they went through the vehicle. It had a first aid kit and a fridge with some food. They were disappointed there were no weapons, as was Leonie because she would've had them already to threaten them with. Jamie regained consciousness and slowly managed to scramble back to his feet by grabbing onto Leonie for support, almost pulling her on top of him. The men were seemingly preoccupied with their new vehicle, so Jamie silently suggested they make a run for it.

They slowly backed off the road into the forest. They swore a few times one of the men saw them, but it turned out he was watching a kookaburra in a tree above them. It actually dropped a bomb that nearly landed on Jamie.

As soon as they were out of the men's sight, they broke into a sprint going deeper and deeper into the forest. Zigzagging through the trees was tough; they almost tripped over their own feet a few times. Leonie was also concerned about finding another one of those damn burning trees again. Luckily so far there were none in sight, but she did accidentally swallow some moth.

After running for a while, it became darker. Maybe it was because it was noon, or possibly because the forest was getting so thick it blocked out most of the light. They decided to stop after Jamie tripped over a large tree root.

"I think we lost them," Jamie announced as he rolled onto his back.

"We lost them ages ago," Leonie said shaking her head.

"What? Then why did we keep running for? My stomach is sore, and I think I pulled my hamstring."

"You poor dear," Leonie replied sarcastically, "So what do we do now?"

"I don't know. I don't know anything about surviving in the forest. We need Leon."

"Well Leon's not here," Leonie stressed, "damn it! I don't know where we are, we could be stuck here until we die!"

"Calm down," Jamie said as he got to his feet looking in pain, "Let's find somewhere to spend the night. Then what comes next. Oh yeah, water? Right? I think. Yeah, we need to find water and then some dinner."

Leonie sighed, "But how do we know what we can eat, Jamie? I mean, all these animals and trees mixed in together, some we've never even seen before. How do we know what's safe to touch or eat? I mean look at what one tree has already done to me."

"Well, unfortunately, it's a risk we gotta take. We can't just starve or die of thirst. We have to try, and if it turns out to be bad, then, we die. Face it, we're never getting out of here."-

"Don't say that!"-

"I'm surprised I've lasted as long as I have! I'm not great at doing anything. Maybe my dad was right. I'm a waste of space. I'll never achieve anything."

With that, Jamie walked off. It was the first time Leonie had ever seen him sad. Not that she's known him for very long. She begged to differ with what he said though. He wasn't a waste of space, not if he could laugh and cheer people up, which he was very good at according to her.

Keeping a small distance, Leonie followed Jamie. She wasn't sure where they'd end up until they eventually ended up at a river. There were three grizzly bears catching salmon in the rain. So it looked like they found food and water before shelter. Hopefully, the bears would leave soon so they could try and catch some fish, somehow. In the meantime, they managed to light a small fire in a dry spot about twenty metres into the forest from the river. So they sat against a large tree in front of the fire together in silence for the rest of the night, neither slept.

By morning the bears had wandered off (thankfully, to the other side of the river), so they could begin their fish hunt. Jamie got a reasonably large stick and tied a very long green leaf to it, then showed it to Leonie who cracked up.

"You can't seriously think you can catch fish with that!?"

"Oh yeah," Jamie said as he threw his invention to the ground, "well what do you suggest then?"

Leonie looked around in the mud and grass; she finally spotted something in a bush beside the river. When she picked it up it, she saw it was a large, handmade fishing net. She showed it to Jamie who just looked blankly at it.

"Oh how convenient," Jamie snorted, "There just *happens* to be a net right there ready for us. It's like in the movies where there just *happens* to be something or someone" –

"Leon!" Leonie yelled as she pushed past a waffling Jamie to get to Leon who had just walked out onto the riverside with a handmade fishing rod on his shoulder. He looked like he'd been in a fight, all covered in cuts, bruises, and mud. He still looked rather relaxed though as he strolled along the river towards them.

"What are you two idiots doing?" He said as he approached them.

"Trying to catch some fish," Jamie said sounding annoyed and slightly embarrassed, "so we can survive. We have no idea where we are, and we could be stuck out here for weeks yet."

"You know there's a Fish n Chips shop just down the road," Leon replied, still looking rather relaxed and watching Jamie try to untangle the net, "why not get a meal there?"

Jamie threw the net onto the ground in rage. "You're having me on, aren't you? You're telling me, there's a Chippy nearby!?"

"Yeah. They're very good too."

"So why are *you* fishing for?" Jamie asked sounding slightly frustrated.

"Because I like to fish," Leon replied looking confused, "it's one of my hobbies."

Jamie sighed, and then he and Leonie followed Leon to the road before continuing on alone for what was hardly a five-minute walk to a nice looking Fish and Chip shop with plain looking tables and chairs outside, closely watched by baboons and seagulls.

"Why would someone even build a Chippy here," Jamie went on as they scanned the menu, "I mean of all the things you could do here, like trying to get out of here, no, let's build a god damn fish and chip shop."

"Please stop whining," Leonie begged, she was starving and just wanted to eat. Inside was nice, nothing flash, just your average plain looking fish n chip shop. It even had an ice-cream freezer.

Leon joined them at a table inside later after he gave the owner of the shop his catch. It was about four fish, Leonie couldn't quite see.

"You guys all good now?" He asked as he fixed up his jacket that he sat on.

"Yeah," Jamie, with a mouth full of food replied.

"What are you doing here?" Leonie asked, "I thought you were heading back to the camp."

91

"I was," Leon nodded, "but I got attacked by some hooligans on the way. I guess that's what happened to you as well?"

"Yeah and Jamie got punched in the face."

"Shut up," Jamie said before swallowing his huge mouthful of fish.

"Anyway," Leon continued, "I was able to kill three of them before getting away. I found this place. I thought it was strange as well, and for a good reason."

"This whole place is strange," Jamie pointed out, "It's absolutely mental. Makes me want to go home, and that's saying something… Wait did you just say you killed three men?"

Leon took them back to the river, later on, to teach them how to fish. Even though they had been lucky this time, in the future they may not be as so and may have to catch food on their own. It turned out though that Leon wasn't entirely interested in teaching them how to fish; he wanted to talk to them alone.

He explained to them how he believed the Fish and Chip shop was not just for food. He said he saw some guards around the back of the shop throwing a man into a shed and killing him. He had apparently found a way out.

Chapter 10:

"How do you know this?" Leonie asked desperately.

"I was listening in," Leon replied, "they were saying something about him getting too close to the edge. Then, the bloke who runs the Chippy filled them in on some more information. He said he found one of the gates. Then they killed him."

"One of the gates?" Jamie asked, "a gate to where? Out of here?"

"That's what I think," Leon smiled, "and I think *here* must be close to it, and that's why I believe this shop is like a surveillance place to keep an eye on everyone. Make sure no one gets out."

"If they didn't want people to get out, then why have a gate in the first place?" Jamie challenged.

"Maybe we're supposed to get out," Leon explained, "remember the room we were in when we were first captured. They only let the best proceed? Perhaps, only the worthy make it out of here too. But they have to make it hard. Killing you makes it hard."

"So, if that's true, then what if getting out of here doesn't lead to freedom," Jamie said, "what if there's something else waiting for us? I think it will be a space war."

"Unlikely," Leon said seriously, "say that's true, that there's something else waiting out there. Then we're still getting closer to some answers. I say we go find the others and tell them and then we plan an escape. Or we stay here forever."

"You said gates," Leonie jumped in, "*gates*. More than one?"

"That'd be good," Jamie said, "means we may not have to come all the way back here if they're scattered all over the place if there really is any that is."

They headed back the next day. Unfortunately, they had to walk. But the guy who owned the Chippy gave Leon directions and gave him a map that had limited details on it. He was probably happy though that they headed away from the possible exit.

They had to rest several times, to begin with, because of Jamie complaining about being exhausted. Leon quickly sorted him out though, and they were able to make greater distance with fewer stops. Leonie was tired too, but it wasn't too bad, something in her made her want to keep going. It was kind of boring walking through all the fields and coming across the occasional cow or horse. She decided to ask Leon why he became a doctor after being in the Navy-Seals. He said his father was a Doctor and he always wanted to impress him. Leonie told him she knew the feeling, but he assured her father was probably not as extreme as his was. Jamie joined in and said all his father ever did was kick his arse to get some kind of job after he was just sitting around the house for months doing nothing.

They made it back to the camp by foot in a few days, thankfully unscathed and they encountered hardly any animals and people, besides cows and horses. Brian greeted them and took several minutes to explain to Leonie how he feels for her suffering and pain. Leonie was thankful at first, but the more he waffled on, she ended up just staring at a tree.

Leon went inside the main tent with Brian and some other bossy people to explain everything that had happened at the chippy. One man wanted to go there just to eat some chips and asked if they had tomato sauce.

Leonie and Jamie sat down on a bench outside watching people work. Several people stared at Leonie, but she'd almost forgotten about what had happened to her to care. Jamie laughed when one guy walked into a trailer after staring as he walked by.

Warren suddenly appeared, running up to them both with a plate of food for them each. He hugged Leonie and gave Jamie high-five.

"How are you?" He asked excitedly.

"Not too bad," Leonie replied, "been a bit rough and things are just getting even more confusing, but other than that... How are you?"

"As good as possible, Max and I had a huge breakthrough."-

"Yeah, Brian told us," Jamie explained, "what's that all about?"

"That was just a small breakthrough," Warren grinned, "which was just finding the layout of the world. Since then we've had an even bigger breakthrough. We've had our own research team you see, and we've discovered ways out of here! Leon told us about that man who was killed trying to escape through one of them."

"Awesome," Jamie admitted, "but why did you say world?"

"Yeah," Leonie nodded, "I was just about to ask the same thing."

Warren had somehow managed an even bigger grin, "Oh guys, it's a scientific miracle. Somewhere in the future, someone has managed to create a whole world! This, right here, is a world, just like Earth is, only it's manmade. There are even volunteers living here from the future, as well as non-volunteers unfortunately. There are people and animals from all different time frames; there have even been speculations of sightings of Homo erectus if you can believe it. Not that there's any proof of that yet though."

"I don't know what to believe anymore," Jamie said looking beside himself, "this is huge. Like, my life was so dull before and now look at it. Mad."

"Unfortunately though," Warren continued, losing the smile, "Max set out with a group of researchers to investigate one of these gateways after we had a theory of a possible location, and well, he's vanished, they all have."

"Clark's missing?" Jamie gasped.

Warren nodded looking sad, "We had a tracker on him, for precautions, like this. But he's completely gone. Jonathan went out after to look for him. We should hear from him soon."

"What do you think happened," Leonie asked looking horrified, "do you think maybe he made it through?"

"Not sure," Warren replied, "I would love to think so, but everyone else seems to think he was killed before he even got close. Unoptimistic twits!"

After pondering for a while, Warren got called back to his team. So Leonie and Jamie were left yet again. It was weird hearing people talk about killing when the only violence Leonie had seen so far was Jamie getting punched in the face by the mongrel they encountered. It made her wonder if she would have to witness something like murder soon, or since she's seemed to have bad luck so far, experience murder herself.

Brian and Leon appeared and requested she go with Leon to the Medical team to get her burns checked again. So she followed them to the medical tent where numerous staff were located. The burns that were healing had healed. That was incredible considering yesterday they were still slightly visible. All that was left were the two bad ones around her left eye and on her right arm, there's an extremely low percentage of them ever healing as it is too late now to use the equipment that was used on her other burns, it needs to be straight away apparently. Leon said he thinks her hair is starting to show signs of growth, but it would be extremely slow, and there'd always be a heap of bald patches. He tried to make it better by opting she either wear long sleeves, sunglasses and a big floppy hat for the rest of her life or just deal with it. Instead, Leonie decided to ignore him and proceed to the Mess.

"JONATHAN MADE IT THROUGH!!!" Came a yelling Warren during dinner time in the big Mess tent, "HE MADE IT THROUGH THE GATEWAY!"

Leon caught Warren as he struggled to stop in time after sprinting through the mess. After making him calm down, Leon asked Warren to continue more peacefully back at his "office".

Leonie and Jamie were lucky enough to be able to follow all the smart people to their tent and hear Warren explain, "he spoke to me through the radio, and he was waiting for a while! No sign of Max or his team anywhere though! He went quiet for a while, but then he started explaining how the gateway appeared! Then somehow he started whispering that it was opening... He got attacked by some guards but said a black panther appeared and killed them!"

"A black panther?" some science nerd asked.

"Yeah! A *big* one!" Warren said, very animated with his hands as he spoke, "I don't understand that either, but what's more important is that he's through."

"Through to what?" Brian asked, "How do we know for sure it's not just some gateway to hell!?"

"Maybe it leads to a Stairway to Heaven," Jamie said out loud hoping for some cheering. Everyone just ignored him instead, and Leonie took two steps away from him.

More arguing went on, it was kind of splendid seeing young Warren shouting and making a huge effort to prove his point. Leonie and Jamie had no idea what to do as they knew nothing of science or smart people things, but they were quite content just watching. Leon had to separate two men fighting as they had a blackboard drawing argument to prove both of their opinions. Warren furiously pointed and yelled at a man twice his height about the facts of teleporting. A small lady with her hair in a plait approached Leonie and Jamie in the hopes of sparking up an argument with them, but Jamie assured her they were both on her side.

The arguing was stopped unexpectedly when a massive explosion went off outside. Within moments, Leonie was knocked over by running, screaming people before it had even registered to her what it was that happened. She looked up to find bits and pieces flying everywhere, there was a huge hole in what was left of the tent, and her ears were ringing. Jamie grabbed her and pulled her to her feet. Together they ran and got Warren, and the three of them ran outside. Immediately, they saw where the explosion had taken place and all the dead bodies that had been caused by it. Leonie started going numb in her whole body at the sight, but they had no time to react as many armed guards came charging in, firing at everyone. Leonie looked at Jamie who looked absolutely petrified as did Warren. They ran off in the opposite direction to where the guards were coming from, only to find that more guards were coming from every direction. Realising escape was not possible at this point, Leonie followed after Leon who was headed to their tent to grab his rifle. He immediately passed one to Leonie and the other two before running off to aid Brian and some others in defending some women and children. Warren could barely hold the gun, and Leonie doubted he knew how to use it, but they ran out anyway, and he did his best to hide behind them. They ran to join Leon, who was like a Terminator shooting guards in all directions. He had great reflexes. Jamie suddenly manned up and joined in the battle after a lady behind him was shot in the chest. Brian and Leon got into a heated argument on which way to take the women and children. In the end, Brian used the authority card, and everyone followed him and his second in command.

"HANSON!" Leon yelled, but it was no use, they had headed into the direction Leon didn't agree with. Soon they were out of sight. Leon continued firing at the guards along with Jamie and several dozen other men before following on to catch up with Brian. When they managed to catch up, most of the women and children were dead. Brian was cornered and desperately trying to hold them off. He managed to for a while, Leon and Jamie shot at the guards from a distance. Then, when Brian saw that now all of the women and children had died, he dropped his guard and then received several shots to his abdomen. His second in command fled the scene like a rocket; his blonde hair was the last thing in view.

After staring at the bodies for a few seconds with a blank mind, Leonie was pushed into a run by Leon and Jamie who were still firing at the guards. They all ran in the direction that Leon had suggested before, Leonie held tightly onto Warren's hand.

They fled into the forest and were pursued by a half a dozen guards, but were in reasonably good distance from them. They could still hear firing and screaming from the hundreds of people still left at the camp.

Jamie yelped as he was shot in the shoulder but kept running. When he was shot in the leg, he stopped running, and his leg gave way. Without saying a word, Leonie and Leon grabbed him and kept going. Warren took over the lead as he knew the best way to where they were heading, the gateway.

When they needed to slow down (but not stop), Leon fired a few shots back at the guards in pursuit. Unfortunately, he's only managed to hit one so far.

The more they ran, the weaker Jamie's leg got, so eventually Leon had to take more of his weight on. This meant that Leonie had to take the role of firing back at the guards, when necessary.

Although it didn't seem like long, although it was a great distance away, they managed to reach the gateway according to Warren. They weren't quite there, but Warren said he could see it. There was no sign of the guards; it appeared they had fallen back a while ago. Definitely still on their way, though.

When they reached the gate, Leon quickly instructed Warren to see to the gateway and for Leonie to keep an eye out for the guards while he tended to Jamie's wounds. His wounds weren't anywhere near any vital organs, but he was still bleeding badly, so Leon did his best to maintain it for the time being.

Leonie had her eyes glued to the forest, any movement and she swore to herself she would shoot. Whether she actually would if it happened was another story though. She had no idea if she actually could or not, but guessed she would find out soon enough.

Warren was pulling his hair out over the gate, not literally though, but he was desperately trying to find a way to open it. They had managed to develop a theory on how to find the gateways but hadn't quite got to the opening bit yet which was why Clark had gone to investigate. He had been quite competitive with Clark; if he had managed to open it, then Warren should be able to better and quicker. If Jonathan had, then Warren definitely should be opening it. Leonie couldn't even see the gateway at first (before when her eyes weren't glued to the forest), but it appears if you know it's there, according to Clark's research.

Two guards came charging through the forest at them.

Leonie panicked, "Leon! They, they're coming!"

"Kill them!" Leon shouted to the seventeen-year-old, "before they kill us!"

Leonie fired at them, but her rifle went all over the place, and she ended up falling to the ground. She got back on her feet and, shaking, she aimed at the guards who had just hidden behind a tree after hearing the shots. She fired with good aim this time, she still didn't hit them, but it was an improvement. It turned into a few minutes of, shoot then hide, between Leonie and the two guards.

Finally, a shot was landed, but on Leonie, on her right arm where her burn was. She fell back onto the ground and clutched her new wound. She wanted to scream but instead made some strange breathing noises. After seeing she was injured, the guards proceeded towards her. Warren was still working out the gateway. Soon the guards were upon her and about to take aim before they were taken by surprise by a huge black panther. It mauled the first guard, received shots by the second, but they didn't seem to have any effect on it. It then killed the second guard as well. Leonie managed to get to her feet and dash over to Leon.

"There's a big panther over there," she said in a fast panicky voice, "it just killed the guards."

Before Leon could reply, he found himself face to face with the panther, its big green eyes staring into his. He almost passed out as it transformed into a beautiful looking lady with long black hair. She quickly got up as they all stared at her with open mouths.

"Do not say anything," She said firmly, "you must go now before they come."

She walked over to the gate where Warren was wide-eyed looking at her. He tried to resist, insisting he could open the gateway by himself, but she was very persuasive.

"See these two stones?" she asked pointing at the gateway.

"No," Warren replied.

"Look closer. One is shaped like a star; the other is just a circle."

"Oh yeah," Warren nodded, "what are they?"

"On the count of three, we push them down. We must do it at the exact same time, or we'll be blown off our feet. Understand?"

"No," Warren replied. But she started counting down from five anyway. Leonie couldn't see, but apparently, they had pressed

101

them down. The gateway opened, and the lady quickly turned to them. She helped Jamie to his feet and forcefully rounded them all up towards the gateway.

Warren went first, then Jamie and Leon. Leonie went to step in, but she had to ask something first.

"What is your name?"

"Emmelia."

Chapter 11:

It was very confusing and disorientating. They were in a little room which Leonie thought looked like an airlock. Warren and Leon were helping Jamie sit up. Then, the room started to fill up with gas, and that was the last she remembered.

She woke up, yet again, feeling dizzy. She was now in what looked like another hospital wing, her being at the far end. It was very bright and clean, but very plain. She looked beside her bed, after hearing a loud snore. Her eyes lit up, and her heart skipped a beat. So much joy filled her at that moment than she had ever had, or at least in a long time. Cody was fast asleep in an armchair beside her bed.

Leonie reached out of bed and poked her in the shoulder. When she didn't wake up, she whacked her instead. Cody jumped several inches off her chair. When she saw Leonie, she sat up and smiled. Leonie was expecting a joke or an insult, but Cody looked a bit sad instead.

"Cody," Leonie said excitedly, "how are you? Where have you been? Are you okay? We were lost and everything! Where are the others? What's going on?"

Cody said nothing, but got up and hugged Leonie. She then started crying.

"What's wrong? Leonie asked as they broke off the hug.

Cody took a deep breath in, "Sorry. Just. Look at you. I can't believe it. What have they done?"

Leonie suddenly remembered her burns and her bald head. Cody hadn't seen it before.

"Oh," Leonie said softly, "it's okay. I'm not worried by it. It's been like this for a while now. I walked into a tree… that burns."

"I know… I just can't believe it, especially seeing you now."

"Cody," Leonie shrieked, pinching Cody's arm, she just recalled what had happened before, "we were in a weird place, and people died!"

"I know," Cody said, and before she could continue, Clark walked in accompanied by Warren and Leon. It appeared Clark had made it through after all.

Warren ran over to Leonie's side, "how are you? Jamie's resting, he'll be okay. Unfortunately, you took in a heap of gas, and you hit your head as you fell. But you're all good now. Your wound is fine."

"Your friend here is quite the character," Leon half smiled as he looked at Cody, "she's filled us in on your life story and everything."

"What happened with the other place? Where are we now? How many people died?"

Clark came closer to the end of the bed and explained everything in detail. They were now on a spaceship, a very big one. There are people from many different time frames, before Leonie's time and after. Because there is a lot of people on board the ship, which is a training ship for war, by the way, they needed a place for people to wait for their turn to go to battle when one squad gets wiped out, another takes their place, for example. The world they were in before was a place the mad scientist (Dr Martens, from two hundred years in the future, with over a dozen degrees in science and other fields), it was created to still keep people thinking and training before boarding the actual training ship. It was like a sort of waiting list, and when people go out from the ship to fight; people from the world are let in.

In regards to why people were suddenly killed by the guards. The guards were actually robots, and someone from the enemy hacked in and took control over them causing chaos. The tree that badly burnt Leonie was still a mystery; they believe it to be a glitch or something because the world isn't entirely real, just a simulation to Warrens disappointment, although it was "still cool".

When Leonie asked about Emmelia Elliston and how she turned into a massive panther, they did not know that either. They had checked with a Cyberteam earlier (because Emmelia had helped Clark get through as well, to Warren's relief) and their records show her to have died within an hour of entering the world. She was bitten by a fierce snake.

They continued filling Leonie in with everything they knew. So the mad scientist turned out to be not bad, just mad. He performs physical and mental tests as well as health checks on everyone before they enter the world. He does this in his lab where they were taken first. Apparently, though, the hackers got the lab as well, and it is now destroyed, which means, no more getting in people to help. Leonie and the others were the last "recruits".

This is apparently the biggest hit they have ever received and possibly the most important hit for the enemy. The worse bit is, they have absolutely no idea who the enemy is. They've encountered some lone spies from the enemy though. Dr. Martens supposedly has a few suspects. But only his top team know that sort of information.

With some things cleared up, and others made more complicated, Leonie was cleared to leave the hospital wing. Cody was going to take her to sign in and find her a bed, but first Cody had other things to show her.

They went into an area called The Apex; it was where the best fighters who fought in the front line lived. It had a sort of black and red theme to it; it was full of exercise equipment and spaces to spar. It was kind of an eerie place, and Leonie had no idea why Cody had brought her here. Or why Cody was acting weird, she was less chatty and more serious. Finally, after standing in a gym and watching people lift weights and work out, Cody pointed at a woman. Leonie had to look hard, and it took a few seconds to click. It was Camilla! Man, had she changed. The once twig figured teenager was now a fit and muscular complete badass looking woman!

"Holy moly," Leonie said as she looked at Cody in disbelief, "that's Camilla!?"

"Most certainly is," Cody grinned going back to her old self-kind of, "She's a beast. She is badass! Just got back from an epic mission. Come on let's go over."

Leonie, unable to take it all in, followed Cody towards Camilla who was annihilating a punching bag. Leonie then realised she was a bit scared to greet Camilla again. Of course, people were staring at Leonie too.

Camilla stopped as they approached; she was all sweaty and looked even cooler up close. She stared at Leonie for an uncomfortable few seconds, still with her attack face on, but when she realised who it was her face completely changed to a mother finding her lost child's expression and hugged Leonie tightly, so she couldn't breathe. Leonie was now covered in Camilla's sweat, she may as well had done a work out herself.

"Oh my word," Camilla gasped, "Leonie, are you okay? I can't believe it!"

They chatted with Camilla for a while at the cafeteria by a big swimming pool with plants in it. They talked about everything that had happened. Camilla talked about how she fell into the fighting side of things and some of her missions she'd been on. It was awesome; Leonie couldn't believe how much she'd changed. She was always tough and confident, but never to this extreme.

Cody, on the other hand, had a tough time finding her place. She had a job of guiding people on missions through their earpiece, but she talked and joked too much that they pulled her out of that job due to the death threats from her colleagues. She couldn't fight like Camilla because she's considered hazardous around firearms and other weapons. She tried working as a cook but was hazardous with the knives and hot things. She secured a job as a cleaner for a while then upgraded to someone who does an agents paper organising stuff.

"Personally," Cody said, "I have no idea why that nutter even brought me here; I can't even do anything useful."

"Everyone needs cleaners, Cody," Camilla chuckled.

"You were great at Chemistry and stuff," Leonie pointed out, "surely there are some science jobs?"

"Yeah I've been trying something with the Chemical engineering people, but they say I need a bachelor in Chemical engineering to join and there is no way of studying here, same with the computer science. They should've got us after we've been to University."

The area was nice; there was no view of space through any windows though. Leonie also noticed that *most* of the people around were from the eighties and there definitely was an eighties vibe going on, with lots of eighties music around the place. Not a bad thing though.

After a nice catch up with Camilla, it was time to leave. Leonie had to sign in to see what her place would be. Everyone brought on board is supposed to have something useful to offer. Otherwise, the Dr would never have summoned them. Perhaps Cody needed some time to shine.

Cody had to wait outside while Leonie went inside the sign-up place. It was currently in the middle of a briefing given to the new recruits by some people who looked like they were in charge of everything in the universe. Leonie found Jamie (Leon, Warren, and Clark were already great and had jobs) and went and stood next to him, on his other side was Jonathan. They said hello through excited facial expressions, but couldn't speak because they'd get into trouble. Leonie was glad to see Jonathan had also made it through. She was glad to know two people who would go through what she just heard to be a twelve-week full-time training course.

Leonie almost fainted. She had recognised one of the boss people talking. That same low, Earthy, English voice was used to captain their soccer team. It was Stacey! She too looked different, not in a buff way, she just looked more like an adult, and her hair was cut to shoulder length now. She looked intimidating though, in her ladies suit, and her voice was so much more assertive. Although, Leonie always thought Stacey would suit this sort of job, bossing people around. Camilla definitely suited a fighter.

After explaining the twelve weeks to them about how it would be a mixture of different things including practical skills and theory, Jamie groaned several times. Jonathan nudged him as Stacey just gave him an evil stare. Leonie almost laughed but wasn't sure if Stacey had become really strict and mean.

The twelve weeks would surely suck. You had to get up at five o'clock and train all the way through until nine and then participate in cleaning up afterwards. No weekends either, it was full on seven days a week, but Fridays finish at two o'clock which was a sort of bonus.

They had to sign a contract, just things like if you get hurt or die, they can't be held responsible. Leonie didn't know who would hold them responsible anyway though. Jonathan was hesitant to sign at first; it is hard to trust these people when they take you without warning and scare the hell out of you by putting you in some random place with people you don't know. Surely most of the people would have been willing to help if asked nicely over a cup of tea right?

"Hey, didn't I tell you, Leonie," Jamie said excitedly as they left the room to meet Cody, "space war baby! Who's a genius!?" Everyone ignored him.

"Wow I just saw Stacey," Leonie said as they reached Cody.

"Yeah I know, she's one of the big boys now."

"Leonie," Stacey said appearing behind her, "are you okay to do this?" Leonie knew she was referring to her burns.

"Yeah of course I am. I guess."

"Okay. Good to see you again," Stacey then turned to Cody and lost her nice tone, "why weren't you at the meeting?"

"Huh. I already did the course with you – remember? Idiot."

"Yeah, but you can't get a job," Stacey said with an attitude, "so I've pulled some strings to get you in for another chance. Didn't you get the email?"

"Wait," Cody gasped, "I have an email!?"

Stacey rolled her eyes and turned back to Leonie, "I'll see you two and Camilla later for a drink, before you're training tomorrow, so not too late."

Leonie nodded, with that Stacey walked off.

They went to find their rooms, Leonie and Cody got to share a room along with two other girls. One was slightly overweight and looked terrified; the other was a young Asian lady who looked like an assassin. They didn't say much to them, so Leonie and Cody had a quick look around their new room then met with Jonathan and Jamie who were just across the hall from them, conveniently. The boys were already waiting for them, probably weren't as interested in their room as they were.

"Your friend is pretty cool," Jamie whispered to Leonie as Cody was trying to release her jacket from the door after closing it on it, "she kind of reminds me of someone. Your other friend is hot, I love women with a temper, dunno why but it turns me on."

"Gross."

They intended on enjoying their last night of freedom as much as possible. The two lads sat with some other lads so that Leonie and Cody could sit and chat with Stacey and Camilla.

"Looking forward to training again Cody," Camilla laughed, "Man that was legendary the shit you did before."

"What did she do?" Leonie asked enthusiastically.

"Oh man you should've seen it," –

"Cody's way of solving things," Stacey interrupted, "is to blow things up. She was reckless... But brilliant!"

The four of them clinked drinks together as they chuckled.

"Yeah," Cody nodded, "the practical stuff was a nightmare, and all the theory was just so boring. Honestly, Leonie, I've worked out that the twelve weeks ages you physically about seven years. It's had a huge effect on these too." Camilla punched Cody in the arm.

"So how did you two get the jobs you got?" Leonie asked curiously, but not that she didn't understand why they got their jobs, she just wanted to know how the process works really.

Stacey explained, "well the training helps to test what you're good at, for example fighting skills or technology, medical to name a few. Most exceed in one area, I was good at everything, but didn't specialise in one thing, unfortunately. But because

I did reasonably well in all areas I was able to land a job in intelligence. My linguistic skills help though as well."

"So if you're good at something, you automatically get work in that?" Leonie asked.

"Not really. At the end, there's a test you do in what you did best at and then you might. Or you have to prove yourself on a mission or something," Stacey continued, "so I had a few different skills in my test, as long as I averaged in them, I was fine."

"There's always testing in bloody everything," Leonie sighed.

"I blew my test," Cody brashly butted in, "I went to throw a stun grenade at a bad guy, but it accidentally got the assessors instead."

Of course, Camilla's test included taking out armed robots in a building, which she aced.

After several drinks and a few curries, joined by Jamie and Jonathan, they headed back in early so that Leonie and Cody could get some sleep ready for the morning. Leonie had no idea what Jonathan and Jamie did though, not that she cared, she was so nervous for the morning. Even with all the stories, the girls told her about the training, she still felt as though she had no idea what it would be like. As Cody collapsed onto her bed and started snoring, Leonie ended up staying awake for hours worrying.

Please don't die tomorrow, she kept thinking.

Chapter 12:

"AHHHH," screamed Tammy and Kumiko, Leonie and Cody's roommates, as they were gassed out of their room. Cody had already warned Leonie of their wake-up call at 0430hrs, so they got up five minutes early and headed to the changing rooms. So that explains why they're only allowed their beds in their rooms and their clothes, and other gear was kept separate. Otherwise, they would pass out trying to get dressed in the gas. They forgot to warn Jamie and Jonathan though who weren't impressed, oops. The training room was just the average one you'd see at the gym, nothing flashy like you'd expect from the future people.

Everyone, about thirty people of all ages (youngest is 16, don't worry), lined up ready, all dressed in their navy blue jumpsuit training uniforms and waited for their commander, Joseph Pratt. He was average height, stocky man who like most people Leonie has encountered was very frightening. After he lined them all up and got through to everyone, he was intimidating and a no-crap-taker kind of guy, he sent them all on a morning run. It was a five-kilometre run, but each day it will increase by one kilometre. Leonie was not looking forward to the eighty-ninth kilometre.

"Is that even legal?" Leonie asked as they all struggled up a hill, "to run that much?"

"We won't," Cody assured, "he says that to scare you, it will increase to about ten maybe, but not that much. That's like a bloody marathon! But he is horrible still."

"So *Pratt* is a label, not just his last name?" Leonie asked, and they both laughed.

Everyone was buggered after the run (except for Cody), but it only got worse from there on in, there were other workouts including weights, and they were introduced to mixed martial arts. Mr. Pratt wanted them all to learn it because so often people find themselves faced with close combat as opposed to just shooting. Mr. Pratt watched as the most intimidating person yet, Debbie Paul, ran them through some moves. Debbie was a tall woman with medium length dark hair and olive skin; she had impressive guns and was overall very muscular. She explained to everyone that by the end of the twelve weeks, they will all look like her; Cody laughed at this and Debbie made her do eighty-seven narrow grip push-ups while everyone watched.

To begin the lesson, Debbie first demonstrated on Cody, who wasn't scared and would giggle with enjoyment when thrown around by Debbie, and then everyone else had to pair up and try.

Tammy, the slightly overweight roommate, copped it a bit, she was quite unfit, "don't worry princess," Debbie yelled, "we'll whip you into shape soon, get some firm abs on that tummy," and she wobbled Tammy's tummy while laughing. Leonie felt sorry for Tammy, she looked like she would cry several times. To be fair, Leonie could barely do twenty good push-ups herself, nor did she have very strong punches.

When Leonie made a mistake one time when trying to sweep Cody over, Debbie came and swept Leonie off her feet really fast, giving her a heart attack, and then made her do it again ten times. For the punishment of her mistake, *everyone* had to walk around for twelve minutes carrying heavy medicine balls in the air, the girls each got twelve kilos, and the men got twenty. Jonathan and Jamie weren't the only men to collapse; in fact, eight did all up. The girls all struggled with theirs, and Leonie's arms were shaking and almost collapsed. She'd only ever lifted

113

a weight once in her life, and that was six kilos, which killed her.

"Don't worry ladies," Debbie shouted, "I'll have you lifting twenty in no time! And lads, don't get me started on what I have in store for you…"

After, they went back to sparring again. Jonathan went to strike Jamie, but Jamie immediately dropped to the ground before contact was even made.

"What are you doing?" Jonathan asked, half laughing half annoyed.

"When I was little, teachers in school told us if someone's going to attack you, to drop to the ground. That way it's hard for them to take you… and I'm still kind of weak from that damn medicine ball…"

"Well, I doubt the bad guys will try to kidnap you, Jamie. I think they'd just kill you where you lay."

Everyone was glad when that class was over and wasn't looking forward to the next.

Theory was pretty bad too; Jonathan was the only one that seemed to be any good at it. A lot of it was mainly, they were given scenarios, and they all had to work out how they would go about infiltrating buildings and things.

"Mr Young," the teacher said pointing to Jamie, "it's night time, you are leading your team into an enemy building to take out some terrorists. What will you do?"

"Ahhh," Jamie said, thinking hard, "I would… Call it a night and take them all for a drink and go back in the morning."

"Why?"

"I'm scared of the dark," Jamie admitted, and all the other recruits laughed.

Other classes consisted of handy things, like finding and building shelters, rafts, finding food and rock-climbing. Then there was science and math class, computer science, medical knowledge, weapons training, vehicle training, swimming and diving, and some history of the war which made no sense as well as etiquette. Every week there was mini exams which were randomly chosen skills of what they'd learnt that they all had to perform, as well as some written exams. Leonie thought they surely couldn't learn it all in twelve weeks, but Cody said everyone thinks that but it all sinks in during the tenth to twelfth week and the anxiety disappears in week four.

This week's exam was very sloppy. They mainly demonstrated some throws and sparring they'd learnt, which looked like a slow-motion fight between drunken people. They also had to complete a huge outdoor obstacle course within thirty minutes in the heavy rain, which no one managed.

When Friday finally came, everyone was exhausted and sore. They finally got some time off in the afternoon. First, Mr. Pratt had them all line up again.

"So, you've survived your first week," he said in disgust, "just. Now you get your afternoon off, I don't want any of you to go getting outta line is that clear?" Everyone confirmed, "Any questions before you're all on your way?"

"Yeah I have one," Cody said. Mr. Pratt glared at her. "Okay, just wondering why do we *actually* need to make our beds every morning? It's hardly important right?"

"Well, Hanson," Mr. Pratt said as he slowly walked up the line, eyes fixed on Cody, "since dumbasses like yourself probably won't achieve much in the day, making your bed is at least one thing you can achieve. It'll also make your momma proud that you are finally making your own bed, and finally, after your hard long day you get a nice cosy warm bed to curl up in. How's that?"

"Awesome. Thanks"

Mr Pratt kept them for two hours longer due to Cody asking that question. They had to run through muddy water with their rifles in the air. When they finally finished, the other students banished her to her and Leonie's room for the night.

The others met in the changing room with some food and talked. Jonathan snuck Leonie a packet of Jelly babies which he'd snuck in somehow. Jamie was busy telling everyone how he would have a Saxon song as his theme or battle song, "I'd have either, "Crusader", "Back on the Streets" or "Sailing to America" I think." He explained.

"I'd have "Everybody" by The Backstreet Boys," Cody blurted out after Kumiko snuck her in. Leonie stared at her in disbelief, "I'm kidding! I'd have Judas Priest! *Hot Rockin'*."

"Kind of irrelevant," Kumiko said suddenly, "we got to get through this damn twelve weeks first before we would even begin to think of music, and that is dumb having a theme song."

It was clear everyone felt the same as Leonie did. So they all agreed to work together and even help one another in spare time on things others struggled on. Leonie thought she would need help with everything, except for weapons, but even her martial arts isn't as good as she thought it was. Her maths and science were definitely at a low standard. Cody said she'd help her with swimming, maths, and science because she was good at those things. In return, Leonie would help her with her weapons. Everything else they'd just struggle through together. Jonathan would help them with a few things as he was rather good at all the theory, but he was tied up with everyone else wanting his help, they all swarmed him as soon as classes had finished that day, Jamie got to him first.

So week one review, Kumiko almost drowned, a guy broke his wrist, Jamie got into trouble loads of times, Jonathan and Cody aced everything (Cody by cheating and remembering things from last time), and Leonie just going with the flow. Oh, and at the end of each day, every student ended up with bruises, wounds or even dislocations and had to report to medical before calling it a day. Leonie had a sprained ankle from falling off a large wall in the obstacle course, she swore someone pushed her, but no one confessed. Luckily, medical had some advanced technology which fixed her ankle up straight away, she just needed to rest it for the night, and it was as good as new. *Finally some good use from the future*, she thought.

Week two, things started making more sense, once they started to expand on what they learnt in week one, in turn, week one made more sense. They had a swimming exam on, where they had to sneak into a house via an underwater pipeline. Everyone made it; they had practised swimming drills every morning. It was a huge boost for Leonie's confidence that she kept up with the others as swimming had never been her strong point. They didn't do so well in taking out the robots yet though; they were very sloppy and needed to work on their communications skills. Mr Pratt suggested they sort out their ranks after yelling and insulting them all for ten minutes. So they did. Naturally, Jonathan was picked to be in charge.

By week five, Leonie had learnt a lot. Her confidence had grown immensely, and she was participating in teamwork a lot more. She spoke up with all her ideas and became a component to some of their success. All the students were working well and were starting to find their strengths. They became more united and dependent on one another while strengthening their own independence as well. Unfortunately, everyone was still reporting to medical at the end of each day, however, mainly due to Debbie, and Mr Pratt making them climb difficult obstacles in the fake rain which felt much heavier than real rain.

Debbie actually complimented Tammy though at one point because she had to put in a request for some new pants as hers were too loose and started literally falling down. Everyone cheered for her and she started to actually become passionate about training, as opposed to loathing it. She became the best fighter and excelled in the studies. Leonie could also see herself understanding the theory a lot more. But the biggest improvement for everyone was physical. Debbie had been drilling their arses with horrible workouts every day, and Leonie had actually lost her muffin top and had some abs, and her arms were stronger, she could lift over fifteen kilos with the medicine balls, and her legs were becoming stronger and less wobbly as well. Even Jamie, who was the weakest man there, was at the top of the pack with Jonathan. Although their sparing was still a barrel of laughs; Jonathan would taunt Jamie who'd reply with "Sticks and stones may break my bones Jonyo" after which Jonathan would grab a Bo and whack him with it.

Things went down in week seven. Cody, who had progressed well in Computer science, of which she was already pretty skilled with, had hacked into the department where Stacey worked and discovered some confidential information. Some people came and took her away for five hours, and when she came back, she was quiet, and Mr Pratt told her she'd have to make up the five hours at the end of the course. Leonie and the others asked her what happened that night, she said they'd throw her in a cell if she told anyone and the only reason she wasn't was because Stacey was able to call in a few favours for her sake.

The rest of the week was a drag, each night everyone begged Cody to talk about what had happened. She wouldn't.

Mr Pratt surprised them on a Thursday night with a drill, they had to perform a MET call on someone as there was no other trained professionals available. Apparently, this could happen in real life, so they needed to be skilled in this sort of thing. The mannequin which was used was very lifelike and had pulses, blood, and ability to vomit and scream at certain points. It was hooked up to a computer that showed its vital signs. It was up to them whether the mannequin lived or died. Jonathan was at the head of the bed and eventually received the Ambu bag and gave everyone else orders. There was another student who was the scribe, and another took the mannequin's blood pressure manually and palpated the pulse to ensure the accuracy of the machine. Kumiko was on the bed performing CPR (as the mannequin had stopped breathing), while Cody was in charge of the defibrillator after removing Mr Jones's shirt and revealing his breasts (multi-gendered mannequin). When ordered to, Tammy administered 1mg of Adrenaline every three minutes which commenced after the second shock with the defibrillator and then after every second loop of CPR. Leonie had fetched the emergency trolley at the start and was handing things to Tammy. Jamie and a few others were watching without blinking.

"Count louder!" Jonathan ordered to Kumiko, "I can't hear you!"

"26,27,28,29,30! Air!" Kumiko yelled, and Jonathan gave the mannequin two pumps of air via the Ambu bag.

Cody was so amazing and serious on the defibrillator, and very assertive as she demanded everyone to *clear* away as she waved her arm over the mannequin's body.

Everyone involved in the MET call knew their places well and handled it ever so professionally as though they did it all the time.

Before Tammy went for the Atropine, the freaky advanced future lifelike mannequin came round. Everyone else watching cheered as they continued to tend to the mannequin. The only bad thing to come of this situation was Kumiko had split her pants, right down the crack, while doing CPR. Everyone laughed at her Captain America themed knickers as she clutched her backside and backed into the wall. A real nurse came in and told her it happens all the time while chuckling herself.

Week eight was the best week by far, they did more drills and things, which Leonie never thought she'd enjoy but it was amazing. They did about five more building breaches, which by the way, was better than when she played video games. Jamie had found his destiny – to be a sniper. He was damn good at it too, considering he was dangerous with firearms in week one and two. He had accidentally pointed his rifle at Mr Pratt, his ammo fell out of his rifle during an exercise, and one time the recoil hit him in the face causing a nosebleed). To be honest, without him or Jonathan, they would all fail miserably. Jonathan especially contributed enormously; he acted as a mentor, tutor and guided everyone through the course well. He also counselled a few people such as Tammy when they found things unbearable. He was truly an inspirational guy, a natural leader, words can't even describe it. Leonie was still unsure of what her skill was, she could handle firearms well, but not much else still, just average really. She had better find a good skill soon. Otherwise, she might have to do some frontline shooting job, and she really did not want that. Killing an actual living thing is not the same as the robots. Unless the enemy *is* robots that is, that'd be good, then she could do it.

Who is the enemy? That's something Leonie, and most likely everyone else has been wondering for ages.

Chapter 13:

Week 10 was a scary week. They were told that things would start being tougher and stricter, ready for the exams in three weeks. Leonie didn't know how things *could* get even tougher, but she had learnt to keep an open mind since starting the course.

Week nine had been a bummer. Leonie finally received the opportunity to get pilot experience and one on one training, but the aircrafts were much more advanced, and she only got as far the simulator (which gives the illusion of the speed a real one would travel), and she threw up all over the cockpit. The pilot that was teaching wasn't impressed at all and explained how expensive it was before throwing her out of the aviation department. Jamie, who had broken another rule before this, had to clean up her vomit for his punishment and he came back to the group looking like a zombie.

But week 10 was good for most people; Cody was already destined to become a nursing officer, even though nursing didn't involve explosives or anything else she was in to, although she could make patients laugh. Jamie was obviously still a sniper and often bragged about it to everyone. Jonathan was probably going to become the next leader of the whole universe. Leonie still had no idea of her purpose, maybe she should just accept the fact she'd be joining Camilla in hell.

The start of week 12, the final week, came too quick. It meant that next week was exam time, and exams had always made Leonie nervous as, especially practical exams.

"Alright ladies," Mr Pratt announced as they all lined up for another day's torture, "this week you'll be left to figure things out on your own. I will throw things at you, but you will be given no warnings, no clues, no help, no support, you will find equipment and supplies by yourself. You won't see anything coming. I will start being mean. Ladies and gentlemen, welcome to life. NOW MOVE IT!"

So training commenced as normal, horribly. But their theory classes had ended, and everything they'd been learning was all thrown at them together for them to try and put to real use. There were now practice drills every day, and each day they seemed more real. A lady in her thirties called Jill broke her foot after she stepped on what looked like a bear trap during a drill in the jungle. She screamed in agony and Jonathan, and another guy had to carry her for the rest of the drill. Cody beat the crap out of a robot at one point, saving Kumiko from a hit in the head from a pipe and Jamie covered everyone with his handy dandy sniper. This is how most drills went down, except Jonathan usually didn't carry people; he would be leading the way.

Halfway through the week, the nerves started really getting to Leonie. It was okay during the day when they were all busy with training, but at night time when things got quieter, she would lay awake thinking and fretting about failing. Cody on the other hand, couldn't wait, she'd done it before, so she knew what it was all about, plus she wanted to get back to partying with Camilla.

Leonie got so worked up; she ended up practising after hours. Even if it was just pulling weights across the pool or going through the rope course, she was determined to be as good as she could be. She felt as though no matter how hard she tried, she wouldn't be as good as everyone else. Whatever happens, she would not let herself repeat the course.

She spent the last evening practising her combat skills on a robot. Mr Pratt and Debbie walked in and chuckled when they saw her. They were wearing Hawaiian clothes and stank of alcohol.

"You don't need to practice that," Mr Pratt said, "you need to work on your brain." Then they both walked off talking about some swimming crisis.

So Leonie's problem was theory, she still had time, it was 2145hrs. She went to find Jonathan; he was the best hope she had. He was getting ready for bed and almost looked annoyed by her request for help, but he accepted of course.

They sat down on the bench at the mess. As Jonathan was about to open his notebook, he looked at Leonie and understood that she was upset.

"What's up?" he asked as he put the book down and swung his legs around, so he was facing her, "nervous about tomorrow?"

Leonie nodded. She couldn't get the words out for a while; she didn't want to cry so she breathed for a few seconds and then blurted out, "I can't do it! I can't, I'm no good, and I have to go home!"

Jonathan looked surprised, but kept his cool, "it's okay, Leonie. You've done well, don't give up now."

"I'm sorry," Leonie said, proud she managed to not cry, "I've just never been good with exams you know."

"Me neither. That's why I always studied so hard, I was scared to look foolish if I failed. But that won't happen to any of us tomorrow, will it? I've seen you, you've done well. Tell me, what do you think is your biggest worry? What usually gets you?"

"Um well, I guess my nerves; I've always found it quite difficult to be confident in myself. I've always been shy, that's probably why I fail so much."

"Bullshit," Jonathan said (first time Leonie ever heard him swear), "that's nothing to be worried about. Many shy people accomplish great things, I studied a lot in history. You know, these days even though we're supposed to be free, we're still judged so much. Being shy is nothing to be ashamed of unless it stops you from doing what you love, and then it's a problem. Come on, I've seen you, you can be an animal when you want to be. Just be passionate about something, and nothing can stop you."

"What if I get it wrong?" Leonie asked, "I hear what you're saying, but it's so hard to get rid of the fear."

"Well. If you get it wrong, you get to do it again, look at Cody, she's blitzing it this time. People are so scared of failing, they never even bother to try. Why I admire Cody is because she doesn't give a crap, some people actually think she's hopeless, but her getting up and doing it again, not worrying what others think or futurising is what I know will ensure her success. You know, when I started University, I didn't think I was that smart. But I said to myself, I'd keep going until the end, even if I doubted myself, I wouldn't quit. I'd only leave if the teachers told me I was no good and couldn't ever come back again. They never did, by the way, I had one year to go before I disappeared. But that's the secret, keep going back until *they* tell you to leave, ninety-nine percent of the time they won't anyway."

"What were you studying again?"

"Physics and computer science, actually," Jonathan said plainly, "my dad wanted me to study medicine or law, but I wanted to study History and English, but he said there's no good future job-wise from studying those, so we somehow got to Physics and computer science."

"But that's great," Leonie beamed, "that means you're really smart!"

"Yeah… But I would still rather English and history," he laughed, "anyhow, come on, we should get some rest before the big day."

"Wait, what about the revision you were going to help me with?"

"I really don't think you need it."

*

"Leonie!!" Cody yelled in her ear, "Uppy duppy doos! Come on, today's the day! Then freedom!!"

Leonie rolled over, "oh no! Damnit, it's morning. I'm going to die."

"No, you're not. Come on, get dressed, you'll be fine."

Leonie slowly got out of bed, there was still ten minutes until the gas would release into the room.

As she slowly walked to into the changing room, Cody was dancing around like a lunatic in her underwear. Kumiko was praying. Tammy looked confident and was already dressed ready to go.

Jonathan and Jamie walked in looking like zombies as they usually did in the morning. Leonie didn't want to know what she looked like, so she avoided all mirrors and other reflections of herself.

No one ate much in the mess that morning, probably because Abhra (an Indian guy who was a law student before being taken) threw up in his breakfast which didn't help, but it was mainly due to nerves.

Cody was the only one to eat; she ate some porridge, fruit, bread, three croissants, and a shake before getting herself another coffee. Leonie managed a tiny nibble on the end of some raisin toast before deciding to just drink her tea.

Jamie kept going to the toilet due to nerves, and everyone heard him farting louder than usual. He came out and then ran back in several times.

Jonathan paced with a bowl of cornflakes while reading something in his revision book.

Leonie almost laughed at everyone's nervous behaviour. It was almost like they were all confused old people wandering around looking for their cars, although, Leonie and her friends used to do that all the time anyway.

The humour of it all relaxed Leonie a little bit, not much though, but just enough to take the edge off.

Mr Pratt walked in with his evilest grin to date, "You all look like a herd of cows ready for the slaughter. No matter, I didn't have any high hopes for any of you." Everyone stared at him and braced themselves when his eyebrows moved again, "but now I believe you could all make a fine living for yourselves in this operation, whatever it may be."

They all piled into the massive, round, theatre-like room which Cody described as the *Def Leppard* concert. It was a daunting place, full of seemingly advanced equipment and lighting that appeared to control themselves as though they were alive. *"A living light?"* Leonie thought, *"what will they think of next?"* Everyone anxiously waited and was relieved when they received the news that they weren't first to do their test, except for one. Sharon, a forty-two-year-old P.E teacher from Delaware, had the unfortunate honour to go first. The rest of the students sat down in their comfy red seats looking down at the stage-like area where they'd be doing their assessment.

Down the bottom filled up with smart-looking people in suits. They'd be the ones assessing them. Jamie gave some of them double thumbs up as they glanced up at the students, but they just looked back down again. Jamie leaned back in his chair looking sad.

Leonie nudged Cody as she noticed Stacey was among the assessors.

"STACEY," Cody yelled, waving her arms around to get Stacey's attention, "STACEY! WE'RE UP HERE! WE'RE GOING TO DO OUR EXAMS! MAKE SURE YOU MARK US FAIRLY! LOVE YOU! NOT, I'M KIDDING!" –

"Shut up!" all the other students whispered as a couple pushed her back into her chair. Leonie regretted pointing Stacey out to her. Stacey ignored Cody anyway, but an Asian guy next to her was staring up at Cody in horror, understandably.

Mr Pratt walked on stage and announced to the assessor's stuff that they already knew. Then he walked back off stage and immediately after, the stage sank into the ground and a set moved forward to take its place. The set was a huge mansion which was bloody impressive. Sharon's assessment would be on how well she communicated to a combat robot going into the mansion to take out gangster robots. Made sense, as the students whispered among themselves, they all agreed that Sharon was a great communicator, very intelligent and had a good eye for detail. It was the perfect job for her, apart from a P.E teacher of course.

The combat robot almost died a few times at the start due to Sharon's exam nerves which gave her a shaky voice, but he made it through alive, thanks to Sharon. She did really well and passed and went through to do her theory exam.

Abhra went next and did really well, he had to disarm a bomb in a toilet (not the disgusting kind) and was covered in sweat by the end of it. For successfully disarming the bomb without blowing up, Abhra too passed.

Kumiko and three others went through next. All did extremely well. Kumiko did a cartwheel off the stage after she passed.

Then it was Jonathan's turn. Everyone was curious to see if they're guess was right, him becoming a commander of an army. They were wrong. Leonie had no idea exactly what his role was; it was sort of like a strategic advisor. Everyone was disappointed; he would've been so epic leaning over a balcony sending thousands or robots off to battle. In fact, no one understood what he was doing; he was explaining complicated things and using big words. He wrote a lot of physics on a board which was like a foreign language to Leonie. She knew a little because, for the aviation course she wanted to do at University back home, she needed to understand some Physics. But Jonathan was going so fast like a kid showing off how fast they can do their five times tables, she could barely keep up and only read the first line by the time he had finished his whole assessment. Jamie didn't even know what physics was, so he was completely lost and unhelpful. Whatever Jonathan did, he seemed to really impress the assessors, who all actually got up and gave him a round of applause.

Cody leaned into Leonie's ear, "don't worry, Stacey seemed to understand, so we'll ask her later."

"Or we could ask Jonathan when we see him next?"

"Yeah! That's a great idea."

Cody's turn was next. Leonie turned to wish her good luck but she was already gone, she sprinted onto the stage looking super excited. Some of the other students didn't like Cody's enthusiasm and scowled a bit, making Leonie laugh. Before Cody could begin, the assessors had to first move back several ten feet (possibly thirty), because last time she accidentally threw a stun grenade at them.

Leonie remembered her dad saying how the military would be great for Cody; she'd be in so much trouble, even just for having a wrinkle in her uniform or a speck of dirt on her shoes. He always said how it would fix her bad ways up quick and that keeping her away from things she was bad at was a terrible idea, fixing them was better. He then told Leonie the same applied to her, especially when it came to communication.

When the assessors were finally ready to begin Cody's assessment, it was no surprise her test was in a hospital setting, and it wasn't like high school where she had to mop the school nurses office either. Cody was a Registered Nurse who along with a doctor robot and some other nurse robots, had to tend to a wounded combat robot who received a bullet to the heart. Leonie, again, didn't understand much of what was going on, she knew pulmonary arteries went from the right ventricle to the lungs to oxygenate the blood and came back through the pulmonary veins and that the Aorta sends blood to the body and it comes back through superior and inferior vena cava. Not that knowing that is as great as what Cody knows, although she'd have to tell Cody all that next time she sees her to show she was listening all those times during anatomy and physiology classes. Okay back to it. After a long while of an intense and careful procedure, Cody and the doctor saved the robots life. Leonie, Jamie and the other students stood up cheering from the stands, Cody had passed! Now she just had to do the theory exam, and she was through! No, wait... She may have just ruined it by break dancing on stage. Mr Pratt yelled at her to get off.

"We shouldn't be enjoying this right?" Jamie asked as he was in stitches on the floor from laughing in front of Leonie, "Oooh my back!"

Jamie had the hiccups through-out the next two assessments. However, the third assessment after gave Jamie the fright he needed to stop them. The youngest student, Andy, had been in a car chase for his assessment when there was a horrible accident. The car he was in flipped and rolled several feet before crashing into a big steel support column. Before everyone even got back up from the floor after diving as a few bits of metal went flying in different directions, an emergency team was already gathering around the car to help Andy.

"Oh my God," Jamie gasped, "Andy! Andy's had a crash; is he okay?"

No one answered, but everyone was gobsmacked and staring at the scene waiting for a sign of Andy. The Emergency team had to cut the roof off the car off to get him out safely.

It was a huge shock to everyone, Andy is a quiet, polite young man and rather sensible too. It was horrible seeing him in an accident.

"There he is," Leonie pointed as Andy was removed from the car on a stretcher, "he's not moving."

"Yeah well, he's kinda in a bad way," Jamie said reassuringly with a hint of sarcasm, "I'd be scared to move too. Maybe his spine is in a bad way and if he moves he might become paralysed."

"I didn't really need a complete explanation, Jamie," Leonie said meanly.

"Sorry. Just trying to help."

"Sorry Jamie, it's just scary. You are right though. Just hope he's okay."

"Yeah me too, he's a great guy."

After Andy was removed from the scene and the crash was cleared. The blinds went down ready to prepare for the next assessment. Everyone was quieter now after the accident and Leonie could feel her nerves creeping back up again. Her heart sank as she was called out next.

"Good luck princess!" Jamie joked, "Go get em!"

Everyone wished her luck as she made her way down to the bottom level, "Good luck Scarface!" someone called from back in the stands.

Leonie prepared backstage, which included changing clothes into a daggy black jumpsuit with a skivvy and a belt with some gadgets that she imagined were there just for display. She felt like she was getting ready for a theatre show.

A man with a shaved haircut with strange patterns in it gave her a couple of pages on what her mission was about. He didn't say anything to her though. Leonie read the paperwork and discovered her task was to rescue four combat robots from her squad who were being held captive. It was very detailed; it told her all the history of the pretend terrorists and the sort of weapons they used. It also informed her of the form of torture they would inflict on her if they caught her. Their favourites seemed to be breaking fingers, drowning you in a bath and using bright lights and loud noises.

Unable to not keep the torture information in mind, she waited behind a door which would lead to her scenario. She was armed with a SIG Sauer P226 Elite Dark with attached Streamlight TLR-1s weapon light, which made her feel ripped off as she'd seen many super advanced weapons in her time of being there. Plus, she imagined the bad robots all had assault rifles.

While she was still in the middle of thinking hard about weapons, the door suddenly flung open. She slowly and carefully leaned in. She could not believe her eyes.

Chapter 14:

The stage was incredibly realistic, there was no sign of a stage, and it looked like an actual building with proper windows that had a view of a city. The Judges and all the students in the stands were nowhere to be seen. It was like she was in a simulator or something. It was so cool.

The room she stepped into had a couch and a bar in it. It was really messy, worse than Alice's or Cody's bedrooms combined, and it stunk of sweat like in a changing room. She looked back at where she came in, the door was gone, and it was now a window. She cautiously looked out and saw she was at least twenty stories high. Thank God she didn't have to go in through the window for real.

She opened the door that led to the corridor after hesitating for a while. She had the same feeling of finding the courage to jump into a freezing cold river.

She stepped out into an empty corridor and proceeded to turn several corners before finding her first bad guy robot. He saw her immediately, but not before Leonie saw him first, and she fired two shots into his head, and he immediately fell to the ground. She was right, he had an assault rifle.

Unfortunately, Leonie had no silencer on her pistol, and she could hear a heap of yelling up ahead. Panicking, she spun around in a circle several times as she tried to figure out what to do. Her critical thinking was certainly not up to speed. With loud feet, she ran down the corridor into the opposite direction of the yelling and dived into a room.

She heard several footsteps running past, and she slowly got to her feet as they faded.

It didn't take much to realise she was in the kitchen. It was rather old too, it had a seventies feel to it. Now she doesn't know why, and she hopes that the assessors won't mark her down for this, or that the other students will judge her, or more importantly that it gets her caught by the bad guys. She was just so thirsty; she opened the fridge and got herself a glass of milk. She could hear Jamie's voice in her head saying, *"Just drink it straight from the bottle!"* as well as Stacey's voice telling her not to drink it in the first place.

As she finished, the door she had come in started to open. She dived behind a dining table across the room. *"Idiot! Why did I do that!? If someone else did it, I would call them a moron."* She held her breath as three robots came in, one looked French. They spotted the milk bottle, so Leonie started to raise her pistol, but there was no need as they simply had a glass of milk themselves. They were there for about three long minutes as they also helped themselves to some sort of slice. Leonie got a heart attack as she realised she was crouched right next to a mirror and revealed a bald girl with a burn on her face and a milk moustache.

"Okay this is weird," Leonie whispered to herself after the robots left, "no more wasting time."

She followed the three robots back out to the corridor quietly and carefully. Lucky she did because they led her straight to the hostages, and they weren't where's she'd of guessed, in the bathroom. She got a quick glimpse of two, one tied up on the toilet and the other in the bath.

One of the bad robots came back out and gave Leonie a fright. Without thinking, she shot him and then forced the door back open before it had even closed properly and shot the other two bad guy robots. She quickly scanned the corridor and after seeing it was clear, went and untied her squad.

"Where's the other two," Leonie asked in a weird voice she gets when nervous, she was sweating like mad.

"I think they kept them in the lounge room," one of them answered.

"Okay let's go, grab their guns," Leonie ordered. One of the combat robots checked if the corridor was still clear while the other searched the bodies of the bad robots. As they were about to leave, Leonie heard something in the window. She looked to find a lady climbing down a ladder on the outside of the building. She looked familiar, but she didn't know where she'd seen her from. She wore glasses and had a huge backpack on. The lady stared at her for a second, before continuing down the ladder. Leonie was about to walk over to the window when the two combat robots ordered *her* to hurry up.

They had just set off when there was a loud voice going through a speaker. It was one of the assessors informing Leonie that her assessment had been cancelled due to complications and to wait for assistance. At the same time, the walls around her had dropped and the two combat robots demeanour had changed to the normal guard robots she sees standing around. They both headed towards the direction of the bathroom window. Leonie thought perhaps that lady was the reason for the cancellation.

Stacey came and demanded that Leonie follow her. She didn't say much just that they were going to see Dr Martens. This made Leonie feel kind of eerie, as she still wasn't too sure about this mad scientist. To be honest, though, she'd almost forgotten all about him in the last twelve weeks.

They entered his office, without even knocking, Dr Martens was standing beside his desk waiting. He showed them their seats and got straight to it.

"We have a terrorist in the facility," he spoke with a German accent which had a slight hint of American in it. He almost looked like a more muscular Sheldon Cooper. Leonie had forgotten what he looked like, definitely not like she remembered. "We believe she is responsible for the hacking crimes we have been experiencing. She must be taken out."

Leonie looked at Stacey who just gave her a look that tried to prompt her to speak.

"So what do I do," Leonie asked hesitantly, "I was doing my assessment?"

"That is not important," he replied, "you are the exception of the compulsory assessment of those who have no qualifications or skills. You had to complete the twelve weeks, but you were always going to be involved in this, Miss Reine... After all, it is your family who started all of this terror in the first place."

Leonie was taken back, "Excuse me? My family started what?"

"In the future, your great-great-grandson makes an immaculate discovery, while on a trek in Bolivia. He found an alien spaceship, one that could time travel, it was not the TARDIS or a DeLorean, and do not talk about Star Trek!" It was as if he could read Leonie's mind. "It wasn't the spaceship which enabled the time travel, it was the large orb filled with red liquid and sparkling jewels that made time travel possible. He, Jacob, took the orb and studied it well. However, he was one of these extreme activists and used the orb to blackmail the government to do things in exchange for the orb. Of course, he never gave it to anyone. Eventually, he was assassinated, but not before his cult had learnt how to create a replica of the orb. The government had the real orb safe in custody, but unfortunately, the replica could not be located. The worse bit is that the replica was dodgy. Humans cannot match the skill of those who had created the orb, and it started to suck in time. Soon, people from as early as 200 B.C were flooding the streets of London. Dinosaurs were charging around cities, causing damage and death. And that was only the beginning. On the bright side, extinct animals came back, including the

Tasmanian tiger, Mammoths, and Spectacled cormorants to name a few. But apart from that, it was… pretty bad. Suddenly, we were visited by angry humanoids that had created the orb and accused us of destroying the ship and stealing the orb. We've been fighting them ever since."

Leonie didn't know how to process this information. This was not what she was expecting to hear at all.

"So… you're saying it's my families fault?"

"No. You can't be held accountable for something your family does in the future. No. Don't worry, your being here is purely coincidence. We take people who had displayed potential in their lives but never used it. You and all your friends were destined to lead a pretty boring life. Why not spice it up a bit?"

"Well, thanks… I guess."

Suddenly he burst out laughing, for ten minutes, he got a sore back from it too.

"I'm sorry," he managed to say, "It's just it's just!" He kept laughing before turning serious, "I'm just kidding. There is no orb or anything. It's from a movie in the future. I just love doing that to people." He handed her a comic book with moving pictures which showed a red orb, a young blonde man holding it and angry aliens, which were blue with red indented streaks all over them, chasing him.

"Oh. Umm okay, so my family isn't bad?"

"Nah, in the movie this girls future grandson becomes evil. In my time, time travel is easy, I still don't tell anyone about how to though. No, the real truth is when scientists found a planet similar to Earth but bigger. Well a long time later, about halfway between your time and my time, they found a way to get there; it was a big secret, and the public was unaware, in case it failed. Well, it turns out the things that lived there weren't interested in visitors and took the arrival as an invasion. They have since attacked us. They look like us, and at first, started the attack by blending in and performing mini terrorist attacks and then built on it from there. They're sadistic and get pleasure from confusing and torturing people. Some say they even eat people, but there is no evidence of that. I apologise for the prank, and I want you to know that I do take this very seriously. The last bit I said about people whose potential was wasted, is true. You were destined to work in retail for five years after dropping out of university and then becoming a stay at home mother of four. I believe, from studying all about you, every angle, that you have the potential to become a leader, a fighter, and a hero. Not as much as Jonathan Morse, but still, you're close up there with him."

Leonie smiled, to try and hide her awkwardness and confusion. She still thinks he's a madman, but what could she do when she's stuck in this place?

After they were dismissed with nothing more said to them, Stacey took Leonie to a big room which was rather nice. It was full of all the other students dressed in suits and dresses.

"Is this supposed to be a graduation party?" Leonie asked.

"Yeah," Stacey replied, "I personally don't see the point to it, but hey, it's nice to have some fun sometimes still."

Cody came dancing up towards them in an embarrassing way, "guess who's going to start her degree in medicine? Me!"

"Your dress is inside out," Stacey smirked.

"Huh? Oh!" Cody giggled.

"Congrats though," Stacey added, "now let's hope you don't get the medications mixed up, hey."

"Shut up you, I'm awesome!"

"Good job Codes," Leonie smiled as she tried to find a way of disguising Cody's inside out dress, "not really chemistry or engineering like you wanted, but it's amazing nonetheless!"

Jonathan walked up looking rather cheerful. Before they could say too much though, Jamie emerged loudly through the huge red entrance doors in his suit which was too small for him. He looked like the happiest person in the universe. Unfortunately, he didn't get his theme song he wanted, but "Let my love open the door" by Pete Townshend was playing, so he worked with that.

"Here he comes," Jonathan cheered, "how did it go, mate?"

Jamie twirled as he got to their little circle, making his shoes squeak, "well, after Leonie's slight delay, which we'll get to in a minute. I was next, sniping followed by interrogation. Man did I rule! And those written exams were a piece of cake right?"

Leonie briefly explained what happened with Dr Martens, leaving everyone's mouths open wide. Kumiko threw a grape into Jonathan's mouth as she walked past. Cody looked thrilled when Leonie mentioned the time travel.

Stacey discouraged Leonie from saying too much though and pointed to several cameras and mics, and anyway, the assessors had come in to give out appointments for job interviews for everyone.

Mr Pratt made another speech on stage, but everyone was more interested in the buffet that was behind him. Cody dragged Leonie up to get some food and hid some in both their pockets as well, including potato bake. Camilla appeared behind them and pushed them into the table, knocking over some punch. She congratulated them, and they all celebrated as though what Dr Martens had said didn't matter, even though it potentially did.

"You must be disappointed after all that training and not completing your assessment," Camilla asked as they ate and watched Jonathan help Jamie take out the coat hanger that was still in his jacket.

"I'm just confused," Leonie replied, "have been ever since we played murder in the dark that night. Life's been crazy since

138

then. I don't know if it's good or bad that no one is bothered by what's happening, we're all just going along with it."

"I love it," Cody said thrillingly, with a mouth full of chicken "it's like a vacation."

"Well considering your vacations were at home watching your aunt's knit jumpers, it's not surprising," Camilla explained.

"I mean don't you all miss your families?" Leonie asked desperately, "Alice? Shani? And Stacey don't you miss Rocco and Rufo?"

Everyone took a moment's silence, as though that was what was required. Leonie calmed down straight away as people started to stare. Cody, who had chicken and grease all around her mouth, smiled at Leonie and tried to cheer her up. Although they were stubborn about being committed to this place, Cody, Stacey, and Camilla did for a moment send a vibe of understanding and empathy towards Leonie. But she wasn't entirely convinced. She guessed she was just feeling a little homesick, but as long as her friends were there with her, she tried to hold on. However, it killed her to think of her parents, to think that her father was probably still working on the case of all the disappearances and now she was added to that list.

The assessors appeared to explain how all the students would be called into rooms individually for a job interview. They also had some news in regards to Andy.

"Andy," one man with not much hair and a blue suit said, "is currently in surgery with a spleen laceration. So he won't be joining us for a while. He will have to repeat the twelve weeks and try again."

There was a whole heap of booing coming from the students, "That's not fair!" they yelled.

"I apologise," the man replied calmly, "but as we are not currently in demand for new recruits, we don't necessarily need him, and as he was so young, we believe he could do with a bit more training to develop his skills more."

"You're a prick!" Cody yelled, and everyone cheered her on.

"Sorry, you feel that way Miss Cody Malice."

Chapter 15:

So the job interviews went ahead really quickly. Leonie's worse fears were realised, she was to be placed in combat like Camilla. That was all she knew so far.

Stacey and Cody were already sitting at a table drinking coffee when they arrived in the worker's Mess (It looked like a half café half club filled with all sorts of people from different times and places, Leonie wasn't too sure when or where though). Camilla had been helping Leonie get her uniform and weapons sorted out, including knives to Leonie's horror.

Leonie spotted Warren and Clark sitting with Jamie and Jonathan and headed over while Camilla was still talking to her about something.

"Hey!" Leonie yelled excitedly, "haven't seen you two for ages! How you been?"

"Great!" Clark smiled as he gave her a hug, "congratulations on your course, so glad I didn't have to do that."

"We've been thrown straight into the deep end," Warren sighed, "working full time, it's hard trying to find an enemy when they won't tell you much about them."

"Wait, they haven't even given you guys any information?" Leonie asked disappointed she couldn't blast them with questions.

"Nah, we're still noobs," Clark said, "we're trying to be kiss-asses at the moment in the hope that it will get us more access."

"But I thought because they let you join straight away without having to do the twelve weeks, they find you important and would tell you everything?"

"Yeah that's what we thought too," Warren said as he sipped his ice tea, "anyway; let's not spoil your celebration. You must be dying for something sweet!"

"Might I recommend the lime cheesecake," Jamie said in a sort of disturbing moan as he flashed his eyebrows at Leonie making her blush (eyebrow flashing was a weakness of Leonie's, even when done by Jamie).

Leonie swiftly headed back to join the three girls at their table. Cody was in a bit of a pickle trying to decide what she wanted to eat and the waiter looked angry.

"Oh damn!" Leonie said as she sat down, "I forgot to ask Jonathan and Jamie how their job interviews went."

"Oh," Stacey said as she sipped her mocha, "well Jonathan is our squad leader.

"Squad leader?" Camilla asked looking confused.

"Yeah, it was going to be announced this afternoon, they've put us all in our own squad. So Jonathan Morse is the squad leader, *surprise*. I, unfortunately, have been placed in the squad as well," (Cody pretended to sympathise), "Camilla, Leonie and a couple of other guys are our fighters, and Jamie Young is a sniper. Leon Tyrell is our head doctor with Cody as the Registered Nurse. And of course, we have Max Clark and Warren Mitchel as our scientists and engineers."

"Wow we've got our own army going on here," Cody laughed, "Aren't they afraid we'll decide to take over!?"

"They should just get the Gurkha's in to sort it all out," Camilla said, "they'll get the job done without all this bull crap sitting around."

"We're not needed yet," Stacey explained sounding irritated, "I keep telling you, Cam, when one squad is wiped out, *then* another goes in to replace them."

"Well I think that's stupid," Camilla stated, "when a squad's getting wiped out they don't send help, and when there's only one person left, they're just left there to keep going alone until they die. It's just cruel!"

"I know," Stacey said understandably, "I want to change that." She lowered her voice to a whisper, "that's why I want to take over one day."

"Oh, I'm sure that's why," Camilla smirked, "well anyone is better than that Dr Martens, I suppose."

"Hey, where's that waiter gone?" Cody asked, looking around, "can't believe he just left while I was still deciding."

"Well that's just such a big problem isn't it Cody," Camilla said as she slammed her mug onto the table, "The world is going to end because poor Cody can't get her slice of cake." And with that, she stormed off.

"I think I want the lime cheesecake," Cody continued, after flinching a little.

"Unbelievable," Stacey scowled before chasing after Camilla.

"I'm sorry," Cody frowned as she looked at Leonie with her head lowered, "I do care I just don't know what to say, that's why I joke."

"I know," Leonie smiled as she shook her head, "don't worry they're just stressed out is all. I'm stressed about becoming a fighter."

"Yeah, I guess I'm stressed about becoming a Nurse and studying to become a Doctor. It's not even what I want."

"Unfortunately," Leonie sighed, "we've got to do things we don't like sometimes. But let's try our best to make sure it's not forever. Deal?"

Cody smiled, "Deal!"

"Now let's get that cheesecake!"

"Waiter!"

*

It turns out that finishing the horrible twelve weeks wasn't the end of training. They are now required to complete a four-week training course specifically focused on their profession. It wasn't as strict though, the hours weren't as long (by about two, and Fridays finish at lunch!), and they still got access to the worker's Mess. The best bit was no gas to wake them up in the mornings.

Leonie was lucky to have Camilla as her mentor. It was great; Camilla apparently had a good reputation amongst all the other combatants.

Today they were going to focus on hand to hand combat. Camilla already knew that Leonie was great with her firearms, but she was a bit too dainty when it came to hand to hand combat and knocking people out.

On their way to the gym they saw Jamie down a corridor being yelled at by his mentor for something, Jamie just had a stupid grin on his face.

They started off with a warm-up run around some fields. It was a great morning which was warm but not too warm. The sun felt good on Leonie's skin, and she had built up a bit of a sweat. She made a note to ask Clark and Warren how the spaceship had a room with an entire sun in it. It wasn't too hard to believe after that strange world they were in, however. The fields were in a room specifically for fitness training, it could do with some doing up, a few nicer trees and better care of the grass. There was a cool water fountain with an Angel in the middle of it. Leonie tried hard not to blink as they passed it. They ran past a beautiful big lake with an island in it and a small boat at the edge. After a while, they passed some other combatants running in a group.

"Hey Lamb," the guy in front yelled to Camilla, "this is the rookie?"

"Yeah Soup," Camilla replied, "don't worry she's a good one!"

"See you soon!"

As the men took a different turn, Leonie decided to ask the important question.

"Lamb?"

"I accidentally shot a lamb on my first day."

Leonie laughed, but was half sad at the same time and wondered why there was a lamb onboard a spaceship, *maybe for milk?* She thought. Camilla explained that Soup was in their squad too and that he got his name because he hates soup and always swaps with someone if he gets the soup sachet while out on a mission. Leonie thought they were both embarrassing names and hoped she wouldn't get one. She did like that Soup was in their squad though he had great energy and had a nice smile on his face. Camilla briefly explained he was from the early nineteen-seventies where he spent time mainly within his African American community, but he was really enjoying his time here mixing with the diverse population and making friends without any discrimination.

The whole day seemed never ending; Camilla worked Leonie harder than ever, she almost puked several times. They did weights and other strength training as well as cardio followed by a whole heap of sparring. Camilla had thrown her, kicked her and punched her over and over as well as grappling on the ground which was loads of fun, *not*. Leonie was aching all over and had bruises almost everywhere. They ended the day with some Tai Chi before Camilla threw her in a hot spa bath with a whole heap of Epsom salts and goodness knows what else. They then ate some chicken breast which had spinach in it, served with some sweet potato, pumpkin, broccoli, zucchini, and asparagus. It would've taken Leonie an hour to eat one veggie previously, but Camilla was very persuasive, and they finished within twenty minutes. After, Camilla took Leonie to get a massage from a Korean lady. She said it was a treat as a friend, for doing so well on her first day. *"Okay, so getting the crap beaten out of you is a good thing? Got it"* Leonie thought to herself. She suddenly had a newly developed fear of Camilla, like she had with Stacey as well as a heap of respect. The nice gesture didn't fool Leonie, she knew that was the last nice gesture Camilla would dish while completing the four weeks.

And she was right. The rest of the week was pretty similar in the fact that it was full on. There were no more massages, although not every day was working out for a whole day, usually just in the mornings and then the afternoon would be either weapons training, infiltrating scenarios, swimming, parachuting or of course more working out and sparring. So actually yeah, all working out.

The second week was much better, Leonie was officially able to join the rest of the squad (as did, Cody, Jamie, and Jonathan along with their mentors) and work under Camilla's watchful eye.

Stacey was Jonathan's tour guide and information giver as he technically required no mentor because he's in charge now. Leonie was blown away when hearing that Stacey was, in fact, their pilot. It was her dream job, and Stacey got it!

"Okay," Jonathan said loudly, and everyone gathered around. "For those who don't know me"—he was mainly talking to Soup and two other guys Jack and Doc who would be working with Leonie, Camilla and Jamie—"my name is Jonathan Morse. I will be in charge." Cody and Jamie cheered. "Thanks. We have our very first mission as a squad. It is just a drill, against some robots, but it will be more intense than anything in our twelve weeks, so we need to go in hard. Clark will go through the scenario."

Clark explained it in great detail, but basically, they were chasing some baddies through the jungle as well as some desert after they stole a chip with some important information of which only scientists understand (Leonie tried, but just couldn't get what they were on about). It was probably just gibberish anyway because it wasn't a real case, this eased Leonie's mind.

So Clark and Warren set up some computers, earpieces equipped with a microphone and explained the plan to everyone. They couldn't risk their aircraft being seen, so they had to drop the fighters off in an area Warren had marked out. They had to move fast to try and intercept the bad guys while guided by Warren's advanced technology, including a tiny flying gem which had a small camera in it to show Warren what was ahead of them.

Stacey's aircraft was epic. The best way Leonie could describe it wisely was like a C-17 Globemaster III, but it was significantly different. It had a sort of bubble on top with a huge machine gun, human-operated, which could spin three hundred and sixty-degrees. It also had a dozen automatic guns on the wings, outside the cockpit, and at the tail.

The inside was much the same as a normal transport aircraft, in the sense that it didn't have a five-star restaurant or anything. But it was a lot bigger with a computer room in it as well as a large weapons armoury. This was the Metal Ark.

"Stace," Leonie said as she stared at the Metal Ark, "

This. Is. Epic."

Stacey smiled and put on some shades before she went to board paradise.

"Ahhh she's even got the cool shades," Leonie said enviously as Cody and Camilla laughed, "even better."

Take off was more exciting than a roller-coaster. However, everyone had to listen to Warren go over things for the third time in his crazy fast maniac voice he gets when he's passionate.

Leonie decided she had better try and form a bond with the other three fighters. So, while in flight, she decided to start with Jack who was sitting on a chair doing something with masking tape. He was an American with short sandy blonde hair, and Leonie got a vibe that he hadn't washed in a while.

"Hey Jack," she smiled, and he looked up at her in an unfriendly way.

"Hey rookie," he replied, "you looking for something to do?"

"Uh, no. Um, just wanted to say that it's uh great you don't have an embarrassing nickname, is all."

"Well thank you," Jack said sarcastically, "but my real name is Connor."

"Connor? Well, why do they call you Jack?"

"Because he does Jack shit!" Camilla yelled from another room.

"Yeah it's true," Soup confirmed, "he never does any work the lazy bastard."

"Oh," Leonie said, and she backed away quickly. Instead, she went to help Doc, the Italian man who was kind of flirty towards Camilla and Stacey. He was checking out the vests they would be wearing. They had a lot of pockets on them filled with stuff that Leonie agreed they should familiarise themselves with.

"Shouldn't we have had a briefing about this sort of stuff?" Leonie asked.

Doc laughed. "Nah, things here are different to the way it was back on Earth. They expect us to be more independent and figure things out for ourselves, there is a huge percentage of fighters who get captured or lost. So I guess they try to prepare us."

148

"Wow really?" Leonie said sounding stunned, "they should have more training for things like being captured and survival when getting lost."-

-"and how to cope with interrogation and torture," Doc interrupted, "yeah. The system isn't really good. Hopefully one day they'll wake up and improve things. You know what they do now if any of that happens? Replace you. They leave you to your fate and replace you. It's disgusting."

"Yeah, Camilla said that."

They landed in the jungle. Warren and Clark explained how their computer scanned the jungle and indicated that the baddies are almost just out of range, meaning they're nearly in the desert.

"There's no way their scanner can pick us up," Warren said, "and don't worry, their scanner isn't as advanced as ours, and theirs only detects aircrafts and vehicles."

"How do you know?" Jamie asked.

"Because I invented this one," Warren said with pride.

"But that's stupid, why would they have one that just picked up vehicles and stuff, but not humans?"

"Because, Jamie, that's just what they have, okay. I guess just try to think. Their logic is, people can't get in the jungle or desert without some form of transportation, can they? And that's all they could make, was one like that."

"Okay hurry up," Jonathan said, "you need to move out now before they get too far ahead. Good luck."

The six of them set off with all their gear. Their vests and backpacks were super heavy. Soup told Leonie that when she runs back at base, to run with the gear on to get used to it. Jamie had on some ear guards like he was going sparring.

"What the hell are you doing?" Soup asked in disbelief. Everyone looked at Jamie and sighed.

"For if we have to do physical combat," Jamie said as though everyone else were idiots, "I don't want to get cauliflower ears!"

"You got your earpiece in?" Doc asked.

"*Duh*, underneath."

As they made their way through the jungle, Leonie tried to spot Warrens small camera that was supposed to be ahead of them somewhere, but it was too small to see. She had something on her mind but wasn't sure if it was a good idea to have a conversation while trying to sneak up on the baddies.

"Is it okay to talk?" Leonie finally asked.

"Talking? Yes," Soup replied, "got to keep sane don't we, but I draw the line at kissing during a fight."

Leonie laughed a little, "okay then. I was curious as to what you all think of Dr Martens?"

"He's a psycho," Doc said.

"Shhh," Jack whispered.

"He can't hear us, dimwit," Doc sighed.

"You don't know that!"

"I don't trust him," Soup interrupted, "I mean he's in charge right? So that means he's responsible for the unfair treatment of the squads when they're sent to battle. Plus he just seems crazy. Whenever I hear him talking, it's like this whole thing a chess game to him."

"Or like he's playing us like a video game," Doc agreed.

"I've never met him," Jamie announced.

"You know that girl you saw during your assessment, Leonie?" Camilla asked, "well I saw her once too sneaking around the base. I swear I've seen her before, but I just can't think where."

"Yeah I felt that way too," Leonie agreed, "what do you think she was up to?"

"I don't know," Camilla shrugged, "but there was one guy who said she used to be like us, a student, but she became a traitor after graduating."

"Maybe she did the right thing," Doc pointed out, "perhaps she found out some things about this *Martens* guy."

"Anyway," Soup said, "we're not sure about him. Now let's get back to it. I think we should pick up the pace through this part."

After going several miles at a relatively fast speed, they received word from Warren, "Okay guys. Can you hear me?"

"Yeah we hear you," Soup said through his earpiece after everyone nodded.

"Great. You're approaching the end of the jungle. Time to start being extra cautious. Now, according to my scanner in Camilla's backpack, as you reach the desert you will walk a mile before reaching a big hill, I've got heavy activity just on the other side of that hill. I'd recommend setting Jamie up on a high point while the rest of you move in. I'll move my camera up further to try and spot them for you. Sorry, my camera's kind of slow; need to adjust the speed after this mission."

"Cheers Warren," Soup said, "Out."

Soup ordered everyone to keep moving at the same pace. As they reached the desert, the first thing they saw was a big hill straight ahead. They made their way to it.

As they arrived at the bottom, Soup gave out orders. "Right, Jamie, you'll go to the top of that high point." He pointed to the highest point of the hill which looked difficult to get to. "Once you're there, you'll tell us and report what you see. I'll take Doc and head around to the right while you three take the left. On the count of three, we will all move out at the same pace and report when we get there. Do not engage until I give the word unless of course you get attacked. Got it?"

"Got it!" Everyone said.

"Okay. One… two… Three, Go."

Leonie followed behind Camilla and Jack without even thinking. It was like she was in automatic. They all had to keep at the exact same pace, the idea was they would try and get there at the same time so not to keep each other waiting with the risk of being caught.

They reached their position at the bottom of the hill, so Camilla spoke through her mic to ask if Soup was in place. Soup confirmed that he and Doc had arrived at their position.

"What about you Jamie," Camilla spoke again, "do you copy?"

There was silence amongst the earpiece's as they all awaited Jamie's response. Suddenly, a loud fart came through Leonie's earpiece. Camilla and Jack both jumped out of their skin.

"Yeah I'm here," Jamie announced proudly.

"Jamie!" Camilla whispered angrily through her mic, "that's disgusting!"

Jamie giggled through Leonie's earpiece.

"Guys, cut it out!" Came Jonathan's firm voice, "we need to focus." They were all listening back on the Ark.

"Alright, alright," Soup's voice said with a laugh. "Jamie, do you see anything?"

"No, I can't. There's not as good a view from here as we thought. They're right down the bottom in close to the hill, and unfortunately, there's a big hole in the hill, and the part near the edge to them is very unstable and might collapse. I don't want to die that way."

"Alright," Soup replied, "Man it's like you're smell's coming through my mic. Okay. Try to get into a position where you can without being seen, we *need* your cover. We cannot advance until we know we have your cover."

"Okay!"

There was a whole heap of moaning and groaning coming from Jamie's mic as he leapt over rocks and climbed up and down.

"Turn your damn mic off next time," Jack said, "that sounds awful."

"Guy's," Jamie finally said, "I'm in a damn good position, but there's another squad there, and they have the baddies in custody."

"What?" everyone said.

Soup decided they should all head down to see what was going on, Jamie stayed up high just in case though. When they arrived, there was one of the assessors from their exams there giving the other squad something Leonie couldn't quite see.

Soup and Camilla stormed up to the assessor who had tried to ignore them, but that was no longer possible. Soup and Camilla both demanded to know what was going on and spoke at the same time.

The assessor gathered Leonie and the others around to explain to them all at once. Leonie turned her mic on so Jamie and the others back on the ship could hear too. It turns out that a new trial had been set in place. On each mission, another squad can join in to compete to complete the mission. For each mission successfully completed, five points are earned to the squad. The points earn you many bonuses" food wise, you can get free meals and drinks. They can also buy you a nice suite for your squad to live in, access to the luxury spa, and much more cool stuff. However, the squad with the most points are also unfortunately next in line for real battle. The squad with the lowest points, although they don't have to go to battle, they also don't get those nice privileges and are on cleaner duty around the base.

The squad that stole their mission snickered as Leonie, and the others began their journey back to the Metal Ark.

"Well that stinks," Doc frowned, "now we have to win missions to get a meal?"

"Well if you think about it," Jack said, "you could avoid both battle and cleaning duties, by doing really well but not *too* well. We could just balance it out."

"You heard her though," Leonie said, "anyone caught slacking off at some point are punished."

"Well I want to go out to battle," Camilla stated, "that's the only way we can find out information."

Everyone else half agreed before Soup pointed out something serious, "where the hell is Jamie?"

"Oh my god," Camilla shrieked, "we forgot about him! Shoot!"

"Well aren't we just the worse squad," Doc laughed hysterically, "so much for no man gets left behind."

It turned out though, luckily, that Jamie had been following them, but was a bit behind. He wasn't too happy about being forgotten, but as usual, he quickly got over it.

When they arrived back on the Metal Ark, they were ordered to line up by Jonathan. It seemed there was one thing he needed to get off his chest and he looked a bit angry too.

Jonathan took a deep breath, "guys, you've got to stop mucking around out there. It's fine to act the giddy goat back at the mess but when we're out on a mission you've got to focus. One day we will be doing this for real, and it's that serious that one mistake could cost someone their life. I don't want anyone getting hurt. So start taking this seriously. No more farting in mics or anything."

As Jonathan went on more, explaining how they should be acting, Jamie held his head down in shame, and everyone else listened respectfully. Jonathan was great at giving stern lectures without sounding like an asshole, probably because of his soft kind voice and his sincere nature.

Leonie could one hundred percent see Jonathan's point and completely agreed with him. But she also could understand Jamie and even Cody too. She knew that pretending was not easy for some people and not everyone is good at acting. It was easy for Leonie because everything scared the crap out of her. She was willing to bet a lot of money that in a real situation, Jamie and Cody (who had apparently been mucking around too during the mission) would have everyone's back and would never let anyone down.

Chapter 16:

By the end of the fourth week, Leonie had been almost tortured by Camilla. She was already in great shape from the twelve-week course, but physically that was nothing compared to what she endured from this scary Lamb killer.

Leonie looked completely different to what she did back home. She hadn't looked at herself much since that horrible burning incident. But when she did, especially now, it was like she was a completely different person, not just the way she looked, but her whole demeanour including her posture, confidence, attitude but the biggest difference of all *was* her body. She was no longer that curvy normal looking young lady, she was so fit and strong, pretty much all muscle. It was in no way a small difference; Cody said she looked like an Amazon or Terminator, so it must be very noticeable. Cody herself looked very different, still quite slender though, but she looked more grown up as if puberty really kicked in over the last couple of months. Stacey, she's changed so much, she's very mature and dresses in business clothes usually, except of course on missions where she wears a green jumpsuit. She's still got a very feminine body, but she's always been quite strong, the sort of person where you don't want to find out what she's like during a fight. Although strangely, her biggest change is her hair, it used to just be long and hang, but it has some body to it now, and it's more blonde, she probably dyed it. The biggest difference of all is Camilla. That lady is like a tank, very intimidating, not someone you'd want to mess with, ever. Her arms, for example, are twice the size of what they were back at home. Leonie wanted to see a picture of them all from before to get a better idea of how much they've all changed.

Even the gents have changed, more strong and fit looking. Jamie gained a bit of muscle and lost his slight beer gut, Jonathan looked the same, but definitely had more muscle on him as well.

Warren and Clark were the only two who looked exactly the same as before. They were allowed to eat pizza and everything. Leon had lost a lot of weight; it was like he was back in the Navy Seals again.

The mental differences were the most significant changes for everyone. Leonie noticed it in Camilla and Stacey the most, but everyone had changed a lot, including herself somehow, but she couldn't quite figure out what exactly had changed about herself in particular.

They went on another mission. It wasn't too hard though. No other squad tried to compete in that one. They basically just had to blow up an enemy building and drop a friendly robot spy off in a city for their next mission. They received their first five points for their success; they were only bronze though which was enough to just buy dinner for them all. The points came in coins of, Gold, Silver, and Bronze. If you earned fifteen points in Gold, it meant that you did expertly well and could buy some really cool things. Stacey explained it as, Gold was like a doctor's wage, Silver was like an average wage, and Bronze was like the weekly pay of a check-out person. *Thanks, Stacey,* Leonie thought.

"It's like being in the Olympics," Cody joked.

"Well," Jonathan said as they all sat down in the mess to eat their hard earnt dinner, "we need to make a plan, so we can save up."

"I suck at finance," Jamie whined.

Jonathan continued, "I say we try and fit in more than one mission a day. Possibly three? Depending on how they go, apparently, sometimes one mission can last a day."

"I've had patients who were on one mission for four days when I worked in the hospital while you were doing your twelve weeks," Leon explained, "they were severely dehydrated, and two were suffering from hypothermia after their boat capsized."

"What was their mission environment like?" Jonathan asked.

"Deserted island," Leon replied, "that's why survival knowledge is important, you never know what your mission will be. Won't always be in cities, and it could be longer than a day."

"Okay," Jonathan said as he grabbed a pen and napkin and started taking notes, "so that's something I think we can agree most of us are lacking in."

"Always catches people out," Leon went on, "I would recommend writing it down and keeping it on you at all times. *Protection*, protect yourself from the elements, be it weather or animals and even emotions. Second is *location*, then *water*, then *food*. People always try and go for food before protection."

Leonie wrote all of that down, she could just imagine herself being lost in a forest and panicking.

Leon agreed to give an educational lesson about survival to everyone. It was strange, in all of the twelve-week training course, Leonie waited for the intense survival lessons, but they never came. Leon explained that the people in charge don't need them to survive, just to do what they're told. He also mentioned how so many people just go along with it without any thought of how much they're not cared for.

"I say we enjoy all this food," Jamie said cheerily, "and worry about them not caring about us when we're in danger."

"That's stupid," Camilla frowned, "you know they could get rid of us at any time, even when we're asleep."

"Don't tell him that," Jonathan said, "now he won't sleep and become a *grumpy* moron."

"How do you even know they're that bad," Jamie asked, "I mean they give us food, beds, and stuff?"

"So do prisons," Leon said.

"We should get back to the missions," Jonathan said quietly as a few people walked past, "I really think we should try and get in as many missions as we can in a day. And aim for gold."

"What if we become the best and get sent into battle?" Leonie asked worryingly, imagining spaceships flying around in all directions and lasers missing them by inches. Not that the real fighting would definitely be in space, but they all hoped so.

"We'll just have to do our best and worry about that when and if that happens," Jonathan reassured, "there's no way around this, we have to do the missions until we find out what's really happening out there."

"I say finding out what is happening out there is a top priority," Camilla announced, "and the only way is to be the best at the missions and get out there."

Leon, Clark, Soup, Doc, and Jack all agreed at once.

"Why can't we just demand Doctor Martens tell us?" Leonie asked.

"Because there's no way of finding him," Stacey explained, "you never know where he is unless he wants to see *you*. And not many people know much information, the ones that do, are just blended in with the rest of us. Like that guy waiting for his cappuccino could be one of his men." She pointed at a random man with glasses waiting for his cappuccino. "So I guess the only option *is* to win and go to battle if we want to find out anything."

After more arguing, everyone came to an agreement. They agreed that for now, they would complete several missions a

159

day to keep them stable and to try and earn a nice suite (Jamie's idea). They would think more about whether or not trying to get into battle was the best idea. If they were right in the fact that it would lead them to answers and potentially a way out, then great. But they still had to consider the fact that, it's a war, and they could die, obviously, and they had to be absolutely sure that that was the only option, before putting their lives on the line. Although this place was indeed very mysterious still, their lives here may not be all that safe anyway, so Leonie thought.

So Leon did a few different Survival classes with them, which made sense, a few light bulbs went off in Leonie's head when he explained a few things. It was mainly expanding on what he said before such as about protection if there's known to be dangerous animals nearby, arm yourself, make a spear, or if it's raining, make a shelter to protect yourself from it and collect rainwater for drinking. As soon as rain hits the ground, it's contaminated and needs to be boiled. Also the importance of keeping a fire going, he explained how it's good for boiling water, cooking food, keeping warm, keeping animals away, and for entertainment; he described it as natures TV. He also had them practice a few things such as traps and weaving for example. She still wasn't too sure how she'd react out in the wild on her own, she had heaps of luck up to this point, but it definitely wouldn't hurt to learn all this. Now she just had to retain all of the information and keep that piece of paper with the priorities of survival written on it.

*

Leonie and Cody had just been to visit Andy, who was recovering in hospital from his spleen laceration and a few broken bones. He was okay, glad to be alive as you can imagine. Unfortunately, though, Andy would have to complete the twelve weeks of training again once he recovered. It seemed another squad had their eye on him already.

160

They ran into a squad who call themselves the Golddiggers, really sums them up. Cody had previously made the mistake of angering their leader, Pip. She was on the course Cody did with Camilla and Stacey and had anger issues. She was small with long brown hair kept in a ponytail, she had green eyes and pale skin and a lot of makeup (she looked like a model!). Cody had gotten into a physical fight with her, unusual for Cody, who usually says some stupid things to people, but never gets physical. Camilla explained that Pip had started it by calling Cody a man. It was just a childish rivalry taken seriously, really.

"Hey Cody Sir," Pip smiled evilly. "Oh, and hi to your boyfriend. Is he an orc?" She was referring to Leonie.

"Shut up," Cody said nastily, "and you smell again, I think you've got a case of sacrificial undies going on their Pippin."

Leonie blocked it all out, she was kind of numb to insults regarding her looks now, she had heard them a lot since arriving here, even had people run away from her. Cody was doing a great job at giving horrible comebacks on her own anyway, even though they mainly involved fart and poo insults.

Pip tried to get in Cody's face, like a UFC stare down, but Cody simply burped in her face. Pip went to smack her, but a really tall handsome man with lovely bright blue eyes and dark chocolate hair pulled her back and said, "leave it. They're not worth it; they'll probably be on cleaning duties for the rest of their lives, anyway. Certainly goes with their looks."

So Pip and her squad of manly men walked off looking proud. Neither Leonie nor Cody was worried about being insulted by the handsome man. Cody didn't know who he was when Leonie asked, but apparently, she and Camilla used to spy on him during their twelve-week course together, like kindergarteners not knowing how to handle having a crush.

They headed back to their squad and prepared for a run with Camilla and Stacey who were stretching after some other workout the freaks do.

Leon joined them on the run and had great pace, he kept up with them easily for an oldish man. Although knowing he was an ex-Navy Seal, it wasn't too surprising. And he even joined in laughing when Camilla pushed Cody into the large water fountain on their way past.

Aside from normal training, it was actually pretty dull and boring. Every mission was fully booked as more and more squads were formed since being introduced several months ago. Leonie found herself watching Cody work in the hospital where she rubbed her knuckles hard on people's sternums if they wouldn't wake up during a Neurological observation. She even acted as a patient so that other students could practice things like log rolls and vital signs with her. It was a really low point and almost depressing time for most of them. Especially for Camilla, Jamie and the other fighters who had nothing to do. Jonathan was really stressed out to the point he was becoming crazy. He'd apply for a mission, get rejected, and then laugh hysterically for some reason. "We just can't get in," he'd say as everyone backed away scared.

About five squads had been sent to battle in the last few weeks, some were quite good friends with Camilla. They were cheered on as they left the facility, like heroes. Leonie and the others didn't cheer as they didn't see the point in applauding for their possible deaths.

The biggest thing to happen other than that was a friend of Warren's, Donovan, another scientist, was arrested. It happened at a café one morning.

Leonie was with Jamie having a free doughnut eating contest when it happened. They dragged Donovan off with moderate force to the shock and fear of everyone watching.

Warren walked in as it happened and simply ordered Leonie and Jamie back to the squad room, along with the rest of them. (Unfortunately, due to lack of points, their squad room was in the Metal Ark).

As they gathered around, Warren and Clark stood up ready to explain.

"My good friend was arrested today," Warren confirmed, "I'm not sure what will happen to him. He was caught making fake Gold, Bronze and Silver coins for squads who were struggling and starving. I told him it was a bad idea but. Anyway, the squads who were supplied the coins will be arrested too."

"What will happen to them?" Doc asked curiously.

"Not sure," Clark answered, "they never discuss punishments much with anyone. All we know is it was a very serious crime to them."

"Who's *they*?" Jamie asked curiously.

"Who do you think?" Jonathan sighed, "the people in charge."

"Oh. I'm convinced they're aliens or robots. Not people," Jamie explained.

"I think they're mental," Cody said.

Chapter 17:

Apparently, not many people got arrested, so this was big news. Stacey explained that the only other arrest she's ever heard of was because a lady got pregnant, so she was arrested and never seen again. No one knew what happened to her, they might have sent her back home, killed her or kept her locked up. For some reason, Leonie felt the second option was what happened. I mean if you think about it, what use is a pregnant woman or a baby to a war? And no one has ever done what Donovan did before. But there was no real law saying not to hack or not to get pregnant, so it is unfair, but what has been fair so far?

As Jonathan, Stacey and the two scientists worked hard on trying to get them a mission, the rest of them continued training in the Apex. Leon had the day off from being a Doctor, so he agreed to help out with the fighters training. Doc and Jack were late for once. So Camilla practised some intense grappling with Soup, while Leon helped Leonie with some weights.

"That girl who interrupted your assessment," Leon said, "apparently she was arrested, but escaped. Not sure what the hell she did, but she's a real handful for Dr Martens."

"Wow," Leonie said as she started throwing a really heavy medicine ball up at a wall and catching it again, "I wonder where she is now."

Leon nodded in agreement, "So... You and Cody are best friends. Meet at school?"

"Yeah," Leonie said as she almost dropped the medicine ball, "It was pretty weird. We met in eighth grade; it was my first day at my new school. We were in history class together, she was sitting behind me kicking my chair, and it became annoying. So I politely asked her to stop. Then we agreed to hang out, and the rest is history."

Leon laughed, "that's how *boys* become best friends."

Suddenly, Jamie and Warren came running in through different doors. They both yelled something at the same time and were out of breath.

"One at a time," Camilla said as she and Soup walked over to see what was going on, "Warren you first."

"Doc and Jack were at a club last night, they were dancing on a bridge thing when it collapsed, and they've both broken both legs in the exact same spot each!"

"WHAT?" Camilla and Soup yelled together.

"Are they okay?" Leonie asked worryingly.

"No they're both in a lot of pain; they've suffered some concussion as well. A total of thirteen people were seriously injured, including an entire squad."

"That's horrible," Leonie said cringing as she imagined the whole accident of the bridge collapsing and people getting crushed.

"That's sad," Jamie said before moving on, "my turn! My turn! Okay, Jonathan found us a mission, we leave at 1800hrs!"

There was no time to visit Doc and Jack in hospital, as their chance to get some gold was upon them. There were now only four fighters which was a strain, but they still needed to go; Leon said in real life they couldn't ask the enemy stop attacking while they throw two men a funeral.

Jonathan gave Leonie a note that was attached to the notes on the scenario.

It read,

Leonie,

I hope this mission gives you the push you need.

DJM

DJM? She thought. *What's DJM?*

Jonathan briefed everyone on the scenario; it's against another team, Pip's team to be precise. They were currently in the lead, so their task was to steal all their gold coins hidden somewhere in their camp. No *weapons* were allowed, and to make things worse, Debbie, their old combat trainer, had joined Pip's team. Probably because there are no more recruits to train as the facility they're first brought into got destroyed, so she may as well make herself useful and join a squad. How terrifying.

"She's a strong fighter," Jonathan said through gritted teeth, "Camilla will have to fight her."

"I'm needed elsewhere," Camilla declined.

"Well, who will take her out then?" Jonathan asked angrily.

"Stacy!" Cody yelled, "remember in training? The only person better than Camilla was Stacey."

Leonie was as shocked as everyone else.

"But I'm needed on here remember," Stacey said, "I'm the pilot."

"Forget that," Jonathan said, "Leon will fly. He's flown before."

"Yeah but nothing like this," Stacey gasped, "this is my baby, and she can be difficult at times."

"I'm sure I'll manage," Leon assured, "if that's what the boss wants, that's what we'll do."

"Fine," Stacey said firmly, "do *not* damage her."

"DJM," Leonie said to herself as they all prepared for take-off, "It must be Dr Martens, he must be tired of us doing nothing."

Once they were ready, they could leave. But first, Jamie had something rather important to sort out. "We need a theme song," he said. "Something awesome."

Everyone groaned except for Jonathan surprisingly, "Jamie you're a genius! I've got it, they expect us to sneak up on them. That's what we always do. That's what everyone does. Why don't we do the opposite?" He looked at Clark and Warren, "can you two build a really loud big speaker?"

"Already got one," Warren grinned, "Max and I were planning a party for the scientists as part of our arse kiss business. But now we're in a squad and have no use for it."

Jamie was still gloating at his *genius* compliment.

"Leonie," Jonathan smiled, "we've never formally heard what your ideal battle song would be?"

Leonie blushed a bit as everyone stared, "well, we haven't heard yours either."

"I don't want a theme song I think they're stupid," Jonathan replied simply.

"Oh okay then," Leonie said, "I choose, *"Bound for Glory"* by Angry Anderson, every time."

And that's exactly what they blasted as they flew in and landed bang dead in the middle of Pip's squads camp. Their squad were definitely taken by surprise, they probably weren't even expecting them for another few hours, and definitely not in this way. They quickly recovered and prepared to face them nonetheless. Leonie managed a quick look out her window at the camp; it was mainly dirt with one big green tent at the back of it and a fire just outside. Other than that it was all dirt and bushes.

167

To surprise them even more, Camilla and Soup were ejected through the top of the Metal Ark, like a whale, and landed on the ground with a padded board held beneath them. Then Leonie, Stacey, Jamie, and Clark charged out of the loading ramp and began fist fighting Pip's squad. Leonie had already punched someone before realising they had reached them; her brain was still taking off her seatbelt.

The adrenaline ran through Leonie, she didn't care that she was beating up people; she just wanted to help her friends, plus it was fun. Camilla and Soup, on the other hand, seemed just genuinely passionate about beating people up and it showed greatly that day. Now, Jamie, that was another story altogether, he was swinging in every direction and made contact only by accident. Cody was amazing, she snuck out with Jonathan while Warren and Leon stayed on board the Metal Ark. Cody was kneeing people in the stomach and dislocating shoulders somehow.

Jamie had just pantsed a guy when Pip and Jonathan called both squads back in line. It was time, somehow, maybe telepathically; both Jonathan and Pip knew that Debbie and Stacey must fight.

So both squads gathered in a circle, with a gap between both ends, and Debbie (who looked bigger and scarier than ever) and Stacey stepped in ready to fight. Leonie had no idea what those two fighting would accomplish, they still have to nick the coins, but she decided to humour the idea for now.

So the fight was to begin. The competitors were Debbie, a former pizza deliverer who was known to have beaten up five men who tried to jump her. Then there's Stacey, known for killing zombies on video games. Really intense.

Cody was given the honour of *ding dinging,* and instantaneously Debbie and Stacey were at it, people cheered and yelled as they quickly went to ground, grappling and punching at each other. It was too quick for Leonie, but she looked, and others appeared to not keep up also. She did know that Stacey was doing rather well, they both had bloody noses, but Stacey's hair looked way better than Debbie's if that counts? Pips squad was cheering loudly as the two ladies fought. After getting back on their feet, Stacey pushed kicked Debbie really hard in the stomach sending her sliding back a bit, but Debbie recovered quickly and sent a right hook to Stacey's face, followed by many more fast hits. It was then that Leonie's heart sank, Stacey was getting hurt. She shot a look at Jonathan who was already looking, he signalled a quick fall back to the rest of the squad, while he stayed behind to retrieve Stacey, who had recovered and was back to landing some good punches. Leonie looked back at Stacey as she ran towards the Metal Ark before she tripped on the ramp, Jamie and Clark grabbed her by the arms before she could smash her face and dragged her into the plane.

Moments later, Jonathan emerged with a bloody Stacey in his arms. Leon quickly raised the ramp, but not before two men had climbed on board. Jamie and Soup quickly went to throw them off, Jamie decided to run up and do a flying front kick and make a retarded ninja noise, but it did send the man flying off. Soup just simply grabbed the other guy and threw him off while the plane was still only a few feet off the ground.

Everyone (except Leon) gathered around Stacey, who was beaten pretty bad but still awake and alert, Cody and Clark tended to Stacey and reported to Leon of her condition ready for when he landed the Ark back at base. She was okay, but Leon did need to monitor her in the hospital for a night. He had access to a private room for her.

"Just in case you didn't know," Jamie explained, "we didn't get the gold coins, which was kind of what we needed to do. So basically, Stacey's sacrifice was in vain."

"She's not dead you idiot," Soup sighed, "she's not sacrificed and not in vain."

"We got the coins, Jamie," Warren smiled proudly as he showed them all the coins in a large trunk, "see, nothing was in vain."

"How did you," Jamie said confused, "why? Who? What?"

"Sorry," Jonathan said before swallowing a burp, "the idea only came to me after you guys went to fight, actually as soon as you left. We realised they'd want Debbie to have a standoff so everyone would be distracted. And Warren was up for it. So yeah."

"You little ninja!" Jamie yelled happily as he gave Warren big tens.

"You sent a little boy out?" Soup asked looking angry.

"Hey," Warren snapped, "I've lived longer than any of you!"

"But how did you lift that?" Leonie asked as she hugged Warren.

"You're not the only one who's been working out," Warren explained looking rather chuffed with himself.

When they got back to base, they were all so happy, even Stacey joined in singing "Eat the Rich" by Krokus along with everyone else. It was only right that that night, they would party, in Stacey's hospital room.

Chapter 18:

The next week, was another loathed dull week. Leonie caught a bad cold and had to rest mostly. They visited Doc and Jack who were in the hospital still; they would be out for months by the looks of things. Apparently, most of their future equipment that could help fix broken bones was out being used in the war, so it's the old natural way for them. What's more to the point, they can't even get any replacements either, so they were at a huge disadvantage when out on missions. They had a few good missions when Stacey got better, none as exciting as the win against Pip's team though. Other than that, Jamie got Jonathan to admit he's a Backstreet Boy's fan and Clark met up with an old friend from the police force.

Leonie walked into their new dormitory just in time to hear the amazing riff from "Love Alive" by Heart. Their dormitory was basically a seventies themed basement with doors leading to everyone's room, most sharing, of course, Leonie with Cody. The kitchen was in the middle of the room at the back, and the bathroom was in the last room next to Clark and Warren's room.

Stacey leapt up to get away from Leonie who still had a touch of her cold, Leonie rolled her eyes at sat on the couch next to Jonathan.

"I like Def Leppard," Jonathan said angrily to Jamie who was still hounding him about music, "does that help?"

"Yes," Jamie smiled as he stared into space, "that does make it a bit better. "Photograph" happens to be the song that got me into rock."

"Mine was "Dream Police" by Cheap Trick," Jonathan said still trying to impress Jamie, so he'd leave him alone.

"Respect," Jamie smiled, "I still can't believe they actually made more *Star Wars*, four years after I was taken. That's what Cody said. What was the last film you saw?"

"*Scream*," Jonathan said as he leaned his head back, "pretty epic. Cody said they make sequels of that too."

"Yeah and one of the killers in the first one plays Shaggy on *Scooby-doo* in the future," Camilla laughed from somewhere.

"And apparently, they've completely gotten rid of those high cut leotards and swimwear. Gone back to that lame sixties bikini bottoms," Jamie went on, "how the hell could they?"

"Among many other things," Leonie chuckled.

"I think that passion is what's missing," Camilla explained as she stepped out of the shadows and joined them on the couch. "Like movies and things, they're all the same. There's no real art to it anymore, just all about the money and having hot, unrealistic looking people in it."

"Unrealistic people?" Jonathan asked.

"Yeah," Camilla replied without explaining.

"Well I'm just glad *The Bill* is still going strong," Jamie said, "my favourite show. Leon told me so."

"Oh that finished in two-thousand and ten," Leonie said softly, "Leon got taken in two-thousand and five, didn't he?"

"Damnit!" Jamie cried into a cushion.

"No idea what any of you are talking about," Soup said as he walked in wearing only a towel.

"What year did you get taken, Soup?" Leonie asked curiously.

"Nineteen seventy-one," Soup said proudly, "I was at a Led Zeppelin concert hearing "Stairway To Heaven" for the first time, in New York."

Everyone jumped up in excitement and gathered around Soup eager for more details. This was the most awesome story Leonie had ever heard. Well, not really but at the time it felt like it.

"This is so stressful," Stacey moaned as she counted up their new silver coins from their last mission in the kitchen, "we need more gold coins if we want to stay up near the top."

"It's so hard," Jamie sighed, "I liked the training course better, it was fun, and we didn't need to worry about coins and things."

"Beats paying rent," Soup pointed out, "I certainly don't miss that."

Clark and Warren walked in giggling like schoolboys, this usually means they have a big idea. They had to wait for Leon and Cody to get back from their hospital shift before they could lay it on them though (There was a shortage in the hospital so while they weren't on a mission, Leon and Cody volunteered in the hospitals for eight to twelve-hour shifts. Leon suggested it to help Cody get some more experience and to help with her medical degree).

"Okay," Jonathan said as he got his lunch out of the microwave, "what is it this time?"

"Smells like chicken and rice, this time" Jamie guessed clueless.

Ignoring Jamie, Clark with a huge grin on his face signalled for Warren to talk, "We know where Dr Martens is," Warren said excitedly.

"That is good news," Stacey said stunned.

"How did you do it?" Cody asked.

"We finally managed to hack"-

"What have I said about hacking?" Jonathan interrupted angrily as he spat a hot bit of chicken back into his bowl, "I don't believe this. Do you want to end up arrested like Donovan?"

"Desperate times call for desperate measures," Clark explained calmly, "don't worry we were very careful. It's obviously an area we've never been in where he is. We managed to tap into messages with his name in it after running searches keying in certain words to track. It doesn't show where the messages came from, but it does show where it goes too. This message appeared to be from his lover."

"His lover?" Camilla asked, "you must be mistaken, Dr Martens has no heart. His only pleasure is from other people suffering."

"What did it say?" Leon asked curiously, and Clark got up on his transportable computer screen a saved message. It read, *"Julian, When can I see you again. We need to talk. Please. I can't hold on much longer."*

"Is that it?" Jonathan asked looking disappointed.

"We've confirmed his first name is Julian," Clark clarified.

"With all due respect," Soup said, "that's hardly anything to go on. Surely there's lots of Julian's around."

"No that's just the one that hints it's his uh lover," Warren explained, "there's actually quite a few messages, two of which included his surname, all leading to the same location."

"We've got him," Clark confirmed.

While everyone else thought Clark and Warren were champ's, Jonathan still wasn't convinced, and he made sure everyone knew just how much he wasn't happy.

"Chill out Jon!" Camilla snapped.

"Yeah chill out Jon!" Cody laughed, enjoying the confrontation that was building up.

"We were doing fine without cheating," Jonathan protested, "we could be in serious trouble now."

"Well technically hacking isn't cheating," Clark stated, "In the FBI and CIA, they hack."

"We're surrounded by cool people," Cody whispered to Leonie.

"I think we need to all calm down," Leon said firmly, "Bickering surely isn't going to solve anything. I agree with Jonathan that we need to work as a team and be more cautious. But I also think, well done you two, that was outstanding work."

Leon helped things a little bit, but there was still some tension especially between Camilla and Jonathan who had completely opposite opinions. Jonathan wanted everyone to be safe, while Camilla wanted to go to war and to rip Dr Martens head off. Jamie was on the couch with his head on his knees and a cushion over his head trying to block it all out. Eventually, things went back to normal after Camilla and Jonathan battled it out at table tennis and darts. Then, everyone was able to reason with Jonathan and convince him to help form a plan to find Dr Martens. Of course first, he had to give Clark and Warren a private lecture first. He then sent Soup and Warren out to determine an exact location and any means of access. They confirmed it to be a space penthouse; they believed it was at the highest point of the whole spaceship on the eastern side. Not that they really knew the layout of the spaceship, there was definitely some skilled people making sure no one knew any of that information. They still haven't had a glimpse of space yet.

So the plan was to that night, sneak into Dr Martens lair, and interrogate him for information and a way out. Leonie went with Camilla to talk to Jack and Doc about the plan, they were all for it, not that they could do much to help. But they would cause chaos in the hospital that night as a distraction to security and other staff.

Leonie then met up with Cody and Jamie who were so excited about the whole thing, they were blowing up balloons. They headed out with a map marked on where Dr Martens lair was, east of the base and it couldn't be a longer walk to get there. They had to familiarise themselves with the location in small groups, so not to cause suspicion. Stacey even took some fellow friends there (without telling them of course) from her old work, so it didn't look like the whole squad was hanging out there. It was a much cleaner area of the so-called space-ship, it looked like a museum, all white and shiny with statues and weird pictures of naked people hidden only by fruit. There was no secret entrance to the lair, it was just an ordinary doorway, similar to the others in that clean area. It's just no one could ever have picked it was that particular doorway to the big guy's home unless they hacked like Warren and Clark did.

"Why on Earth did you blow up balloons for?" Jonathan asked at the group meeting back in the basement.

Soup was the last to arrive; he had collected some cool looking electrical equipment for Clark. Warren had already hacked into the CCTV of the lair area. And he had prepared a loop of them all for the CCTV operators to watch ready for when investigations began.

Clark had made Jamie a funny looking fake pencil moustache to go with his disguise as a butler for the evening. Warren was in luck because Dr Martens real butler just got fired and was looking for a new one. With his excellent hacking skills, he managed to put in Jamie who was beside himself with joy to do some undercover work, except he was certain the penthouse he was going to was the magazine version.

Stacey combed Jamie's long brown hair and made a neat part in the middle, it naturally curled a bit towards the ends at his chin but looked reasonably presentable. She washed his face with a face washer and even plucked his eyebrows a bit. He wore a snazzy black suit with a black bow-tie. Leon and Soup then gave him some advice on mannerisms and voila! Jamie actually looked surprisingly attractive, to Leonie's shock, it made her feel uncomfortable, but he did look quite handsome. Cody said he looked really gangster, and Leon said he looked like a proper butler fit to serve a rich and powerful person, like Dr Martens.

After going through the plan over and over again, Jonathan decided it was time to send Jamie on his way to the penthouse to begin his undercover work, especially since he kept on singing "Ooh, my, you do look smart, you do look smart," whenever he saw himself in a mirror.

Meanwhile, Cody was preparing herself to be a cook for Dr Martens and his guests that night. No hacking required for Cody, she managed to convince her old boss to give her another chance and pretended to be jobless without a squad.

Stacey got herself invited to the penthouse for dinner. Dr Martens had thrown a dinner party for his top agents. Stacey still worked a bit in the big office, but she was invited mainly because she was very pretty, so.

Leonie, Camilla, Soup, and Leon were in charge of storming in, once Stacey gave the word through her earpiece. Then once the penthouse was secured, Warren and Clark would join in for the interrogation. Of course, somewhere in there Jack and Doc would be causing a scene in the hospital. Good on them.

Stacey and Cody had now also taken their places at the lair. Back in the basement, everyone else was watching through Jamie's bow tie which had a hidden camera in it. Unfortunately, his bow tie was completely sideways. So they had to get Stacey to try and sneak up to straighten it so they could get a better view.

Stacey's camera was on her necklace, the pretty shiny bit. All her footage revealed so far though was that men liked looking at her cleavage.

Cody was set in the kitchen preparing food; her camera was hidden in her chef's hat (that technically she didn't need to wear). Jonathan had to yell at her to stop dancing around at one point as it ruined their view. There was not much excitement going on in the kitchen, however; it was mainly just a precaution in case the Cook had mad skills like Steven Seagal in *Under Siege*.

While Stacey was keeping all the guests busy at the dining table, Jamie managed to beat the crap out of four security guards (not at the same time) and hide their bodies in Dr Martens walk in robe. He then relaxed on a couch in the living room with his legs crossed together, a cup of tea and a tart.

"Jamie," Jonathan said through the mic almost scaring Jamie into spilling his hot tea everywhere, "make sure they don't wake up. And you have to take out Martens company. She's in the study room. Go."

Hesitantly, Jamie put his tea down and proceeded to the study room. Leonie was worried; Jamie didn't seem the sort to knock out a lady. Taking out those men was a surprise in itself. As he entered, the young woman, who had mahogany hair and a round nose and wore a black lace dress, was currently up a ladder trying to reach a book. Jamie looked scared but kept approaching. She turned around and smiled at him, before walking towards him and checking him out. As she started to say something in Dutch and pulled out a knife, Jamie punched her in the face, and she fell backwards, landing unconscious on the ground.

"Jesus Christ Jamie!" Soup yelled through the microphone in disbelief, "you hit her?!"

Jamie swore, unable to believe it himself, and went to try and wake her up by slapping her some more in the face, "I'm sorry! I'm sorry!"

"Leave her," Jonathan said, "she'll be alright, just hide her somewhere and get back to it."

After hiding the woman behind the curtains, Jamie left the study and returned to his cup of tea, shaking with fear.

"I can't believe it," Soup said, "I don't know about your time, but in my time, we never punch women in the face unless we're scum." Soup was a gentleman, who still stands up when a woman enters and leaves the room, and he even opens doors for all the ladies too. But everyone *was* glad Jamie didn't get stabbed.

Cody had brought out the dinner with some sleepy stuff in all the other guests" food. She almost gave Stacey a sleepy meal, but quickly corrected the plates and covered herself by saying to the man who she gave Stacey's too that she was allergic to pepper.

To avoid suspicion, Stacey asked Dr Martens to step out into the living room with her for a chat, he accepted with a disturbing smile. As soon as they left, the other guests fell asleep into their food.

Jamie managed to sneak out of the living room with his tea as they entered and was greeted outside by Cody.

Stacey sat with Dr Martens by the fire in the living room; with Jamie's half-eaten tart still on the coffee table. He was dressed in a nice black suit and bow-tie with nicely polished shoes. His hair was full of gel, and it almost looked as though he wore foundation on his face.

"So," Dr Martens started, "you have done exceptionally well haven't you, Stacey. I must admit, I was rather disappointed at you turning down my offer to join my personal team."

"Well I'd rather be with my friends," Stacey replied as she sipped her port.

"I see. You're friends. Leonie Reine, Cody Malice, Jamie Young, Jonathan Morse, etcetera, all destined to make history doing wonders. And yet, you are all still confused. What is taking you so long? None of you has any idea about anything. You blindly follow my orders, like every other squad. I'm still waiting for that big moment when you all blossom. I gather you've worked out about your missing friend? Or... I'm sorry, not."

"What missing friend?" Stacey asked looking confused (from Jamie's camera poking through the door).

"You know. Your friend, the lost one. You haven't seen her for a while, she disappeared when you did though." Dr Martens smiled and looked as though he took pleasure in Stacey's confusion. Leonie had no idea what he was talking about either; she looked at Camilla who just shrugged. Even Cody expressed her confusion through her microphone, "Huh?"

He laughed, "Yes. You are all so confused. Tell me, how you can possibly win a war when you are confused. How can I let you go out there if you can't even find the information you need. Is that why you and your *friends* are here? Wanting to ask me personally for information? You could have just called you know? I would have sat down with you... You know, you are the worse team we have ever had, which is disappointing as most of you I had hoped would achieve great things for us."

"Technically we're a squad," came Jamie's voice before his Stacey's and Cody's mics and camera's all went dead.

"Shit," Clark gasped as he and Warren madly pressed buttons on their computers, "Excuse me, sorry."

"What happened?" Jonathan asked sounding panicked.

"I think he was on to us," Leonie said as she was still processing what Dr Martens had said.

Everyone panicked; they didn't have time to think so naturally, Jonathan led the charge into Dr Martens lair. Leon and Soup tried to advise against this on the way many times, but everyone else was with Jonathan for once.

When they got there, the place was an absolute mess. There was smashed glass all over the place, tables were broken, and there was a large plant hanging from a chandelier. Blood was up one of the walls in one of the rooms and a body on the floor underneath a couch. Leonie immediately dashed over to see who it was. It wasn't one of theirs, which meant it was one of Dr Martens' men. Perhaps Stacey managed to pummel, and goodness knows what else to one of them before they were taken, kidnapped by the bastards.

Then, Camilla called everyone into the dining room. Leonie quickly raced in, and had a huge sigh of relief when she saw their three pals sitting on the floor looking exhausted but all in one piece. A few more men were lying on the floor around them, and to Leonie's horror, they were also dead.

Stacey was bleeding badly on her arm, and her dress was no longer a dress, it was ripped to shreds and was now even on backwards.

"He got away," Stacey managed to say, "we were taken by surprise, we managed to fight them off but he dived out the window, and we heard a helicopter."

Jonathan was the last to arrive in the room, "oh thank whoever in this damned place has given us yet another chance for God's sake!" He shouted.

Leon, who was tending to a large cut in Jamie's head, was already concerned about what would come next, "this isn't over. They'll attack again, or get someone else to do it for them. We need to get the hell out of here."

"Are you okay Cody?" Camilla said as she joined Leonie on the floor next to Cody, "you're all bruised."

"Yeah I'm alright," Cody replied with a distant look in her eyes, "I really, was not expecting that at all."

For once, Jamie said nothing. Stacey confirmed that she had killed most of the men, but Jamie had killed one of them who was slumped on the table on top of one of the still sleeping guests. It was not long ago when Jamie was upset over punching a woman, now he had killed a man.

"Oh no wait," Stacey said, as she suddenly remembered what happened, "don't worry Jamie, I remember now, I killed him, not you. You're off the hook."

And with that, Jamie had piped up back to his old self again and started speaking really fast in gibberish. Although now Leonie was stunned at the fact that Stacey is okay with killing. Stacey could apparently read minds.

"I know what you're thinking," Stacey said, "I'm upset too, but it was either them or us. It was chaos in here."

Leonie smiled and gave Stacey a hug; however, they had to leave now. Warren and Clark had been investigating the rest of the penthouse but found nothing. Leonie helped Cody on the long walk back to their basement. Clark and Warren ran off ahead to start packing things ready for their departure.

When they made it back, Leon continued to tend to Stacey, Cody and Jamie's injuries and everyone else began madly packing things that were important. They passed things through the doorway and Soup, and Jonathan chucked them onto the Metal Ark.

They all crammed onto the plane, and Leon quickly made his way to the cockpit ready for take-off.

"Right we have everything?" Jonathan asked impatiently.

"Yeah, Warren's just getting a few more things for our radar," Clark replied as he brought in a whole heap of computer stuff.

"Where the hell are we going?" Camilla asked, "Do we even know how to get out of this place?"

"Yes," Clark replied blankly.

Leonie was about to leave to give Warren a hand when she saw Pip and her team heading towards the plane with Warren in custody.

"Oh shit," Leonie whispered, "guys, Pip's here!"

Jonathan came storming out of the plane with Soup right behind him.

"What do you want?" Jonathan asked bitterly, "let him go, or I swear to god, I will." –

"We're here to escort you," Pip smiled as the rest of her squad gathered around her, "you are lucky enough to be the next squad sent into battle. Congratulations."

Chapter 19:

"Excuse me?" Jonathan said as the others peeped out of the plane.

"Didn't you know?" Pip gasped sarcastically, "your little trip to the boss's lair was a mission, you performed really well, and it's put you on the top *right* at the end of this season."

"Of course, we didn't know," Jamie yelled out from the plane, "no one bloody told us!"

"No matter," Pip nodded, "you must prepare now. I'm *so* jealous of you."

"You're enjoying this aren't you?" Camilla said bitterly as she stormed up to Pip.

"Of course not, I envy you. Really."

Hundreds of security came in to back up Pip's team, so resisting wasn't the smart option. They followed them to yet another unexplored area, where there was a really nice gym like looking room, equipped with a Dojang for Korean martial arts, as well as heavyweight machinery. Not that any of that mattered as they would not be training, in fact, they would not be there long at all. They were told by the head security that training started since they first arrived on planet Zenith, which turns out to be what they call the place they were in with the burning tree. Not a real planet of course, but they're trying to work out a way to keep the human race in fake places like that to avoid threats like the one they are currently facing. So there was no need to train anymore, it was a quick briefing, access to new information, and then they were thrown into battle.

Dr Martens arrived looking rather excited and crazier than ever. He sat down at the head of an ugly kitchen table, still in his suit, and told Leonie and the others to join him. Most of the security either left, stood guard, or went to use the gym equipment.

"I don't know about you lot," Dr Martens grinned, "but I rather enjoyed that before. Oh, Stacey, you were wonderful. I really hope you last long when you get out there."

"Me too," Stacey said mumbled.

"Anyway," He continued, "*finally*, you may know some information. Well, useful information at least. So, the aliens, I gather you all want to know about them the most right? They were first discovered by a scientist called Alfred Izoto, reminds me of risotto. He was an arrogant prick… We haven't formally given the Aliens a name yet, but Izoto called them amalgams, but he was a prick, so we're not calling them that. Not even sure where he got that *stupid* name from, silly man. So, in about year thirty-one thousand and thirty-two, we started noticing these strange things that blended in with humans but weren't. Most of them were found in normal circumstances, such as married with kids, at university, cleaning facilities manager, paramedic, oil rig engineer, you name it. But also, in secret, they were doing things, hacking into our governments, having secret scarification of humans, and just plain old murders. At first, they were discarded as just psychotic humans until my father, Dr Martens, Senior, looked deeper into one of them. He wanted to know why one of them was so crazy. As he examined them deeper, physically through scans and tests, he made an *incredible* discovery. These people were not of Earth, they were aliens. He did some more research, and slowly uncovered the truth of how that dumb scientist landed on their planet giving them the impression that *we* as the human race *all* wanted to experiment with them. They did not like this. So, of course, they had to invade Earth and kill everyone. But I saved humanity because I'm just so generous." He then looked at Stacey who seemed on edge, before leaving the room.

185

"What a complete tosser," Jamie sighed as he leaned back in his chair, "I mean, this is why we have Special Forces. Why the hell, would you get a guy like me who spent most of his time in the pub, to help save the world? He must be smoking something, or he's completely deranged."

After pondering for a while, Leonie and the others jumped out of her skin as Stacey, who was sitting right next to her started twitching.

"Are you alright Stace?" Leonie asked, very concerned as she put her hand on Stacey's shoulder.

Stacey turned to Leonie and then began to talk really fast about planes. It was quite scary; she kept getting faster and faster the more she spoke. You could hardly understand her, Leonie managed to catch something about packing parachutes properly, but still, her words became more muddled as she kept getting faster. Cody walked around the table ready to slap her, but before she could Stacey leapt out of her chair, and starting racing around the room at top speed, it was impossible to keep up with her, it was surreal. She started picking up objects such as pens, lamps and even chairs and investigating them before putting them back down. She then began getting into people's faces, saying things no one could understand because it was so speedy. In the end, Leon had to give her a sedative which Warren had retrieved from an office on the other side of the gym thanks to a freaked out rookie guard who told him. As Stacey went out to it, everyone just stared at each other hoping one of them had an explanation. Meanwhile, the rest of the guards were still using the gym equipment as though nothing had happened.

Clark managed to persuade a guard to give him access to a lab. Seeing as Dr Martens had been gone for hours, they may's well tend to Stacey. While Warren, Clark and Leon were in the lab trying to figure things out with Stacey, the rest of them naturally used the gym to take their minds off things. Jamie used the treadmill, Jonathan and Soup did some weights, Camilla boxed, Cody and Leonie used some skipping ropes.

Some dinner was brought in by a robot, and during dessert, Clark and Leon came out with results on Stacey. Test results revealed someone had been spiking Stacey's food for months with an unknown drug, probably from the future, Leonie imagined. Over time, Stacey had some crazy outbursts, increasing as time went on, only the three of them knew until finally, the full effect took place as they saw earlier. It had caused her to become hyperactive to the extreme. Neither Leon nor Clark had ever seen or heard anything quite like it in their lives. It had to be either futuristic stuff, or alien.

"Why didn't you tell us?" Camilla asked sounding irritated. "Because that, before, was scary. A little warning might've helped."

"We know," Clark nodded, "but we didn't want to tell you about a condition Stacey, a friend, has, without knowing anything about it first."

"We still don't know much about it," Leon added, "but Warren has been working on something to help Stacey control it."

"Well, it's still scary," Camilla said.

"What have we said about secrets," Leonie asked, remembering all of Jonathan's speeches, "Jonathan, are you hearing this?"

"Ahh," Jonathan said, scratching his head, "I kind of knew, and agreed it would be best not to say anything."

"You tosser," Jamie said half-heartedly, "What a waste of time listening to you. I could've been relaxing somewhere, or sleeping."

"What do you mean?" Jonathan asked in disbelief, "you sleep through my speeches anyway! Look, we know you guys; we needed you to stay focused and keep working while we figure it out. It was Stacey's idea; she didn't want you moping all around her instead of training and trying to figure out a way out of here."

"Which we haven't anyway," Camilla snorted.

"Has she been infected by something?" Cody asked.

"Yes," Clark said.

Warren came out looking chuffed with himself. He explained how he managed to create oil, filled with plenty of calming ingredients that he invented. He also made a necklace with a pad in it. He put two drops of the oil onto the pad and closed up the necklace with it inside. He had to wear a mask because it was really strong, in fact, he warned everyone not to get too close for a while and to keep at least an eleven-inch distance otherwise they would get knocked unconscious. Only Stacey was able to take the smell of the oil without any side effects, it would calm her down instead and stop her from becoming hyper. Leonie could smell the necklace from twelve feet away, so she believed Warren when he said not to get too close. Warren placed the necklace around Stacey's neck and then woke her up. She slowly sat up, looking dizzy and her face was a bit puffy. Camilla put a mask on before sitting next to her and rubbed her back. Stacey needed some time to recover, so Leon ordered everyone out back to the gym area. Luckily, Clark got the TV working, and they were able to watch *Bottom*, one of the girl's favourite comedy shows. If they *were* in space, Jamie's laughter could probably be heard back home.

"How's Stacey?" Came Dr Martens voice, making everybody jump. They were so into the show they didn't know he and several guards had entered the room, "*Bottom*? Interesting, old TV show hey?"

"Hey! This can never be beaten!" Cody shouted pointing a mars bar at him.

"What have you done to Stacey!?" Both Camilla and Leonie asked as they furiously threw their chairs back and marched over to the Dr with the stupid grin.

"So quick to blame, the real question should be what's wrong with you. Ever since you first arrived, since you became a team, you've done nothing but muck around. You were taken to a place you knew nothing about, are told you will one day fight in a battle you know nothing about and blindly follow orders. Yet, despite knowing all of this, here you are watching *"Bottom"* where your laughter is bothering everyone in my headquarters."

"So?" Cody shrugged.

"It's fascinating, I want to know why."

"We don't mean to," Cody shrugged again, "just ends up that way. It's actually a good point. I have *no* idea what's wrong with me."

"We're just waiting for word on Stacey," Jamie announced.

"What do you care?" Jonathan asked, "You're worried about people *mucking* around when the real problem is what on Earth is wrong with you?"

"Or what on Spaceship is wrong with you," Jamie corrected as he winked at Jonathan as though he just saved him from the utmost embarrassment.

Jonathan did the usual and ignored Jamie and continued, "It's because of you that we're even here. Nothing you've done with us makes any sense. It's only natural for us to rebel and demand answers, which by the way you've done a piss poor job at. Jamie and Cody are two of the most annoying people I have ever met in my entire life, but they're two of my best friends, and their humour is probably what has kept our squad going strong."

"So what is the deal?" Soup asked.

"You guys are pure gold," Dr Martens said, still smiling this whole time, "I think I might keep you."

"What do you mean?" Leonie asked, not sure how to take any of what this madman said.

189

"Keep us?" Cody checked, "what's wrong with you man?"

"Cody," Dr Martens said softly, "did you know that at first, I thought you were a part of the band Hanson? But I know now, wrong time."

"I'm a girl!" Cody said almost offended.

"It must be the clothes you wear."

"What the hell has that got to do with anything?" Jonathan snapped, "you're not wriggling out of an explanation again!"

"Wait," Jamie said as if about to say something important, "Hanson is guys?"

"JAMIE!" Jonathan roared, and Jamie ran behind Soup to hide.

"I think we all need to tone it down," Dr Martens said with his hands in the air, although he did seem to enjoy the tension. He then turned to Leonie, "so, where do you stand in all of this? Still not come out of your shell yet? What will it take?"

"You leave her alone," Camilla ordered, "you're still avoiding Jonathan."

"I'm sorry *Jonathan*," Dr Martens said as he turned to Jonathan, "but I'm afraid I have something rather important to attend to now. You'll have to come up with something better, something clever if you want answers. I don't think anyone in your squad is worthy at the moment, but I am very patient and have faith. Auf wiedersehen."

As Jonathan attempted to tackle Dr Martens to the ground, three guards did just that to him instead. "Where are you going!? Come back!" Jonathan bellowed from underneath the three guards. Dr Martens and the guards left leaving everyone unsettled and angry.

It was so infuriating; Leonie could see it in Jonathan. They just couldn't get anywhere and haven't moved forward with anything for ages. If anything, things have gotten worse, what with Stacey's crazy show and everything else that's been happening. It's as if they were going around in circles, perhaps Dr Martens really just wants to mess with their minds. Leonie felt quite fearful as she quickly remembered every bad thing that had happened since they first disappeared, from her getting burnt, to all the people being murdered, to being kept in the dark, conflict with other squads, being told they were going to war, secrets.

"Weren't they going to send us straight to battle?" Leonie asked after that memory clicked in her mind, "we were only going to be here for a little while, and then they were going to send us out, remember?"

"Yeah maybe because of Stacey, they've given us some time or something," Jonathan said in a much calmer voice as he leaned onto the table.

"Wait," Soup said, "no one is scared at that thought of going to a real war? You know, not even a little terrified?"

"Somethings playing with our minds," Camilla said as she looked up from her coffee, "I mean, when he taunted us about mucking around and not having a clue, maybe it's a trick question."

"You mean you think something's making us not think properly?" Soup asked.

"Yeah like happy gas," Jamie nodded, "like at the dentist."

"Or maybe they sneak drugs in our food, and we're all just high all the time?" Cody suggested after thinking about it.

"I don't know," Camilla said, "just a thought, but it seems like we *haven't* been thinking straight this whole time. I mean we have been watching too much TV and eating at the café instead of worrying about, for example, being sent to war."

"I think we've been thinking fine," Jamie shrugged as he bit his strawberry doughnut, "maybe *you're* on drugs."

191

"Actually, I think Camilla may be onto something," Leon said as he entered the room. "I did some more tests on Stacey, and there are some weird chemicals in her body I've never seen before. I tested it on Warren, Clark and myself as well and we have the same. No idea what it is but, my opinion of Dr Martens is getting worse and worse by the minute. We need to get the hell out of here. ASAP."

"Agreed," Jonathan said at the vending machine, "we need to get to the Metal ArK. Before that, we need to take the guards out."

"No shit," Camilla said as she took up a position next to the door which led to the main headquarters.

"You know they probably have the room bugged and know what we're up to, right?" Cody checked.

"We're mad and not thinking clearly, remember? So it doesn't matter," Jonathan assured.

"Oh yeah," Cody said.

They decided that Jamie should be the one to get the guards attention, so he started knocking down all the gym equipment and threw weights at the door. A large gun then appeared from the roof and shot a dart at Jamie's face; he immediately collapsed and started snoring.

"Well that's not gonna work," Soup said as he stared at Jamie in disbelief.

"Where was that dart gun when Stacey was going nuts?" Cody asked.

"Okay, new plan," Jonathan said, "Leonie, Warren, remember in the room before planet Zenith? Say something smart."

"I don't think that's going to work," Warren smirked as he shook his head, "I think we need to ask for something."

"Like what?" Clark asked curiously.

192

Warren walked up to the door and with a soft voice said, "Excuse me could I please have a word, I have something rather embarrassing to talk about."

After three seconds, the doors opened and four guards walked in, "what is it?" one of them asked.

"Hey I said it was embarrassing," Warren said, "I didn't need four of you."

Camilla leapt out behind the door and took out two guards with some sort of cool grappling where she flips them, Leonie heard a bone break but she's not sure what and she wants to forget about it, plus the guards are supposed to be robots. Meanwhile, Soup knocked out the third guard after about ten seconds, and Warren kicked the fourth in the groin before Camilla finished him off. She then grabbed their guns and passed them around to Jonathan, Soup, and Leonie.

Leon and Clark came running out with Stacey holding onto their shoulders, Jonathan had to help Jamie up who was now awake but drowsy. So Leonie, Cody, Camilla, Soup, and Warren were the only ones left empty and free to fight. Although technically, Warren had his iPad thing that guided them through the headquarters, so he wouldn't be much help in defence. But the good thing was four guns, four people so everyone with free hands got a gun.

After Warren gave the all clear, they quickly dashed through the door and made it through the first two corridors before more guards came at them, at least ten. Again, most of them were taken out by Camilla, but Leonie and the other two managed to get one or two.

"We should find a door at the end of this corridor," Warren said as they continued running, "It should lead closer to where the Metal Ark is unless they moved it."

"Moved it?" Soup asked, "man we didn't think of that."

As Warren was busy looking at his iPad, and trying to explain things, he, unfortunately, ended up tripping over his own feet and falling to the ground, his iPad went flying along the corridor and nearly hit another guard. Leonie grabbed Warren and threw him to cover just as the dozen more guards started firing. Leonie and Cody were split from the rest of the squad who were on the other side of the corridor behind a corner. As the guards kept moving closer, and their ammo was starting to run out for them to just madly spray rounds, they agreed that the rest of the squad would keep moving through the corridor on their side, and Leonie and Cody would go their separate way for now. They sprinted as fast as they could, without thinking, they ran around corner after corner for at least five minutes until they came to a big luxurious looking set of doors.

"It could only be," Leonie said as they slowly approached the doors, "Dr Martens main office, maybe."

"Should we go in?" Cody asked sounding unsure, "he's kind of scary, what if he's in there?"

With the sound of many fast footsteps approaching, they made the plunge in through the office door, which was unlocked; in fact, it had no lock.

It didn't take a genius to realise once inside that it was Dr Martens office, as there was a picture of him on the wall graduating from a degree; the picture had a three-second motion on repeat. There were also many certificates on the wall with his name on them, his first name *was* indeed Julian. Most of the office was full of bookshelves filled with hundreds of books, at least. Cody went straight to the desk in the middle of the room and started looking on the computer which seemed pretty similar to one in their time, disappointingly. Leonie observed the books, to see which genre is most popular to him. There was a lot of science, physics and medical ones but also history, and many on literature. He had Charles Dickens books, even some Roald Dahl. There were many Leonie didn't recognise, but there was a lot of fun reading material that was mixed in with his nonfiction. This man loved literature.

"Leonie," Cody said in a tone Leonie had never heard her use before, it was a very flat and fearful sounding voice, "look at this."

Leonie walked over, worried by Cody's voice as to what it might be, her facial expression was even more worrying, it was pale and blank.

Cody let Leonie sit down, there was a folder on the computer filled with images. The first image was hard for Leonie to see; there were many more. And the pictures, like Dr Martens graduation photo, had a three-second motion on loop, with sound.

The images showed Dr Martens with patients, or victims, each with their own gift. For instance, the first, a woman, had just had all of her nails removed, in a gory way. The loop showed her looking terrified and jellylike at the sight of her own fingers, "Julian" was observing her with his hand on his chin. The second picture was more intense, where another lady had all of her fingers broken, she made noise in this image, a sobbing noise, again "Julian" was observing, he was not looking satisfied with something.

Leonie looked up at Cody; they both were horrified, before clicking on the next image. This time it was a man, he had cuts all over his body, "Julian" appeared to be rubbing something painful on the cuts, but the three seconds was too short to make out much to find out what.

The images got worse as they went along, for instance, this next image, in particular, made both Leonie and Cody shriek. It was a step further, a dead patient, it was split into two images, in fact, the first showed him alive and screaming as they started to chop him up in on a kitchen bench. The next image showed the end of the chopping up. And yet, "Julian" simply looked

195

disappointed, as this was apparently not what he was after either.

"I can't watch anymore," Cody said as she turned away almost crying, "Leonie I'm scared, I think I have been all this time... What is he doing? Why is he hurting them is that going to happen to us? Maybe when people get arrested, this is what he does to them. Torture them as a punishment."

Leonie was just as terrified, but she knew she needed to be strong for Cody who was obviously scared out of her mind. Before Leonie could say anything, however, the doors flew open making both girls jump out of their skin.

Chapter 20:

He entered, reading a piece of paper. He looked up and smiled at the sight of Leonie and Cody. Dr Martens, the same man who they had just seen torturing human beings, entered the room undoubtedly unaware of what they had just learnt about him.

"Hello," He said, "what a pleasant surprise, finding you here. How close are you to escaping?"

Both girls said nothing. Instead, they were shaking in fear of what they just saw, petrified of the fact that the man that did it was right in front of them, smiling.

Noticing their faces, he walked over to see what they were looking at, when he saw, his face, for the first time Leonie had seen, wasn't smiling. Instead, it showed more of a panic and anger.

"No!" He shouted, "No, no, no! You weren't supposed to see *this*!" He paced around the room with his hands on his head before turning back to them, "Things were starting to get there, and your team was starting to become perfect. I will not let anything ruin it now!"

"You tortured people," Leonie stammered.

"No," Julian said as he firmly grabbed Leonie by the shoulders, digging his bony fingers into her bone, "It isn't like that at all. *You* must understand, they were only drafts, they're not it anymore. I realised how things should be."

"How?" Leonie asked hesitantly, her voice high and with a slight tremble at this point.

"War," he replied confidently and gently as he released her leaving a slight bruising feeling on her arms, "and *you're* the hero Leonie, don't you understand that? You're the hero. You just need some help to get there. That's what this is. The great Leonie Reine is an ordinary, shy, anxious young girl who becomes a hero, but she needed guidance to get there... But things keep trying to mess it up! Like that goddam four-eyed girl! I knew that she was a threat. I knew she could potentially become the hero, but *I'm* the boss, and I say it's YOU! So I tried to get rid of her, but she keeps coming back, sabotaging *everything*! And now these images are found and are going to ruin it again. I deleted them! I even gave you a computer from your time to make it easier, but she put them back!" He then screamed really loudly and knocked over a globe of Earth making both girls jump back. They waited a few seconds for him to calm down again.

"I don't understand," Leonie said as she looked at Cody who looked even more confused, "w-why did you call those people drafts?"

"They're from another draft I-tell me. What is your biggest regret?"

Leonie was curious by Julian's sudden change in energy and furious by his latest change in topic.

"Uh. Wait. Alright. Well, I suppose the whole gun stealing incident that went on back home."

Julian raised his eyebrows, "You still think that was real? Wow. Must be weaker than I thought."

"What's that supposed to mean?"

"God you're dumb. Okay, two points. First. Extreme, even for you two. Second point, not *even* a slap on the wrist. In Australia?"

The doors burst open again, this time Jonathan and the others were all there, taking cover from all the guards who quickly broke into the office behind them. A fight broke out, Stacey, who had seemingly made a complete recovery, was fighting alongside Camilla and were both making short work of all the guards. Jamie had recovered too and was fighting alongside Jonathan.

Without warning two bullets made their way to a trembling Dr Martens chest. He fell to the ground, and then ear-piercingly loud sirens went off along with many red lights all around the place. Everyone paused for a moment.

"To the Metal Ark!" Jonathan ordered, and they all ran for their lives. Leonie quickly looked back at Dr Martens who was lying motionless on the ground in front of his desk. She had hoped to hear the end of what he was talking about but was glad to witness the monster finally being taken out.

Warren had found a successful route to the garage where the Metal Ark was, now they just hoped it was still there. But Warren assured if it weren't, there'd be plenty others to steal, much to Stacey's despair. They weren't sure even if they did find the Metal Ark if it would be tampered with, but Leonie was focused on the confusing fact that all the time, the guards try to kill them, but their boss called her a hero and wants them to succeed.

They reached the garage which was full of many different types of aircrafts, including some type of automatic car wash for aircrafts. Fortunately, the coolest aircraft there was the Metal Ark. This meant their chances of escaping were relatively large again and with boosted morale, they immediately boarded Stacey's baby and prepared for take-off.

Stacey raced to the cockpit before anyone had a chance to protest with her being unstable still, Leonie buckled up in her seat next to Cody and Warren. She was excited by the fact that they were finally going to escape. *What would space be like?* She thought to herself, *What if they're greeted by aliens out there?*

"If we do escape," Warren quietly said to Leonie, "I haven't the faintest idea as to where we'll go. Or if there is anywhere to go or if we'll even survive for too long. Just saying."

"Thanks, Warren," Leonie said awkwardly. Her good feelings she just had quickly disappeared, but he made a great point. Where would they go if they *did* succeed in escaping?

It's not like there would be a space motel floating around, although everything had been crazy and weird so far so that probably wouldn't blow their minds too much. Cody quickly voiced her views on a space Putt-Putt and had at some point made herself an astronaut's helmet entirely out of cardboard.

Clark got the garage doors open, and Stacey started to take off, right as the garage started to fill with guards either shooting at them or hopping into their own aircrafts ready to pursue them.

One of the guards managed to get on board and started strangling Clark. Leon pounced on the guard and choked him to death, although his head did come off confirming he was just another robot causing everyone to cheer at the fact that they weren't murderers.

Leonie noticed something strange about the outside of the "Spaceship" through the garage doors. It looked like space, but it had a huge sort of tear through it which kept getting bigger really fast. They flew through the tear only to find themselves squinting from the bright sun in their faces. When her eyes adjusted to the brightness, Leonie was able to realise, they weren't in space at all. They were flying over an ocean.

Leonie looked back to find only the garage doors were visible, floating above the water. Once the doors shut, after several other aircrafts flew out, they disappeared.

There wasn't any time to discuss the fact that they weren't in space or anything at all. First, they had to avoid the persistent guards chasing after them and firing from their aircrafts, missing them by inches.

"What sort of planes are they?" Cody asked curiously.

"I don't know," Leon answered, "Never seen those before, must be from the future or something."

"They look a bit like Messerschmitt Me 262," Soup suggested, "but more advanced maybe?"

"Yeah, they do," Leon agreed, "Hey! We need another tail gunner. Jamie! Get your ass into that turret, because they're going to start shooting again!"

Camilla was already in her turret, but Jamie had to quickly race into his. Camilla's turret was located in the really big looking bubble on top of the Metal Ark.Jamie's turret was at the rear end and was really small, so he could barely fit. They hadn't started firing yet, but when they did it was a really unnerving feeling. Stacey was an exceptional pilot and did well at keeping her beloved plane unharmed while Camilla and Jamie were in their turrets firing back. Leonie had to cover her ears, and even so the guns were still really loud, and her whole body vibrated. *Surely the future could've come up with something to prevent this?* She thought. Then Warren handed her some earplugs and winked at her. It helped the noise immensely.

Leonie decided to focus back on the ocean; it was very beautiful but not what they had expected. More questions would be raised when and if this fighting was over.

"I just saw a Megalodon!" Cody announced at the top of her lungs. Leonie and the others didn't see it, they were all too busy either panicking over being chased, scratching their heads over why they're not in space or in Leonie's case, staring at the ocean. Then again, nothing really, since they first disappeared had made sense. Cody suggested, at top of her lungs, perhaps it was another world like planet Zenith they were on. Or even back on planet Zenith itself Leonie couldn't quite hear her with her earplugs in but managed to work out what she had said. Cody started crying hysterically after the plane dived suddenly at top speed, it sounded like a sarcastic cry, but her tears were real. Stacey had done it to avoid an enemy aircraft which had gotten too close; luckily Jamie then took it out. Everyone was frustrated that they just couldn't catch a break. Life back home was kind of boring and dull, but Leonie definitely would give anything to be there right now, away from all this hassle and fear. But perhaps home won't always be just "boring" maybe one day, this here, what they have been experiencing will become home.

"Guys I saw a Meg!"-

"Shut up Cody," Stacey yelled as she rolled the Metal ark to the right, "no one cares!"

"There's one in our blind spot Jamie," Camilla yelled, "I can't get him! I'm busy with the one at the back!"

"Leave him to me," Jamie yelled back, "I'm pressing as hard as I can. It's all I can do for now."

Camilla then managed to blow up an enemy plane right next to them, Leonie swore she felt the heat on her already burnt face. She snuck a quick peek through the window and saw there were still at least four flying after them. But for some reason, it was alarming just looking at them, so she quickly hid back again as if it made her safer.

"Why do they always try to kill us, and then, want to have a friendly conference with us?" Leonie asked as she leaned back in her chair.

"Because they're morons" Cody answered proudly as if she had just answered a really hard physics question, "let's just hope they don't succeed in killing us this time. Camilla, Stacey, Jamie, our lives are in your hands. Good luck."

"There's an island! Three o'clock!" Stacey yelled.

"Get us there!" Jonathan yelled back.

"You got it!" Stacey replied, and she fiercely turned the Ark to the right. Leonie thought her flying was almost as scary as her driving.

Jamie had just taken out two enemy aircrafts within the space of thirty seconds. "*I* am a *beast*!" He roared in his Thor voice.

They had reached the island and were trying to find a place to land which only caused more arguing as there were many trees and Stacey couldn't find a decent spot.

"Just land!" Soup yelled.

"I can't!" Stacey shouted back.

Leonie looked up at the wrong time, to find Camilla's turret, right above her, had been hit hard and literally detached from the plane. The blast was painful on her body as she watched in horror as it crashed onto the island tearing through several trees before sliding to a halt.

Leonie yelled at the top of her lungs, and Cody, Warren, and Soup looked to witness the crash as well before they flew off to attempt a landing that Stacey and Leon had found in a field. Jamie then took out the last enemy aircraft, and they landed brutally but all in one piece.

Immediately, Leonie, Cody, and Stacey undid their seatbelts and raced out of the plane to go find Camilla's turret. The others yelled out after them and tried to keep up. They found Camilla's half flattened and beaten up turret, it wasn't exactly hiding. Leonie jumped onto a bent tree to peep into the turret, she saw Camilla not moving at all.

"Don't touch her" Leon ordered as he ran up, "we need to cut her out."

Leonie had no time to ball her eyes out as she was in charge of fetching the hydraulic rescue tools with Jamie. Clark then perfectly cut off the roof of the turret, and soon Leon and Cody were securing Camilla on a stretcher, being extra careful with her spine. Leonie couldn't quite hear, but Leon seemed to express great concern for Camilla's spine. She wasn't okay, but she was alive, just. Leon was *very* eager to get her back to the Ark.

Stacey hugged Leonie, none of them spoke, but they slowly trailed along behind as the others helped with carrying Camilla's stretcher.

Once back at the Metal Ark, which was scratched and had a few other damages that Clark needed to attend to, Leon ordered Cody to stay with Leonie and Stacey. Instead, Warren would help Leon look after Camilla.

Leonie managed to convince Cody it was a good idea, by going exploring. Stacey came too, it was nice just the three of them. Not that it was nice without Camilla of course, but without the guys hanging around, it was great to be together with old friends in this horrible time.

"Leon's great," Stacey finally said as they strolled along through the trees, "he'll make sure she's okay."

"Yeah," Cody said in a different voice to usual, "I still feel like I should be there helping."

"You wouldn't think clearly," Leonie said with a slight brittle voice, "at least you got to help with the log roll. Making sure Jonathan and that did it right and in time."

"Mmm," Cody agreed, "I hate when people hold the head wrong. Lucky Leon is a professional, I guess."

"How do you hold the head?" Leonie asked, wanting to keep Cody talking and distracted.

"Well... you're supposed to sort of hook your hands in so that your thumb is on top of their shoulders and your fingers on their scapula. Then, your arms squeeze their head really, really hard, so it's secure."

"And Leon did that?" Leonie asked.

"Yeah of course he did, he's great," Cody laughed, wiping some tears. "You know a head can weigh from three to five kilos? So it gets heavy when holding it in a lateral position for too long."

"Interesting," Leonie smiled as she patted Cody on the back, "you're a great friend Cody, and Camilla knows it."

"Thanks, Leonie," Cody smiled, slightly.

"Guys!" Soup called as he came jogging through the trees, "we need you back, sorry."

They quickly followed Soup back to the Metal Ark where a man with long dark hair and leather jacket stood. Everyone except Leon and Warren who were tending to Camilla stood around to listen to what the man had to say.

"Welcome," He said, "Congratulations, you have made it out alive. Everyone on this island has done the same. You should come into town, we have a café, a nice restaurant where they sell curry for breakfast, and I wish I could say more, but unfortunately, I'm late for something. Good luck with your friend, we don't have a doctor or anything here. Maybe when your friend's done he could open up a Medical Centre. Oh and, my name is Jeff. "

And with that, Jeff walked off to a motorcycle, which Leonie hadn't noticed and by the looks on everyone else's face nor did they, and rode off doing a wheelie.

"I feel like tomorrow we're going to wake up in candy land," Jonathan said shaking his head, "I need a drink. Come on, let's go find this town, I've got my earpiece in, if Leon needs anything we're straight back. There's not much else we can do."

"You're not twenty-one yet," Jamie snickered.

"Actually," Jonathan pointed out, "I might be because I have no idea how long I've been away from home."

"I'm going to stay here and begin repairing the Ark." Clark said, "bring us back something?"

"Sure," Jonathan said.

They found the town after a thirty-minute walk through the jungle and a few English looking fields. The town had a couple of little buildings on each side of the dirt road that went through the middle, nothing over the top though. On the right were buildings that had a beach on the other side of it. The buildings on the left were in front of more forest. They found a restaurant through a walkway on the right side which had a great view of the beach which looked like it was being set up for a beach party. There was a stable next to the restaurant full of horses; some with carriages even, at the end of the pathway which led to another smaller dirt road before the beach, as well as many parked motorbikes. It seemed really smoky so you could barely see the ground and there were lots of bright lights of different colours everywhere and a neon sign on top of the restaurant called *Rebel Joint* with a scary skull.

Inside the restaurant was not what Leonie expected. It was a heavy metal themed bar, not bad looking either, and it kind of had a touch of Hawaiian to it too. Most of the customers looked like typical eighties rockers with their long hair and leather or denim clothes, they were most likely the owners of the motorcycles outside. But there also seemed to be a few cowboys from way back in time, which explained the horses and there were some customers from the eighteen hundreds, thus explaining the horse carriages.

"No Sleep in Hell" by The Angels was playing from the jukebox. Rocking out to it were a Geisha, an Egyptian Queen, some Maori men and some male rockers. Leonie found herself blinking a lot.

They sat down at a booth, Soup and Jamie had to pull up a chair each. On the wall of their booth was a picture of the band members from Def Leppard. One of the guitarists, Phil Collen, was wearing a shirt which said *I love going down on Jamie*. Jamie assured everyone that Phil Collen had *never* gone down on him before, he then laughed at his own joke.

Realizing they had no money to pay for anything, Leonie and Cody volunteered to go up and ask the barmaid for some water.

The barmaid was very beautiful; she had alluring dark brown eyes, with her dark blonde hair pulled up into a tight bun and a white flower in her hair which matched the flowers on her long dark blue sarong which was tied up around her neck at the top like a halter dress. Her smile was her best feature, if the other features weren't enough, she looked so kind and gentle, and her voice was even more so.

"What will it be my loves," She said as the sunlight coincidently shined on her through a window. Leonie couldn't tell what her accent was.

"Ah, just some water thanks," Cody replied, "we haven't any money."

"Haven't you met Jeff yet?" The woman asked, "Not to worry, every new arrival gets their first meal for free. So I'd suggest you all really *pig* out."

"Are you serious?" Leonie asked stunned, "that's really nice of you."

"It's no trouble at all," the woman beamed, "just try and use the rest of today to try and find a job."

"A job?" Cody asked going pale in the face, "we need to work?"

"Yes, unfortunately, it's the only way this place can function, do your piece, collect a coupon after work and you get food... Don't worry there are all sorts of jobs, such as fishing, hunting, waitress, cleaning. Or if you're really confident and smart, you could apply for a job at the big mountain, that's where all the scientists and other hot shots are." The lady saw the confused and probably distressed looks on their faces, "don't stress, just enjoy your food for tonight. You escaped, so celebrate, and go for a stroll along the beach. My name's Ingrid by the way."

The girls introduced themselves and ordered many foods such as curry, pizza, fish n chips, potato bake and lemon squash.

"Thought you'd gotten lost," Stacey said as they returned to the table.

"We got lots of food coming soon," Cody grinned as she slid past Stacey into the booth.

"Remember we need save some for Leon, Clark Warren," Leonie said, "and Camilla."

When the food came, they dug in. It was delicious; Jamie got the hiccups from the spicy curry and snot was dripping out of his nose, yuck. They all laughed and exchanged many stories about themselves and tried to cheer each other up about Camilla. It also reminded Leonie about how close Soup was to Camilla as well. They had worked together for a while before she finished the course. It was nice to talk about Camilla, it really helped.

They had almost finished eating, Stacey had packed some food up to take back to the others, and Jamie farted really loudly, and it vibrated off his chair so that the whole restaurant almost shook, disgusting many. Then the owner of the restaurant, a Maori man with big hair, came over and leaned over the table to remove the picture above them.

"You have a call," he said with a friendly smile.

"A call?" Jonathan asked.

"Phew," Jamie said looking relieved, "I thought he was coming over to yell at me for letting one rip in his restaurant."

Suddenly a screen appeared where the picture had been. On the screen was the girl they had heard about for ages, ever since she had interrupted Leonie's assessment.

"Hello," She smiled, "great to see you all again. Where's Camilla?"

Chapter 21:

"She's hurt," Jonathan said, "badly."

"No way!" She shrieked looking upset, "Will she be alright?"

"We're waiting for our Doctor to tell us," Soup replied.

After appearing sad for a few moments, the girl took a breath and got on with what she called them for. "Thanks to you, we have taken out Dr Martens. He is the worlds most wanted in his time. I'm afraid he has been filling your heads with lies. There are no aliens. He is simply a mad scientist."

"Are you for real?" Jonathan asked looking worn out.

"I'm afraid so," She replied, "What it is, is he is, was, an intelligent man, with several PhDs" in science. But he was also an aspiring author. He couldn't catch a break in his novels he wrote. No one wanted to publish his work. Many of the plots in his stories were that of the lies he told you about aliens. It seems, if he couldn't get the world to read his work, then the next best thing was creating it and putting the people of the world in it. Using his science, he managed to create simulated worlds where he could bring real people in and manipulate them to suit his story. Unfortunately, we have no idea how to get out of here. We had hoped to capture him, for interrogation, but I guess things just don't work out in this place."

"You mean we're stuck here?" Soup asked.

"For now, yes, I'm afraid so, unless we can figure out a way of escaping, you may as well call this home."

"Who are you?" Leonie asked, unable to hold the question in any longer, "I know I know you."

The girl readjusted her sitting position, took a moment and replied, "My name is Tracy. I used to be friends with you girls, I was on your soccer team. I had to wipe myself from data to escape from Dr Martens. This meant wiping me from your memories as well though, unfortunately. It feels like a waste now, knowing that we're stuck here for good. He's dead, but I am optimistic and have confidence that one day we will find a way out... All the best, I truly hope Camilla recovers."

The screen disappeared again. The restaurant manager had been standing there the whole time waiting to put his Def Leppard picture back up (Leonie wanted to nick it).

"I need more than lemon squash to take this in," Soup explained, "I really need a Scotch."

"So he was a crazy psycho after all," Jonathan stated, "unbelievable, he was just an author."

"With several PHDs," Cody added.

"We should head back," Leonie said, "The others would want to hear about this. And we need to check on Camilla."

Everyone agreed and packed up for the short journey back. They thanked Ingrid who was still smiling and happy and headed off.

"I was really hoping to meet aliens," Jamie said disappointed, "this is actually worse, it not being real. It's like it was all for nothing."

"Consider yourself lucky," Stacey said, "an alien invasion is nothing to be glad about, really. I know, I've seen *Independence Day*."

They arrived back to find Warren sitting on the grass outside looking really worn out and down. He led them inside ready for an update from Leon. They all sat down and waited for the news.

"Camilla is not in a good way," Leon explained, all red in the face, "she has a few serious injuries, now the worse one which even I have hardly ever seen before, is, she has an Internal decapitation." –

Leonie, Stacey, and Cody broke down in tears. Leonie had no idea what an internal decapitation was exactly, but she knew what "decapitation" was.

Leon continued, reading from a screen, "basically, in short, the ligaments of her spinal column, the Atlas or C1, have been separated from the base of her skull, or the occiput. Now we need to perform surgery, in the hope to prevent her from becoming paralysed. At the moment she is stable, she has a few fractured ribs as well, a fractured clavicle, dislocated left patella and laceration on her right thigh. That's it for now. We must get going."

"We need to find jobs," Jonathan said trying to hide his sadness.

"Well go and do it," Leon snapped, "leave me alone you're all no good just hanging around here. Sorry."

Cody stayed behind this time to help with Camilla's surgeries. Leonie had never seen inside the medical area of the Ark, but it was apparently quite impressive. So in the meantime, Leonie, Stacey, Soup, Jonathan, and Jamie were to go and find work.

Leonie felt quite numb inside, she imagined Camilla's parents blaming her for their daughters" injuries. A massive whack on the back by Jamie soon snapped her out of it.

"I can just sense you're worrying," Jamie said in an unusually soft voice, "it's not your fault, see they're going to do some surgery… I think it's time we learnt how to fish properly, there may not always be a chippy around the corner to save us."

So Leonie went with Jamie to seek out a job in fishing.

They met up with a lovely old Welsh man and his crew of two other men, his sons; they had just finished for the day and had hauled in a huge load of Salmon and Rainbow Trout. The man agreed to give them a trial the next day. So they celebrated by Jamie pushing Leonie into the ocean.

They found Stacey who had had no luck in finding a job; she tried waitress and security guard. So they helped her and soon she had a job as cleaning up after the cowboy's horses.

Much later, they met up with Soup who had a job as a hunter which started later that night. He looked quite pleased with his job, more pleased than Stacey.

After not being able to find Jonathan they went into a local café and found him working as a barista.

"People love their coffee here at all hours," he said. He sat down with them all, after making coffee for them each. Soon, everyone got on with cracking jokes and mucking around, but there was a vibe and a sense of gloom amongst them all. They were all worried about Camilla.

They tried to head back to the Metal ark, but upon arrival, they were ordered to find somewhere else to stay, by Leon. They would only be a distraction. So they went back to the café where Jonathan was a barista at and hanged out there. As Jonathan closed up the shop, the restaurant behind them where Ingrid worked had music blaring really loud. So they all decided to duck over to see what was going on.

It was the beach party; everyone was dancing on the beach dressed in sarongs and bikinis. Leonie spotted Ingrid who was carrying a tray of cocktails.

"Hey!" Ingrid grinned, "Leonie right? Want a drink?"

"No thanks. I'm underage," Leonie replied, as Stacey took one, "what's the party for?"

"It's the anniversary of the day Donovan escaped," Ingrid said, "he started this and quite frankly we all owe him one. Maybe you saw him when he snuck back to the ship?"

"Donovan?" Leonie muttered, "I've heard of him, I think my friend knew him."

"He's a scientist; he's up in the mountain at the moment, brilliant mind. Did you find a job yet?"

"Yeah, fishing."

"Oh good. Hey relax now, have a good time. There are many handsome men here." Ingrid walked off tittering.

Jamie walked up next to Leonie with a quiche in his mouth, and one for Leonie.

"You know Warren's friend Donovan?" Leonie asked.

"Yeah," Jamie nodded, "the one who got into trouble."

"He founded this place, Ingrid said, we have to go find him. He's on a mountain somewhere. I wonder if Warren Knew…"

"Cool we'll go first thing tomorrow," Jamie smiled.

"Why can't we go now?"

"Because there's a party going on," Jamie explained, disgusted at Leonie's suggestion, "Man you're no fun."

Leonie told Stacey and Jonathan what Ingrid had said as well before finding a place to sit while unwillingly watching Jamie dance with three Chinese girls.

The party finally ended with everyone singing and dancing along to "Slice of Heaven" by Dave Dobbyn, of which Leonie was forced to participate in by Stacey.

Jamie decided to ignore the flirting Chinese girls and instead went and tried to pull Jonathan in with an imaginary rope. He then took the spotlight along with some Maori and a Mongolian

Shaman, singing along to the song. Cody had arrived in time to participate.

Not wanting to wait until morning for answers, Leonie waited until the others were asleep back in the café until she snuck out ready to journey to the mountain of which she had no idea where to find. But she felt it was a great idea because she believed if anyone could help explain things to her, Donovan was it. She made it out of the café and halfway down the road when she heard someone behind her.

"Oy! where you going?" Stacey whispered loudly behind her.

"Going to the mountain," Leonie said bluntly before continuing.

Stacey quickly caught up, "I thought we were waiting until morning?"

"I can't sleep," Leonie moaned, "not now, there's so much going on. It's all well and good to hide it when partying but what happens when the party stops? It comes back again."

"It's not easy for anyone," Stacey snapped, "you need to quit whining about how hard it is for you, well it's hard for everyone else too. Just because we're loud and not afraid to dance and try to put it out of our minds for a few hours, doesn't mean we're not coping any more than you."

"I know," Leonie snapped back, "but this is *my* way of dealing with it. If you don't like it, then go back to sleep."

Leonie stormed off along the road. Five minutes later, Stacey caught up again, and they continued on together without speaking.

They weren't angry at each other, or at least that's what Leonie hoped. Sometimes silence seemed to be the best thing somehow.

They made their way through grassland and Leonie didn't even register how they made it to the road on a cliff overlooking the ocean. They had a great view and the stars and Moon shined brightly over the water. It looked so real it almost felt like they were on Earth sometimes. Although every now and then you got the sense of something fake, such as scenery mixed together that you wouldn't normally find, or stumbling into an African looking wilderness before unexpectedly finding yourself in a Japanese looking wilderness.

The silence between them finally broke when Leonie thought of something she had completely forgotten about, but thought might be important, "what did Cody find when she accidentally hacked into something during our course?"

Stacey almost laughed, "oh that? That was just... How can I put this? Dr Martens was into Phil Collins."

Leonie looked confused.

"A famous singer, Leonie..."

"I know. What it was just a clip or something of him dancing to Phil Collins?"

"It was "Something happened on the way to heaven" to be exact," Stacey nodded, actually laughing this time, "he loves some singer called John Newman too.

They came to a heap of open land; it was very dark, but in the distance, they noticed a heap of cows and some horses. There was another dirt road running through the middle, and there were fences at the end of the open land near the road which indicated it could be farmland.

They made their way to the road and continued on down it, they had spotted a mountain in the distance, so they thought they had better check it out. Their water was running short, so they hoped they were on the right track.

At one point they had a huge fright, of which made them finally realise the stupidity of travelling at night. They heard a terrifying, ear-piercing scream that sounded like a woman or possibly a child screaming. It sounded like they were getting attacked. After looking at each other in utter horror, Leonie and Stacey undoubtedly decided to go and help. They came to where the terrifying screams came from; as they got closer, they ended in a sort of deep evil laughing. After seeing nothing in sight and hearing the laughter, the girls wondered whether it was a trap. Then, Leonie noticed a big Owl in one of the trees above, the moon shining upon it. Then she suddenly worked it all out. It was a Barking Owl. Leonie had heard a similar screaming once back home one night at about two o'clock in the morning, which went on for an hour. It was the same terrifying screaming which sounded like a woman being murdered right outside her bedroom window, followed by an evil laugh. She was fortunate to learn that it was just the screams of a Barking Owl which is known to Australia. They can make barking noises like dogs, but on occasions, they can make this terrifying scream similar to a woman or child in pain. It is very loud, like a siren, and it is often nicknamed "the screaming lady". She heard a story once of a man camping who drove himself mad trying to desperately get to the woman to help her. However, on a positive note, hearing these owls scream is supposedly very rare, and you're only likely to ever hear it once in your life, if ever at all. Leonie's heard it twice now. She wondered if these owls just have a dark sense of humour, imitating women and dogs. After cursing a bit (nothing too rude), Stacey calmed herself, and they continued onwards. However, they hoped there were no more spooky surprises for the rest of the journey.

Eventually though, after walking for a few more hours, they came to a rather disturbing sight after noticing a sickening smell. At first, along the road was a couple of dead chickens, it looked like most of their feathers were missing, and they were a disgusting purple and red colour. Some of them had been run over, and guts were all over the road. Retching, they continued on, only to find more and more of these dead chickens the further along they went. They eventually had to be extremely cautious not to step on any. Finally, they came to a huge pile of dead chickens in a deep part of the road. Up ahead they noticed a large truck, parked under a lone tree with its back door hanging by one hinge and an even bigger pile of chickens at the bottom. There had to be hundreds, if not thousands of them. Leonie had to stop by the side of the road to puke up the chicken curry she'd had for dinner.

There was no one in sight so eager to get away from the awful scene, the girls continued on.

"What a random sight to come across," Stacey said still recovering from her retching, "I've never seen anything like it... Of all the crazy things that have happened to us lately, this one, I'm afraid, blows them all away."

"I see a gate," Leonie said as she noticed a gate with another road leading into it. They quickly made their way to the farm, and after a long journey down the driveway, they came to a house. It was an old looking white farmhouse with a barn right next to it. On the veranda was a man wearing jeans and a checkered shirt holding a shotgun. The girls stopped dead in their tracks upon seeing this. He noticed them and lowered his weapon before waving them over.

As they approached, the heavily whiskered man greeted them warmly, "sorry to give you a fright, lass's," he said with his strong American accent, Leonie didn't know quite where about he was from though, "always got to carry a gun with me. Lots of unexpected surprises around here, but you have nothing to worry about. Did you by any chance see those dead chickens?" The girls nodded, "ahh, they're me neighbours those are. They're supposed to have gotten rid of them by now. Dumped the lot right out front of my farm, the bastards. It reeks. Don't worry though, I got em back, my dogs took a great big dump on their land on our walk this morning." He then laughed hysterically for a few seconds, "so what can I do you for?"

"We're looking for Donovan," Stacey said.

"Ahh you want Donovan," he replied, "I knew I couldn't be that lucky, to have two beautiful girls interested in me." Leonie blushed a little, mainly because it had been so long since a stranger complimented her looks, not that anyone really did before, but it was nice to have someone not look repulsed by her. This was obviously a man interested in any woman who'd have him. "Yeah he's up on the mountain is Donovan. You'll want to keep heading down the road, and once you come to an area with a heap of Maple trees, you're getting warm. You'll find an opening with a beach and a stone entrance into a Japanese garden. There will be guard dogs, but just call out for Kazuki, he's the caretaker or security, and he monitors who goes in and out of the facility. His garden is right in front of the mountain, and he has a secret passage in his garden that leads into it... Now I hope you're not evil women. Otherwise, I shouldn't have told you all this. But you see... I'm a sucker for beautiful ladies."

After receiving some more water from the man who they had learnt to be called Pete from North Carolina, they set off again hoping the Maple trees weren't too much farther ahead. Unfortunately, they were, in fact, an hour's walk farther. The Maple trees were beautiful and old looking, they're orange and red leaves spread out making the road like a tunnel. It was a fairly long stretch of Maple trees before they found the opening overlooking yet another stunning beach. There were some manmade unstable steps led down off the road onto the beach which they followed as instructed by Pete. Once down the bottom, they gazed around for a sign of the rock opening, they found it after a while. It was massive and went all the way from a mountains edge to the ocean shore. They walked through its big unevenly round shaped opening. On the other side, they found another rock opening sitting diagonally a bit further ahead which this time led into the mountain via a short rock tunnel.

The tunnel was filled with puddles from when the tide comes in, and there were some big holes in the roof letting in light. There was also a nice reflection on the walls coming from the water. When they eventually made it to the other side, they experienced their biggest most pleasant gobsmack to date.

Imagine the most beautiful Japanese garden you've ever seen, with lots of trees, flowers, a big pond with a bridge over it, lovely statues and colourful lighting. Not to mention a lovely waterfall in many of the ponds, and to top it off lots of big pretty goldfish in the ponds. While this Japanese garden has all of that, it's still immensely better than your favourite Japanese garden.

Leonie and Stacey were so captivated by the sight, it took several minutes to realise all the barking dogs up ahead behind a fence which led to a gorgeous dark grey Japanese house.

Once noticing the dogs, both girls naturally freaked out. Stacey, in particular, was used to big scary dogs like Rocco and Rufo. But a pack of big scary dogs was another story. Leonie spotted at least a dozen dogs before even more came running over. There were many including, German Shepherds, Rottweilers, Irish Wolfhounds, Dobermans, Carpathian Shepherd Dogs, several breeds of Caucasian Shepherd including two tied up Sage Gorgy, and a Dachshund. This was the ultimate security system. They reminded Leonie of some videos and descriptions of dogs back years ago, for instance, the German Shepherds seemed more of how they used to be originally without the overbreeding problems. And the Irish Wolfhounds looked different, which convinced her that these dogs were taken from back in the days where they hunted wolves and deer before they became people's babies. They were in no way your typical pet. If not for the tall gate, they'd have been shredded.

A whistle blew which got all of the dog's attention immediately, then a man's voice yelled something in Japanese, and the dogs quickly took off to a nearby barn out on a grassy area past the garden.

Both girls looked up beyond the trees at the house to find a young Japanese man wearing black cargo pants, a big dark blue puffy jacket and an orange beanie head their way. He had a warm smile on his face and as he reached them extended his hand for them to shake through the gate.

"Hello, I'm Kazuki! Pete told me you two were on your way," he said as he unlocked the gate, "sorry for the dogs, I've been a bit behind today and couldn't sort them out earlier. Don't worry about them though, I already ordered them not to attack. Please, do come in."

"It's a lovely garden you've got here," Stacey said still staring around at the garden.

"Oh thank you," he blushed, "it definitely is a hit that's for sure... You, uh, deserve to be in a place like this, uh, miss...?"

"Oh sorry," Stacey said as she took her eyes off the scenery and paid attention to Kazuki, "I'm Stacey. And this is Leonie."

"Pleasure to meet you both," Kazuki said rather excitedly.

Chapter 22:

Kazuki showed them around his garden, it was so amazing, Leonie wanted to have a garden just like it when she went back home. Stacey didn't want to leave; Leonie had never seen her so mesmerised before. Even some of the dogs were allowed back to say hi, unfortunately not all of them though because they were there for a purpose. He didn't go into much detail, but Kazuki said there is a lot of danger around, from wild animals to thieves and just plain old hooligans. He told them they were very lucky not to have encountered any on their way there.

"I'm very sorry," Kazuki said, "but there are certain time frames for visitors. Once in the morning, once in the evening, I think they are very busy, is all. Hehe."

"That's okay," Stacey sighed, "the only thing is our friends will have been looking for us all day."

"One of our friends is badly injured," Leonie explained, "we just can't do much back there so we thought we'd get started on finding Donovan and seeing if he has any information for us."

"Oh, I see," Kazuki replied, "I am very sorry to hear about your friend. I hope Donovan can provide you with the information you need. In about an hour I can let you in."

"How long have you been in here for?" Stacey asked curiously.

"I'm not too sure to tell you the truth," Kazuki said as he thought about it, "I know it's been a very long time. I have a dog here who's about twelve, and I've had her since she was a puppy. But I've been here way longer than that. I like it though. I was the same as you, I went to the ship and did the training, hated every minute of it, and they were worse back then, abused you and everything. I guess they've toned it down a bit."

"That's awful," Leonie said, "I didn't think it could get worse, but that just proves me completely wrong."

"Yeah," Kazuki laughed a bit, "I remember when I got taken, I was about to start University in Tokyo."

"What were you going to study?"

"Architecture actually."

"Good choice," Stacey smiled, "if you don't mind me asking, you said you were about to start university, but you've been here for over twelve years. Yet you still look like you're about to start university."

"Is there still a time freeze or something?" Leonie asked, seeing Stacey's point.

Kazuki laughed, "perhaps Donovan will explain it more to you. You know a week back on Earth is equal to a year here? Figure that one out."

"Then wouldn't we age fast?" Stacey said looking confused, "I don't understand. Then again I'm not the brightest when it comes to that sort of thing."

"Just ask Donovan. I don't want to confuse you."

They chatted more about each other, Kazuki's dream was to move to America to experience life, and he was worried he'll never be able to get that chance, but he's glad he gets to stay in a beautiful place like he is. Although he explained to them how it's everyone's fantasy to live in a place away from home, from their world even, but they've been unlucky to experience how bad that can be.

"Perhaps," Kazuki continued, "one day if we can't leave, we can maybe make it like a dream place that everyone wishes it to be in their dreams back home. I guess it's good to experience something bad though, to become stronger."

223

"Yeah you're right," Leonie said, "I still just wish nothing happened and we just continued with our slumber party and finished year twelve." Everyone laughed in agreement before realising it was now time for them to head into the mountain.

Escorted by a few dogs, they made their way through Kazuki's garden, past the barn and down a stream which was connected to the pond by a small waterfall. They came to a pavilion, which was hanging over the stream. On the other side of the stream was the wall of the mountain which the pavilion was connected to.

They stepped into the pavilion which was beautiful, grey like the house but with red and gold patterns through it. There were more statues and plants all around it and a comfy looking lounge. Leonie found herself again wondering where people get such supplies from.

On the other side of the pavilion, there appeared to be an outline of a door on the mountain. Both Leonie and Stacey looked at Kazuki in disbelief.

"Simple right?" He said as he walked towards the door, still smiling, "why do things have to be complicated? I have the best security and who in their right mind would want to break into here? Besides, the door only opens from the inside..."

After having to look twice, Leonie noticed a small camera engraved on the mountain wall. The lens had moved a bit, probably to check out who exactly wanted access. The door suddenly opened... slowly, making an awful sound as it did. Kazuki, who was still smiling, signalled his hand for them to go in.

"Don't worry. It's safe," he assured them, "Donovan knows you're coming."

They walked in through a dark hallway which was carved through the mountain rock, which felt unstable and very claustrophobic. Leonie found herself hiding behind Stacey.

"Oh, it smells!" Stacey said bluntly, screwing up her nose, "like yucky water and mould and rusty metal, it's awful. Let's go back to the garden." She joked.

It was a bloody long way, but finally, they made it to another door, similar to the one beforehand. There was another camera checking them out, and then this door too opened slowly but sounded tolerable this time.

They were immediately facing several men all yelling orders at them in what Leonie thought to be Russian. They immediately became frustrated with the two girls for not understanding them and ended up shoving them along to a room where there were two women who could speak English there ready to search them for weapons. The lady searching Leonie was big and scary. They ordered them to strip off their clothes so they could check if they were hiding anything in awkward places, not that *they* worded it like that. When they were cleared, after a whole lot of embarrassment, they got dressed again and went back to the men outside who were now confirmed to be Militsiya from Kyrgyzstan. Apparently, they'd had an attempted breach a few months ago (even though Kazuki didn't mention it), and they're not taking any chances, not even with two clueless looking teenage girls.

They were ordered to sit down on the ground against the hard, pointy rock of the mountain wall. They finally got a chance to have a look at the place. It was quite dull, it was basically just the inside of a mountain, with dirt and stone for the floor, a few weird big looking equipment everywhere and serious men and women in uniforms. It was really messy and looked dangerous, one man almost got run over by a forklift and started yelling and abusing the driver in Russian, the driver then started yelling back and waving his fist.

"Okay, I'm sorry we came now," Leonie said as she looked in all directions at the chaos, "I can't believe we walked all this way just to witness all this madness and be stripped and yelled at. Not to mention shoved around like prisoners."

"It's all good," Stacey shrugged, "I'm actually quite pumped, I feel like if anyone comes at me again, I'll thump them one. It's awesome."

A tall nerd suddenly approached them with his arm already stretched out to shake hands from twelve meters away. His glasses got knocked off when a crazy man came charging past, and he had to stop to pick them up while trying to avoid a stampede.

"Greetings," he said as he was finally able to shake their hands, "you must be Brandon and Ebony?"

"Stacey and this is Leonie," Stacey corrected.

"Oh sorry, Stacey… My name is Donovan, I'm a good friend of Warren as we were together a while in the changing rooms… Actually, that sounds bad, but you know what I mean. I'm from the year twenty-sixteen."

"Wow, thirteen for us," Leonie smiled, "anything interesting or good happen in between our two times?"

"Ah well, interesting? Yes. A lot of bad things too, unfortunately. But there is a new *Star Wars* movie late twenty-fifteen!"

"Epic!" The girls both shouted excitedly.

"Cody and Camilla would be beside themselves!" Stacey cried.

"Not to mention Jamie and Jonathan!" Leonie said, "they're still waiting to see episodes one, two and three."

After spending five minutes trying to even get Donovan to tell them the name of the new *Star Wars* movie, they all agreed to get on with the purpose of their visit. So they went for a walk up to Donovan's lab. On the way, they chatted.

"So how'd you get here?" Leonie asked curiously.

"Well, it wasn't easy at all, to get here or to get our hands on any decent and useful equipment. It took ages of sending in people to steal things from Dr Martens' base. After, of course, I managed to first escape, much like you did, with a little group of my own. Word got out to our friends, and they soon joined us. Then there was trouble for the Dr and things started going terribly wrong for him. Tracy, another vigilante, managed to destroy the lab where they bring people in. And she managed to keep sneaking into his base undetected which made him furious. She's amazing and inspires everyone, more than I do in fact; she's a pioneer for us, a legend."

"We believe we knew her," Stacey explained, "she told us she used to play on our football team, but she had to wipe herself from data which unfortunately included all of our memories of her."

"Ah," Donovan nodded as though recalling something, "that is what you'd call an adverse effect, she wouldn't have known that would happen, no one did until she did it actually. A real shame it is, she's such a nice girl. I think she could do with some friends right now."

This made Leonie feel sad. She couldn't imagine how it would feel if suddenly Stacey, Cody or even her parents had no idea who she was. It would be depressing and lonely she imagined.

"What about this whole time thing?" Leonie asked, "Kazuki said you could explain that to us."

"Did he now?" Donovan asked as he halted after they went through an archway. "Well let me see if I can without overcomplicating it for you. Now, a week back on Earth is equal to a year here. This is due to a few theories, such as no one really knows whether time here is the same as on Earth, perhaps time goes a lot slower, so perhaps our year is even less than a week on Earth. It's all complicated stuff, don't worry, just be glad you haven't any grey hairs yet."

Leonie wanted more, "But Kazuki's already said that his dog is at least twelve."

"That is because he is counting day and night like we'd do on earth, so therefore it is as if the days are the same as on Earth, hence adding up to twelve years like he did. But realistically, we're not even sure if this place was invented any more than a year ago. It's hard to explain with words, but if you think hard about it sometime, when you've nothing to do, it should click."

"How can time here be more here if we're not aging?" Stacey asked looking confused, "or have I got it wrong? Wait, how does it work?"

Donovan laughed, "it's okay, it's tricky. No matter, we needn't worry about time right now, especially when it seems to be to our advantage here."

None of it made sense, so they quickly moved on to more important things.

"Here, we mainly study this place and of course, try to work out how to escape… It's very tough, you got to remember, Dr Martens is from a long way in the future to us. We don't know his exact time, but it's at least several hundred years in the future to us. So obviously they have smarter technology and equipment." Donovan explained as they arrived at his lab. "To be honest, I'm hardly impressed with the stuff I've seen from his future. But then I must realise after a long time here, I still haven't solved anything, so I'll give him that."

"It's like his strategy was to just disorientate you," Leonie sighed as she stared around Donovan's massive lab, "it's probably very simple, everything, but he complicates it for us."

"Cruel bastard," Donovan nodded.

"Wow this lab is amazing," Stacey said in awe of the remarkable lab. It was so big and full of incredible equipment that both girls wisely decided to stay right away from as they hadn't any clue what any of it was used for. Leonie only recognised a lab scope on Donovan's desk, some stationary and a computer which he later explained was to keep him in touch with his time. He showed them some futuristic computers which were like a screen that appeared when you clapped, much like the clap lights.

After many questions, Donovan finally told the two girls that what they were currently doing was right, as in laying low, getting some jobs and waiting for word on an escape chance and to even prepare for a possible attack from some of the dead Drs "team".

"We don't know how long we will be here for," he continued, "but one thing I think we have *all* learnt here is that nothing is impossible. That means, it's possible we can escape, it is also possible we could be attacked somehow. We're currently working on setting up a sort of order so that people can still work and things, but also have a schedule so everyone can have time to train ready for this thing we have plans for."

"And what is that?" Stacey asked hesitantly.

"Well we're thinking either every six months or every year, uh, Earth time, we have a few days of tests for people after we've placed them into teams. It will be set over a couple of days, where there'll be swimming races, running races, obstacle courses – we have a forest which would be perfect for teams to be given maps and try to find their way to the finish line while avoiding traps and animals. We'll even have a Search and Destroy competition, which is kind of like Laser tag. Teams will compete against one another until two winning teams are left to battle it out. Just an idea, we're still working on it. We want to keep people on their toes, I don't think we're quite out of the mist yet, it'd be too easy. Everything else is complicated, so why should escaping to this island be any different?"

"Good point," Leonie agreed, "I guess that sounds fun. I just don't like competitions too much."

"Don't worry; we'll try to make it fun, like a school carnival. As long as people still remember how to use a map, can run well, swim well and use weapons, that's it really." Donovan explained.

Donovan was very busy, so he had to quickly shoo them off, but not before introducing them to his lovely wife, Rhiannon, a beautiful Lebanese woman. She was seven months pregnant and allowed Stacey and Leonie to feel the baby kick. It was rather nice to see something beautiful like this after all the horrible things in comparison that they have. Stacey was almost in envy of the young couple, who were in their early thirties. They told them they had met during their twelve-week course and that she had invented his hearing aids that can translate up to fifty languages.

Donovan brought in two tall men. One was called Ryan, he had very pale skin, which randomly went red at times without warning. He had short sandy blonde hair and spoke with a Swedish accent.

The other man was Austrian, his name was Marko, and he had brown hair which was styled in a top knot with an undercut. Both men were in their late twenties and appeared very unhappy with their new job, which they both called, "Babysitting two teenagers." Marko was a very aggressive and angry man. He didn't hold in his feelings about the job and made sure the two girls knew how much he hated it. Luckily, Ryan was more polite, he still wasn't happy, but at least *he* remained calm.

Ryan and Marko had to watch the girls *all* the time. They started with a tour of the mess hall where many more guards, mostly Russian, were eating lunch.

"Go on then," Marko said bitterly, "go have some grub then, I want to watch your faces when you taste it."

Leonie nudged Stacey after her fists clenched up. Marko and Ryan saw this and laughed hysterically. They obviously had no idea there was more to Stacey than her princess looks. Then again, Leonie and Stacey had no idea what these two hooligans could do either.

Before things could escalate more between Stacey and Marko, Leonie felt a hard whack on her back, which made her body flop forwards in a ripple. She turned around furiously, and saw a stupid grin, from Cody...

"You idiot! What are you doing here?" Leonie asked, in pain from Cody's attack.

"I saw you two leaving," Cody said smartly, "I knew where you were going."

"Yeah, but the genius went back to sleep and didn't tell us until the morning," Jonathan said as he appeared from behind Cody.

"Why panic?" Cody pointed out, "anyway I was knackered from the party."

"Where's Jamie?" Leonie asked, noticing the lack of chaos, despite Cody being there.

"We sent him back to the ship to tell the others," Jonathan replied, "I could just foretell the outcome of sending those two up here by themselves. Figured it'd end badly and couldn't risk it."

"Good thinking," Stacey nodded along with Leonie.

"So did you find Donovan?" Jonathan asked, "has he got answers?"

"We found him," Stacey said, "he has answers, we can't make much sense of them. And he's really busy, so he's got these two dorks looking after us."

"Steady," Ryan warned as he put his hand in front of Marko's body to stop him from getting into Stacey's face.

"What's with the crazy welcome from the Militsiya," Cody laughed, "they sure meant business."

Chapter 23:

The next day, Donovan organised for the Metal Ark to be allowed to arrive. Leonie thought it couldn't possibly fit into the mountain from anywhere, and she was right, it got teleported inside.

Immediately, without permission, Leonie and the others raced into the Metal Ark. Leon and Warren led them into their own little hospital room where Camilla lay, still unconscious.

"We've made progress," Leon said, sounding exhausted, "but I need better equipment. Warren suggested we ask Donovan if he has any."

"If anyone can help us it's him," Warren said with a small smile, he too looked exhausted, "I'm Jolly hungry though. Could sure go a hot meal right now."

Soup and Jonathan went to fetch Donovan while everyone else discussed the stupidity of Leonie and Stacey's actions.

"Not just from you two," Warren admitted, "but from Cody not telling us until the morning. And Max had to go and find Soup."

Clark was nodding off in his chair; the poor things all looked so tired. They had tried their very best to save Camilla. Perhaps Donovan can come up with some miracle from one of his cool equipment. It felt like that was the last hope of saving Camilla.

Donovan returned; spoke with Leon, Warren, and Clark before they got a Medical team in to transfer Camilla to one of their wards. He then instructed everyone to leave her to his team. Leonie got a glance at some of the tech, there was actually a lot of big tubes moving around the room attached to a large machine on wheels.

That night, Donovan formally invited the squad to join him at a table in a private pub for dinner. It had another space feel to it, but Leonie was so disappointed in having not been in space before, that she didn't care. "The Things We Do For Love" by 10cc was playing as they sat down at their table. Only a few other people were sitting at some tables. They all looked tired from a hard day's work.

"You know, this pub just appeared one day," Donovan explained straight after everyone sat down, "Incredible isn't it? Woke up one morning and it was just here."

"Along with the food and alcohol?" Jamie asked seriously.

"No."

"What is your plan?" Leon said bluntly, getting straight to the point, "I mean what's the whole deal with this place? You're trying to achieve something?"

"The whole deal with this place," Donovan replied, "is to provide sanctuary to all that escape the ship. The plan? Is to catch Dr Martens."

"He's dead," Clark said softly as he buttered some bread.

"No. He is not." Donovan said, staring at his plate. Rhiannon held his hand, "One of our spies spotted him in a newly discovered part of the simulated world. Or possibly, a newly added part of the simulated world. As much as it pains me to find this out, we must realise, how good it would be if we could capture him. He's the only one who can get us out of here. I'm relieved and feel guilty about it."

"And how are we going to do that?" Leon asked.

"He will be in hiding for a while. Recuperating. It will be extremely hard to get to him at the moment. I thought about

233

it and believe the best thing we can do is to continue making this place stronger and preparing everyone to face him. It's not nice, but it's the only way. I have seen his worse, trust me, you don't want to take any chances. I just hope he doesn't want to find his wife."

"His wife?" Jonathan asked, "What are you talking about?"

Donovan sighed and took his glasses off to clean them on his sleeve, "his wife lives here, well their divorce never got the chance to be finalised... She's the sweetest person you'd ever meet. Perhaps you saw her down on the beach? I believe she works as a waitress."

"Ingrid?" Leonie asked, remembering the heart-warming smile of the waitress, "no sorry how silly of me to think that."

"Yes! Ingrid," Donovan said as he pointed his fork into Leonie's direction, landing some potato bake onto a disgusted Stacey's plate. "Ah, she's been wonderful to have here. Was a bit apprehensive at first, being that she's married to the madman. But she's the complete opposite of him."

"I don't believe you!" Jonathan shouted, "that can't be his wife!"

Stacey laughed, "Jonathan thought she was *hot*!

Jamie started singing "Hot Girl" by Sabrina, which was ignored by everyone.

"Don't worry about Ingrid," Donovan assured, "she's no trouble and simply wants to live in peace and even help others. And before you ask, we've had her tell us everything... You know, about him."

"So is it true he was an author who was really passionate and wanted to make his story real?" Warren asked.

"Yeah, I guess," Donovan replied, "he was really just simply psychotic, crazy. Apparently, they were going to send him to a secure unit in a mental facility right before the final touches of building this place were put into effect and they missed him."

"Poor Ingrid told me about how different he is from when she first met him," Rhiannon said, "he hid it all from her for years. She described him as free-spirited in those years. Until one day she… Walked in on.. a murder.."

After no one knew what to say to this, Donovan changed the subject, "So, let's discuss your new *temporary* lives here. In two months there will be the new job opening trials. I thought perhaps you lot could remain as a squad and tryout for a patrol unit. I can't push the date forward I'm afraid, but enjoy the beach in the meantime. Leon, Warren, Max, I'd love to have you join *my* personal team if you're interested."

The three of them grunted, not saying yes or no. Leonie and the others looked at each other uneasy; worried they'd lose them from the squad. That'd be right, the three smarty-pants leaving them to fend for themselves. Even Jonathan was offered a role as some strategy person, but that wasn't until eight months" time. That would mean all that would be left was, Leonie, Stacey, Cody, Jamie, Soup – and Camilla. Leonie tried not to think about it too much, even though Cody complained out loud right next to her. Thankfully, a loud vibration from Jamie's chair ended the dinner quickly.

Unable to stay any longer due to a drill starting that night for the guards, they were escorted back to the Metal Ark by Marko and Ryan.

"Well I must say I am utterly disappointed," Jamie announced, "I mean again, not many answers, and you lot might be leaving us. Not that you would though, eh? I mean we're a fun bunch. We like to boogie."

"I can't believe we weren't even allowed to see Camilla before we left," Leonie said sadly as she watched Cody burst open a packet of crisps. She did ask before they left if they could see

235

her, but they assured that they were really busy and as soon as something changes or she comes round, they'll be in contact.

"She's in good hands," Leon said gently, "there's not much more I could do for her. And Donovan's team seemed really impressive, and their equipment was out of this world. I'd love to wor- learn more from them one day."

"You want to work for them?" Leonie asked, trying to hide her sadness.

"We're not sure," Clark answered, "it is a great opportunity."

"And think about it," Warren added, "we could really be of use to them."

"Don't lose any sleep over it," Leon said, "it's not going to happen overnight, or even in a week for that matter. We'll just take it one day at a time alright."

Leonie and the others nodded, still looking unhappy.

"What about Jonathan?" Jamie asked, "Strategy guy?"

Jonathan made some moaning noises and then headed straight to the toilet in a hurry. He didn't want to talk about it, which was a bad sign Leonie thought.

When they landed, it was morning tea time, so everyone agreed to go into town to grab a bite. Donovan had given them some coupons to buy some food and toiletries and things. It was Leonie's idea to go into town as she wanted to see Ingrid again. Donovan had rushed up to them before they left and begged them not to draw attention to Ingrid as he was afraid if word got out about whom she was, she could be in danger.

Soup, Jonathan, and Stacey decided to go to work and earn more coupons. So the others found a table at the *rebel joint* and had a coffee and some cake. While Cody reviewed the story about Kazuki again, Leonie snuck off to Ingrid as she spotted her pass by with a tray of empty glasses to put behind the bar.

"Hello! Leonie isn't it?" Ingrid beamed as she held out her hand to shake Leonie's, who accepted with a smile. Leonie couldn't get past Ingrid's manners, she was so kind, and she wondered how she could possibly have been married to such a horrible man. "Settling in are you all?"

"Yeah thanks," Leonie replied softly, "just took a friend up to the mountain for some medical treatment."

Ingrid's smile shrunk ever so slightly, not much but Leonie's good eye could just spot it. "Oh, the mountain. Is she okay?"

"I hope so. Their advanced tech should do the trick we hope. Donovan was very helpful."

Leonie watched for Ingrid's response to Donovan's name. She didn't know why she was trying to get reactions from her. Maybe she was checking to see whether Ingrid *had* a dark side to her.

"Donovan's a good man," Ingrid said with her smile back to full stretch.

"Yeah, he is," Leonie said before taking in a deep breath. She was going to do it, she had to ask. "Ingrid, he said, you were married to Dr Martens... I... uh."

"I was," Ingrid replied calmly, with her smile slightly shrinking again. "But I'm not anymore."

"So... what was he like? Did you."-

-"Look," Ingrid said, raising a finger, "Leonie. I like you; I think you're a nice young lady. However, that was a period of my life of which I don't like to discuss. I don't know him, really, I have no idea what goes on in his head. Now if you would excuse me, I must go and serve these other customers."

Leonie watched as Ingrid walked over to serve some ancient Roman people. Leonie felt guilty and embarrassed, so she just sat back down at the table to hear Jamie talk about a stingray he almost caught.

Later, Leon sent Jamie, Leonie, and Cody on a run down the long beach, mainly because Jamie was annoying him. Leonie was amazed at how quickly she'd gotten out of shape; she was out of breath and panting heavily with a stitch in her side. Jamie had slowed right down and was actually praying for it to end as he slowly ran in a weird looking way. But Cody was out of sight, she could run fast. Leonie was amazed and angry because all she thought Cody did all day was stuff her face and lounge around.

Leonie decided to stop after her stitch became unbearable. Eventually, Jamie caught up with her, walking like a zombie. He tried to hold himself up by placing his hand on Leonie's shoulder, but sweat was pouring off him onto her, so she stepped back and let him fall flat on his face. Leonie got to watch the sunset, it reminded her of when she was little, and her mum, dad, and she would sit out on the back veranda and look out at the view while eating cheese balls. Her mum even painted a nice picture of the sunset once and it hung in their living room. She wished she could be back home with them, but as each day goes by, she loses hope in the chance that she'll be able to hug them again.

"What's the matter?! Did you choke on my dust!?" Came rocket Cody and she jumped onto Jamie's back yelling, "Stacks on!"

Jamie yelled into the sand. Leonie laughed as they helped Jamie to his feet, which took several attempts. They dusted the sand off him, but couldn't do much for the sand stuck to his face from all the sweat.

"GUYS!" Came a high pitched yell. And they turned around to find Stacey racing up the beach to them. But the voice came from behind Stacey… It was Soup with an unusually high pitched voice, "GUYS IT'S CAMILLA! SHE'S BACK!"

Immediately, Leonie's stitch was gone, Jamie was fully charged again, and Cody was still Cody. They raced back to the

Metal Ark and piled in noisily with their shoes squeaking and thundering on the floor.

Camilla sat in a wheelchair with a large head brace on, a cast on her left leg and a large wound dressing on her right leg. Camilla had a big smile on her face, and Cody broke down in tears. Jonathan comforted Cody, while Leonie approached Camilla.

"Can I hug her?" Leonie asked.

Before Leon could answer, Camilla pulled Leonie into her and hugged her as tightly as she could. Unfortunately, Leonie noticed little strength in Camilla's arms. Cody and Stacey came over and hugged Camilla as well.

"She'll need to wear that head brace for a few months," Leon explained, "and gradually build up her strength after that. She's a strong one."

The girls all jumped up and down around Camilla, laughing and cheering.

They then asked Warren to help set up a PS4 that some guy from two thousand and fifteen gave Jamie along with *Black Ops lll*, *Tom Clancy's Rainbow Six Siege* and *FIFA 15*. Leonie and the others were angry that Giggs and Rio were no longer playing for Manchester United. But at least now Camilla would have something to do while she rested.

The girls had a quick deep conversation about life.

"Camilla," Stacey started, "what happened to you really scared me."

"Me too," Camilla snorted before turning sensible and serious, "thanks, Stace. I was, uh, actually emotional too when watching you guys set the PlayStation and that up. You know, just about everything that's happened. I guess now that I've stopped and am able to actually think, it's hit me... We probably won't be seeing our families again, will we? Even Clark said if we do get back, our families could be long gone."

"Eh Clark Shmark," Cody said loudly, "I personally was more concerned with the fact that we were *so* close to finishing grade twelve, but now, we probably will *never* get the chance to play "School's Out" by Alice Cooper. We'd been waiting years for that!" After Leonie and Stacey gave Cody a look of *really? Camilla's sad!* Cody noticed Camilla's slight teary face. "Don't worry guys… It'll be okay, you'll see. In the meantime, we've got each other, eh?" Leonie smiled and gave Cody a nod of approval, and in return, Cody put her feet up and took a controller as if her work was done.

Camilla wasn't the same teenager she once was. The next day she was wheeled outside ready to help Leon command the workout to everyone which she continued to do every morning for the rest of the week. And when everyone ran laps, she read a book.

"Stephen King?" Jonathan asked as he and Leonie ran passed.

"Enid Blyton," Camila replied.

An example of some torture she gave them. 75 pushups, 75 situps, a sprint across the beach, heavy kettlebell exercises, 60 swimmer starts on each leg, 2-minute plank, 50 flutter kicks per leg, 50 pull-ups, then start again. They did this for over an hour, and Leonie lost count of how many times they went through the reps.

They all spent the rest of the day working at their jobs. Leonie and Jamie had to give up their fishing jobs as it coincided with their workouts. Luckily they managed to get another job picking crabs and stuff off the beach ready to be delivered to the restaurants. They were able to play music from a stereo as they scavenged. After work, they would do another workout before bed. This was mainly combat training and more running. Every second day, Camilla swapped the sprints along the beach for heavy swims in the ocean. Cody freaked out about Megalodons every time. Leonie started to notice her muscles coming back again as they had started to fade since escaping the ship. Leon explained how even just a week without exercise can set you back four weeks.

"My arse is just killing me," Jamie moaned as he bent down to pick up a small crab at work one day, "my goodness it's bad! Must be from all those squats with the kettlebells."

Leonie was opening up a letter she received that morning at breakfast at the café Jonathan worked at. It almost blew away in the wind, but she managed to steady it and have a read.

Leonie,

I know I said I don't like to speak about it. But I thought perhaps I could try and write about it. After all, you seem like a decent person. Not that I'd know, experience has shown me.

I met Julian when I was at University. We met at a club he owned. He was a flamboyant, overconfident being who loved to wear and talk about things from all different countries and time frames. Everyone hated him. I used to work part-time at a bar while I studied English Literature and German Literature. He used to come to the bar and talk to me a lot and help me with my German. He would blast all different kinds of music from his vehicle and got arrested many times; music isn't as appreciated in the future. I don't know why, but I really liked him. I never imagined for one second that he was capable of doing the things he has indeed done. I feel ashamed and only wish to end this madness and to help people. I hope someone can find him and make him end this all once and for all. It can't be me I'm afraid. As I'd kill him the moment I saw him. I don't care who I once thought he was, I assure you, I just know what he has done and how much it has affected people. I fully support his capture and sentence when it does happen. Justice needs to be served. It is long overdue.

Thank you for not revealing who I am, I assure you it is worthwhile.

Ingrid.

241

The wind was then too strong, and the letter blew out of Leonie's hands and into the ocean. Leonie stared after it.

"Come on, you slacker!" Jamie called from several feet away. "Hey look at this big oyster!"

The sound of "Sorrento Moon" by Tina Arena, her mother's favourite song, playing from their stereo faded from Leonie's ears as she stared across the water. She smiled and then began to laugh. She was overwhelmed with a mixture of emotions as usual. But one thing was for sure, she had close friends by her, and she felt safe knowing that. What better time to have friends with you than when you're stuck in a senseless simulated world with people and animals from lots of different eras surrounding you and a mad scientist playing with your mind. She could not think of one.

www.ingramcontent.com/pod-product-compliance
Lightning Source LLC
Chambersburg PA
CBHW051427170626
46809CB00006B/2348